R P SNOW

Turning Point

ISBN: 1484878132
ISBN-13: 9781484878132

DEDICATION

For Steven, Kevin, Patrick, Karen and Kathi, all of whom have experienced turning points.

ACKNOWLEDGEMENTS

Once again I've had the good fortune to benefit from invaluable editing advice and mentoring from noted author Lesley Poling-Kempes, who took time from her writing projects to nurture me along. Ongoing gratitude to my life partner Suzanne who not only makes me a better person, but also a better writer and storyteller. Many thanks to friend and neighbor Tracy McBride for both nuts and bolts editing and style suggestions drawn from her training in journalism. Also, thanks to friend and bee keeping partner Bill Page for his sharp-eyed editing and suggestions. Any shortcomings that remain are entirely on my shoulders.

This story follows chronologically from the first story **Folsom Point** in both time and place (Abiquiu, New Mexico several years after 9/11). The author has taken liberties with geography, certain place names and distances. Any resemblance of characters in the story to persons living or dead is purely coincidental.

1

December 24

The last rays of the stark winter sun knifed through the ancient Taos Pueblo. People hunched against the cold wind sent long shadows ahead of them as they made their way silently into the plaza for the annual Christmas Eve procession of the Virgin. Some were relatives of pueblo residents, a pueblo actively inhabited before the Norman conquest of England and well before Spain — the ethnic heritage to many northern New Mexicans — sent Christopher Columbus on his voyage. Most onlookers were local folks and a few tourists who came to witness an event unlike any other holy-night ritual in the Catholic world, an event eagerly anticipated, like a circus or a magic act captivating unbelieving eyes. As an amalgam of pagan folk dance with classic Catholic Mass, the ritual graphically portrayed the compromises missionaries made with folk cultures to achieve conversion.

Abigail Romero, along with best friends Carmen Tafoya and Nick Trujillo, stood on the north bank of Rio Pueblo, an intermittent river dissecting the village into a plaza and work buildings on the north side and the main pueblo on the south. To a first-time visitor, the structures probably look like a movie set, and it would seem inconceivable that people today actually live in a place built of mud with no running water and use ladders to get to upper stories. From the elevated bank of the river, Abby, Nick and Carmen had the vantage to watch the procession begin at the Chapel of San Geronimo to their left, proceed through the pueblo's north side and return to the chapel by way of the main plaza to their right.

The crowd easily exceeded several thousand, spread throughout the grounds. Cars lined the two-mile entrance road from Taos to the pueblo, and natives directed late arrivals to dusty adjacent fields, making their vehicle's location a challenge to find in the darkness later in the evening. Nick had tied an orange ribbon to the communications antenna on his truck and extended it as far as it would go. Ever the Boy Scout, Nick also had wisely brought a flashlight. Both he and Abby had marked the location in their minds; each picked out different markers and would joke about it later.

At dusk, the first of many *luminaria* bonfires ignited throughout the plaza sent orange flames dancing upward through the latticework stacks of pitch wood. Black acrid smoke belched in all directions as wind swirled around the buildings, and more than a few visitors put on protective masks or pulled scarves over their mouths. The tallest of the *luminarias*, at twenty feet, stood in the main plaza and was reserved for a dramatic climax to the end of the procession.

The first of the fires signaled the end to vespers in the chapel and the start of the procession. Anticipation mounted in the crowd, as though it were waiting for the curtain to rise at a theatrical event. The newspaper said the procession would begin at four o'clock; it was now after five, but everyone understood this was "Indian time."

Piercing rifle shots from white-shirted guards announced that the statue of the Virgin — the bride of God — was about to leave the chapel, the only time this would occur during the entire year. Bells pealed and the statue emerged on a platform carried by six brown-skinned men in white tunics. Mary rested on a bed of green pine bows, protected overhead by a billowing white canopy, and from a distance, she appeared to float above the crowd as if on a gently rolling barge carrying a fairy princess to her waiting prince. A priest followed the virgin carrying the sacred crucifix from the chapel, while drummers followed close behind chanting in their native Tewa, adding to the pagan character of the scene. The crowd milled around the procession and pressed close to soak in the magic of the moment.

The mixture of contrasting rituals along with earsplitting rifle shots and rolling black smoke punctuated with shooting flames created one of the most surreal religious scenes imaginable. By contrast, Catholic churches elsewhere in the world offered serene services accentuated and exalted by angelic choirs. Not here. In the midst of Taos Pueblo, a frail statue of the Virgin Mary under a white shroud bobbed above the throng, while clouds of swirling charcoal smoke and rifle shots peppered the air. It looked like a grotesque comic opera, the perfect setting for the outburst of evil, or the triumph of virtue.

Nick had witnessed the procession twice in past years, but it was new to both Carmen and Abigail. Despite growing up in nearby Española, neither had attended this long-standing event. Family rituals had always come first, as they did for the majority of *norteños*. This year, all three had no family members nearby and Nick suggested they do something completely different. He had briefed them as they drove to Taos from El Rito, but nothing could really prepare Abby and Carmen for the drama that gripped the pueblo plaza with numerous blazing *luminarias*, and thick rolling smoke that engulfed the procession as it weaved through the village.

Nick, Carmen and Abby stood huddled, hands buried in jacket pockets, necks scrunched into jacket collars watching the crowd and the procession, which now was at the north end of the village, about eighty yards away. Smoke was not yet a problem for them. Carmen waved to several friends. Abby noticed several former clients in the crowd and walked over to wish them Merry Christmas. While they were talking, Abby saw a short, stout middle-aged man stop and talk briefly to Nick.

"Who was that man?" Abby asked Nick. "He doesn't look like a local."

"Oh, that's Silas Mendoza. Haven't seen him in a few years. He's a mover and shaker behind the scenes. I'm surprised you've never heard of him."

"I've heard of him," Abby said, "but never have seen him. But then you said he worked behind the scenes. *Oculto, que no?*"

Nick nodded while staring out at the spectacle. "I haven't seen him since he tried to buy several ranches in El Rito for one of his dubious developments." Abby shot a quick look at Nick, surprised by his candor given the sanctity of the evening.

As the Virgin moved toward the center of the plaza, the main *luminaria* was lit from the top, and people standing on the high river bank moved toward the warmth of the fire. Abigail found herself separated from Carmen and Nick, carried along by the energized yet respectful crowd. As the procession continued along, Abby noticed a priest or monk in a Franciscan-style cloak move quickly behind a tall well-dressed man who Abby thought she recognized. As another volley of rifle shots shook the air, Abby heard two pistol shots.

Suddenly ahead of Abby a woman screamed. The crowd parted as the well-dressed man crumpled to the ground. Quickly people rushed toward the man who was gasping and bleeding from the mouth. More screams and yelling, but the procession moved on toward the chapel. Tribal police appeared from nowhere and surrounded the wounded man. Someone yelled something about blood. Abby saw Nick and Carmen push through the crowd. Instinctively, Abby looked around and saw the monk disappearing toward the pueblo entrance.

Abby raced after the fleeing monk, fighting her way through people now rushing toward the scene with typical morbid curiosity, trying to find out what happened. For an instant she caught sight of the monk running along the main entrance road, then lost him in the jumble of parked vehicles. Abby continued a hundred yards more, and then stopped and looked back thinking she might have passed him. A dark SUV barreled out of a driveway twenty yards back and roared toward her. In the instant before diving out of the way, Abby saw that the driver wore a hood and dark glasses. Several people yelled at the vehicle to slow down, but in a cloud of swirling dust it was gone. Abby only got the three letters of the New Mexico license number . . . MLR.

Ten yards from where Abby, Nick and Carmen had been standing, a middle-aged man of medium build wearing an expensive fur-trimmed coat and a Russian-style fur hat calmly watched the proceedings. Despite the ban on photographs for this event, he had taken a number of shots with his phone camera, as had others in the crowd. However, this man's photos were only of the man who had been shot.

Braced by the cold air and her close call, Abby walked rapidly back to the plaza and found Nick and Carmen standing by the low adobe wall that surrounded San Geronimo. The statue of the Virgin Mary and the crucifix were safely back in the chapel and pueblo police had cordoned off the shooting scene. Sirens in the distance grew louder.

"Where did you go?" Nick and Carmen both asked anxiously, Carmen clutching Abby's arm.

"I think I saw who shot the man," Abby said trying to regain her breath. "You won't believe this, but it was a monk, or someone disguised as a monk." Abby stopped and breathed deeply. "I followed him out to the road, but he got away in an SUV. Bastard almost ran me over. Is the man alive?"

"We don't think so, but no one can get near him." Nick said, looking back toward the crowd. He walked over to a small group of people he recognized.

"What did you think you would do if you caught him?" Carmen asked Abby, standing tall with hands on her hips.

Abby shrugged. "I don't know. Come to think of it, it was kind of dumb since he had a gun and I didn't. Anyway, he got away and I never saw him. But I need to tell the police," Abby said craning her neck to see over the crowd.

Nick returned waving his hand. "Those folks I talked to said the man is Alfonso Salazar."

Both Carmen and Abby gasped, putting their hands over their mouths. "*Díos mío,*" Carmen said, eyes wide. She reached to grasp Abby's arm.

"I thought I recognized him, but wasn't sure," Abby said to Carmen. "This is huge."

Both the state police and the Taos municipal police arrived at the same time. After a flurry of intense discussion between tribal police and municipal and state authorities, the state police took charge of the crime scene and crowd control was handed over to the locals. Abby made her way through the crowd to one of the state police officers and handed him her card (**Abigail Romero: Research and Recovery**), while telling him she thought she had witnessed the shooting.

"Stay here," the young officer told Abby. "I'll get the sergeant," and he disappeared running.

Feeling a bit awkward, Abby stood amidst the milling crowd and smoke that still swirled overhead. A minute later a middle-aged uniformed officer appeared and introduced himself as Sergeant Duran. He asked Abby to come over to the cruiser where they could be away from the crowd.

As they walked he said, "I understand you witnessed the shooting."

"I think I did," Abby said. "I noticed a fellow dressed like a monk walk up behind the victim. When the procession guards fired a volley of shots I heard two small-caliber shots. The man fell and the monk disappeared. Was it Alfonso Salazar?"

"We're not releasing a name yet," the sergeant said quickly. "Please go on," Duran motioned to Abby with his hands, all business.

"I saw the monk moving fast toward the entrance of the plaza and followed. The crowd was thick and I couldn't gain on him. Just past the entrance, I lost him, turned around to see if by chance I had passed him, and was almost run over by a hooded man driving a dark SUV. I think he knew that I was following him."

"Any identifying characteristics, like build?"

Abby put up a hand to pause and think while she watched the ambulance arrive. She turned back to Sergeant Duran gesturing with both hands. "Medium build, looked like he was wearing running shoes, and the robe was the kind that Franciscans wear. There is one more thing. There was something different about his movement. I can't put my finger on it, but it was distinct."

"You mean like a limp?" Duran asked.

"No, not a limp." Abby moved her head and shoulders back and forth searching for the right words.

"Okay, thanks for your help," Duran said hurriedly. "I see your phone number is an Abiquiu exchange. What does this mean on your card, 'Research and Recovery'?"

"I'm an investigator. I find people and things. In a word I guess you could say I'm a hunter." Immediately, Abby wished she hadn't used the term hunter.

Duran looked puzzled. Abby thought that he probably wondered if she was a bounty hunter, which she detested.

"Do you plan on being home next week?" he asked.

Abby nodded yes.

"We'll be in touch. If you think of anything else, please call." Duran handed Abby his card.

The sergeant walked back to the crime scene and Abby found Nick and Carmen still standing near the chapel, both looking impatient.

"You find out any more?" Abby asked.

"Yes," Carmen said. "They put the guy in a body bag." Carmen rolled her eyes upward.

"And it was Alfonso Salazar," Nick said.

"Who would want to shoot Alfonzo?" Carmen said shaking clenched fists. "And Christmas Eve of all times."

Just as Nick was about to say something, a young woman rushed up to Abby. "Excuse me, but I'm from the Taos News," she said excitedly. "I saw you talking to a police officer. Do you know what happened? Did you see who shot the man?"

Abby shook her head and held her hands out to calm the reporter. "I saw someone leave the scene in a hurry, but I never got a good look. I'm afraid I can't tell you anything." Abby backed away.

"Can I have your name?"

"No, please, no names now. Give me your card, and if I remember anything I'll call you."

The young woman frowned, but pulled a card from her bag. "Okay, but please call," she said handing her card to Abby. The card read Mali Reznick, Reporter, Taos News.

Nick interrupted. "If you don't mind Miss., we are on our way to church," and he steered Abby and Carmen toward the parking lot.

People continued to mill around the plaza feeling unsettled by what they had witnessed. This was to be a night of religious drama. Instead, a drama of evil had tainted a temple of God. As they walked toward their truck, Nick suggested they still had time to take midnight mass in El Rito and have a light dinner at his house. Abby and Carmen nodded in silence as they trudged heads down toward Nick's truck. The biting wind sharpened the tragedy of the evening and they all turned their shoulders in for protection.

Just after nine o'clock on Christmas eve, Lupe Garza parked the SUV near the spot where she found it and left the keys in the ignition. She had been surprised to find a vehicle so easy to steal, and on a quiet street. A short block away, she found the beat-up Nissan truck she had borrowed and drove south toward Santa Fe at an easy pace. She was hungry after her mission and stopped for takeout at a generic taco stand near one of the four casinos along the way. She also picked up a six-pack of Mexican beer for later, that is if she was fortunate enough to find a companion for the night. After a shower at the economy motel on Cerrillos Road in Santa Fe, she put on a faux biker outfit complete with a Brando-style motorcycle cap from the classic fifties film "The Wild One" and headed out to her favorite gay bar. From a distance she was a dead-ringer for Brando, only thinner and now with jewelry in her nose.

Alfonso Salazar had been only her second job of the year, but she now had enough money to spend the rest of the winter comfortably in Puerto Vallarta on Mexico's west coast. She'd check later to make sure the money had been deposited in her account in the Caymans and tomorrow she'd fly south. The only minor problem was putting the gun back into circulation with some unsuspecting punk in Santa Fe.

On Christmas day, with the temperature resisting double figures, Nick and Abby ate blue corn *huevos rancheros* for breakfast and exchanged gifts before Nick left for Albuquerque to spend the day with his son, daughter, their spouses and four grandchildren. Carmen drove to Pagosa Springs to visit a friend and ski at Wolf Creek. Abby's mother, Mary had taken a cruise with Abby's estranged brother Raoul, and would not be back in Española until after New Year's. Abigail returned to her home in Barranca, near Abiquiu, to spend a quiet day. She always saved the Christmas cards she had received to read on Christmas day, and she always called her grandmother, now in her mid-eighties, who lived in an intensive-care facility in Las Vegas, New Mexico. Abby thought about driving over to see her, but snow was falling and she did not feel up to fighting weather on a long drive. After the call, which always left her feeling a little guilty, she and Duster, her Maine coon cat of four years, watched snowflakes float past the windows while holiday music played in the background.

2

When the day after Christmas falls on a Saturday in Santa Fe, only commercial businesses offering door-buster prices bother to open, and Abby was not one of those hungry shoppers. She opted to stay home and give Duster some company. It was one of those slate-gray days of flat light that offers no incentive to venture outdoors unless you're a stalwart fly-fisher looking for absolute quiet and willing to freeze while getting little or no action from sluggish trout. Abby decided to read, and settled in with the art book on medieval Spanish painters Nick had given her for Christmas. By mid afternoon she was restless, having fallen asleep twice while reading, and decided to go for a run along the back road that paralleled Rio Chama.

Abby jogged along the dirt road with the confidence of a woman eager to get on with life. It had been six months since Myron Galton, aka Myron Galt, met his doom in the raging arroyo that crossed this back road, following his attempt on Abby's life. Except for a recurring dream of a hooded figure with a grinning skull, Abby had worked through most of the emotional trauma of Galton's revenge over losing his brother Martin to a federal prison, thanks to Abigail's testimony. Martin — the love of her life three years ago — was mainly a memory of bad judgment.

Abby jogged easily along the rutted road that flanked the south side of Rio Chama below the large earthen dam built years ago to store water for the city of Albuquerque. The entire community of Abiquiu now wished it hadn't been so generous with its water rights. Chamisa bushes in their sorry-looking winter state lined the road along with scrub juniper and the noxious salt cedar that had done its job of flood control far too well. Despite the coarse appearance of the road, the towering cliffs on both sides of the river near the dam gave the gorge a look of majesty that Georgia O'Keeffe captured in several memorable paintings.

After thirty minutes, Abby was past the point of being warm and unzipped her heavy sweat suit jacket part way to let steam escape into fifteen-degree air. She kept moving and turned her mind to the murder she had witnessed less than forty-eight hours earlier. Why, she wondered, was a popular politician with a promising future shot down in a crowd observing a long-standing religious ritual in a peaceful native pueblo? Why him at all? Why there and then? And who carried out the deed? Was it really a monk? And what was it about the way the fellow moved? When she reached the base of the high dam she chuckled, as sure enough, there was a solitary figure casting a fly rod on this cold gray day, no doubt enjoying him or herself immensely. Abby waved, turned and headed back for the warmth of the wood stove and kiva fireplace in her adobe home, and some lap time with her twenty-pound affectionate cat.

On her return trip, a young couple jogged toward Abby, waved a smile, wished her a happy new year and continued on. Suddenly, Abby stopped, turned, and watched the couple jog toward the dam. The movement of the woman captured her attention — and then it hit her. A woman's running movement is not quite the same as a man's. The person in the monk's robe was a woman. Abby was sure of it. She watched the couple grow smaller before resuming her way back home.

Abby turned on the small television, which sat on the kitchen counter, just as the evening news started. Abby sat on the edge of her favorite wooden chair. The comely anchorwoman promised late-breaking news on the death of state legislator Alfonso Salazar. Minutes later, film showed the SUV that had tried to run Abby down, parked somewhere in Alcalde, a small agricultural town north of Española. A very young woman reporter, standing on a deserted street flanked by old adobe houses and a few curious children and adults, said that a partially burned monk's robe was found in a trash barrel near the vehicle, which had been reported stolen by its owner who lived in Alcalde. Apparently the assailant had stashed a car near the spot where the SUV was found. Police were questioning neighbors, but no one saw anything suspicious. Film showed neighbors talking to police while the reporter's staccato voice rattled on trying to make it sound urgent.

Abby stared blankly at the television while the story segued into a commercial. It was one of those moments all people have for no apparent reason, but this one felt like something had come up from her blind side and tweaked her lightly. As a hunter, Abby was ultra sensitive to slight changes in the environment, and she recognized that something in her house was different. She knew she didn't need to understand it yet; simply recognize it and file it away for later, which she did just before Duster snapped her back to reality with the trilling sound all Maine coons make to announce their arrival. In one graceful leap Duster was on the kitchen table looking quizzically at Abby.

Abby reached for the phone parked on the end of the kitchen table, found the card for Sergeant Duran and entered the number. She didn't expect to reach him on a Saturday night but left a message that the assailant might be a woman. She popped a frozen casserole in the microwave oven to thaw and sat down to construct a file on the Salazar case. Abby wasn't sure what piqued her interest in the case, but her curiosity was up, and with nothing on the front burner, Salazar would fuel her attention for a few days.

An hour later the phone rang; it was Bob Janovich. The holiday period was the doldrums for scientific work at Ghost Ranch where Bob worked, and he wanted some company. Abby and Bob's friendship went back six years. Bob played a large role in helping Abby heal after the failed relationship with Martin and his criminal trial, and Abby had worked with Bob on the Folsom artifacts theft last summer. There had always been the possibility of romance between them, but both had been overly cautious and no spark was struck.

"Abigail," Bob said, a bit loudly, "would you be interested in having dinner at the inn tomorrow night, purely social, no agenda?"

"Well, yes, but let me check the calendar to be sure." Abby glanced quickly at the calendar knowing it was blank, but force of habit and a woman's prerogative led to that response. "I'm free. What time shall we meet?"

"I'll pick you up at six," he said with pleasant authority.

Hmm, Abby thought, this is sounding like a date. "Okay." Abby let that word rise in anticipation to show she understood the implication. "I'm looking forward to it. See you at six."

"Good, six it is. I think I can find your place."

"Barranca Road, up the hill and I'm on the right just before the road makes a sharp left. Look for my 4Runner in the driveway."

"Right, 'bye"

Abby put the phone down grinning and did a little pirouette. She hadn't had a real date since Clay Crawford wined and dined her following the showdown with Galton last summer. Clay was a fly-by-night kind of guy who was great fun, but that's as far as it went. Bob, on the other hand, was the kind of guy mothers urge their daughters to marry: solid, stable, employed with a future, handsome enough, pleasant to be around and occasionally funny. In short, Bob had no negatives, at least from a mother's point of view. But he wasn't the kind of man that women follow with their eyes, and ask "Who is that?" Still, after several extended work sessions with Bob at Ghost Ranch, Abby felt very comfortable with him and this was an opportunity to get to know a different side of the dusty scientist.

Abby started to think of what she'd wear. The Abiquiu Inn was very casual, but she was ready for a "dress-up" evening. Her reverie was interrupted by the phone. Caller ID said Duran.

"Ms. Romero, I got your message. Why do you think the perp in the Salazar case was a woman?" Duran wasted no time getting to the point.

"Remember I said there was something about the way the person in the monk's robe moved?"

"Ah — yes. Go on."

"Well, it occurred to me that this person moved like a woman. She's possibly under forty and probably in good shape."

Duran paused for a moment. "I think I understand, but you didn't actually see this person's face, correct?"

"Well, yes, I mean no, but my intuition . . ." Immediately, Abby realized it was a mistake to use the word intuition. "I mean I observed a woman jogging today and the movements were the same as the assailant's." Abby realized she was just making it worse.

"All right. I'll note in my report what you said. I appreciate your call. If you think of anything more, please get in touch. Thanks again." Duran hung up.

Abby sighed. No way did Duran take her seriously. So much for that, she thought. Abby sat down at the kitchen table, and while eating, made some notes and labeled a few file folders under the heading Salazar. Duster had moved from the table to the floor, and with Abby busy eating and working he decided it was time to join in. He hopped up on a chair, and beamed his big green-gold eyes at her.

"Okay, buster, you deserve some me-time," Abby said. "Let's get that fire built and put on some music."

Abby spent Sunday doing odd jobs in and around the house while Duster romped back and forth. The snow was gone, but the gray weather and cold temperatures persisted, which meant she needed more wood for the stove. Adobe structures work well in sunny winter conditions, but not after several cloudy cold winter days in succession. Abby called one of her wood suppliers for a cord of piñon that would last through the spring winds. Geese honked up and down river, and Abby looked for eagles that came this time of year to fish in the low water. Nick and Carmen would not be back until tomorrow night, so the phone would be quiet.

At four-thirty, Abby showered and dressed in a Santa Fe-style black skirt with black boots and a colorful blouse she had bought in Barcelona last summer. Turquoise hoop earrings set off her cobalt eyes. In a five-foot-five frame, with straight ebony hair, light brown skin and strong facial features, Abby was accustomed to being described as a handsome mid-thirties woman; not pretty and not gorgeous, but definitely not plain. Duster took this all in with interest, and was satisfied when his bowls were properly filled.

Abby was looking out the bedroom window when Bob's blue Prius pulled into the driveway five minutes early. Like most northern New Mexican males, he had a truck for work, but unlike his peers he drove a hybrid whenever a truck wasn't needed. He climbed out of the car with an athletic grace that Abby had not previously noticed. Suddenly, six years of familiarity with the archeologist from Ghost Ranch were ancient history. He was new and intriguing in his six-foot slim frame, sheepskin jacket, gray Stetson, and polished brown dress boots. Duster was at the door to inspect the stranger and pass judgment, which was favorable. Bob's normally tossed salt-and-pepper hair was neatly combed and he wore a tan dress western outfit that Abby had never seen. He kissed her lightly on the cheek and Abby felt a warm glow run down her spine. He held the car door for her as she climbed in and adjusted herself feeling a bit awkward. They were off, with Duster watching from the kitchen window.

The inn was fully booked for the holidays, and the cozy restaurant was nearly full. Abiquiu Inn always looked festive during the holidays, with *farolitos* lining the outside earthen-colored walls, crystal lights strung from trees, and various folk art decorations placed strategically throughout the classic adobe interior. Bob had wisely made a reservation and a candle-lit window table was ready when they walked into the small lobby.

They draped their coats on the back of their chairs and Bob put his Stetson on a hat rack in the corner. The inn had recently transferred ownership, and thanks to a new law it now had a wine and beer license. Bob picked out a reasonably priced wine from locally grown grapes, and they chatted easily while looking over the menu and glancing around the room. They ordered predictably with blackened salmon for Abby, sirloin tip for Bob and a shared a corn cake appetizer with red chile-sauce.

Abby looked at Bob inviting him to start the conversation. He complied without missing a beat. "I haven't had the chance to find out how your trip to Spain went." Following her return in August, Bob had briefed Abby about the resolution of the theft of the artifacts, but they had never taken the opportunity to sit down and talk.

Abby leaned back, relaxed her shoulders and raised her chin. "As you might imagine, it was more than I expected. You know I went with my friend Carmen?"

"Yes, I heard."

"She was a perfect diversion after all that trauma with Myron Galton. I still can't get over the extent of his hate for me and his elaborate plan." Abby looked away briefly remembering the events. Her face reddened slightly as she looked back at Bob. "I mean, stealing those artifacts just to play me like a puppet. And then tossing me in the pit on the mesa to drown; a real madman!" Abby had balled up her hands and the muscles in her neck stood out. The waitress brought the appetizer and Bob made small talk about the origin of corn cakes to get Abby off the morbid subject.

"Well, I'm glad you had Carmen with you. She must have been a hoot at times."

Abby felt a little embarrassed by her tirade and put her hands up, palms out. "Yes, absolutely. I couldn't ask for a better friend; and a great traveling companion. Unless, of course, it was a knowledgeable archeologist who could talk about Spain during the period of the Moors." Abby tilted her head and winked. "But we talked, laughed, ate constantly and even danced a little. I found where my father's ancestors lived. Frankly, I don't know why they left, other than politics. Catalonia is beautiful country. And the people," Abby raised her hands in a gesture of amazement, "really friendly."

"Were your father's ancestors part of the early migration to New Mexico?" Bob asked.

Abby knew that Bob was not simply trying to make small talk. With his scientific mind, he was genuinely curious.

"No, they came in the mid 1800s. They were part of the early settlements around Peñasco. My father was raised on a small farm and sheep ranch. My brother and I used to spend part of the summer up there. My grandparents were simple folks and very traditional. I learned to cook from *mi abuela*, but my grandfather thought that little girls should be little girls. Me, I wanted to ride horses, and fish and hunt. He tried to shift those activities to my brother, but it didn't take, and *abuelo* never understood it. He's gone now, and so is the farm." Abby looked out the window with damp eyes and changed the subject. "Have you ever been to Spain?"

"No, but I'd like to. I passed up a chance to do some field work near Toledo after graduate school, and I regret it." Bob's eyes widened and he raised an eyebrow. "Although had I gone, I might never have come to Ghost Ranch or met you."

Abby reciprocated the smile, and asked, "So how is the new climate-research program coming?"

Bob adjusted himself in the chair. "Well, it's developing, but much slower than I'd like. Several large grants are in limbo due to a federal budget crunch. But the ranch is supportive. The best thing is that all of the Folsom material was authenticated, and we do have a grant for more excavation. In fact, Caitlin O'Brien has already asked to work this summer." Bob paused, waiting for a reaction from Abby, as Abby had severe doubts about the young graduate student after the Folsom theft.

"I'll admit I was wrong about her. She's crafty, but I no longer doubt that her intentions about the artifacts were honorable." Abby scratched her head, looked away and drummed her index finger on the table until Bob came to the rescue.

"I know you worked for NASA Ames for two years, but you never talked about it when you were at the Ghost Ranch after the trial."

"It was an interesting experience. They had a half-dozen anthropologists in that unit, and two of them were PhDs with lots of ideas. NASA gave them free rein to design models to examine living in isolation. For reasons I can't explain, I volunteered to spend several months as a guinea pig in one of those closed environments." Abby took in a breath, looked at the ceiling and then back at Bob. "Thinking back on it, I feel it may have retarded my social development."

"How so?" Bob asked.

"Well, at a time in my life when I could have been exploring relationships away from my family's eyes, I was stuck in a bell-jar. I think it was one of the reasons that I fell so hard for Martin. I was ready for some action. But, I don't want to rehash all of that." Abby took a fork-full of salmon.

"So then you came back here to settle the family ranch affairs," Bob said, and immediately wished that he hadn't mentioned the loss of the Romero ranch. A large man accidentally bumped Bob's chair, spilling Bob's wine as he was about to drink, which erased the awkwardness of Bob's comment.

"That's another bad memory," Abby said, as Bob wiped up the spill. "We took care of Raoul's problems and he hasn't spoken ten words to me since." Abby sighed, "Enough about me, Robert. As much time as we have spent together I've always been too self-centered to find out who Bob Janovich is besides a dedicated scientist. So tell me, *señor*, what's the other side of that 'ah shucks ma'am' personality?"

Bob laughed. "Well *señorita*, there are a few things you probably don't know, although with your curious mind you may know everything."

"Try me," Abby said opening her hands and leaning towards him.

"I'm a train buff, especially steam. I'm not a foamer or even a yahoo."

"Wait," Abby said. "A foamer . . . You mean like foaming at the mouth? And yahoo? What's that?"

Bob chuckled in a deep pleasing tone. "A foamer is some-one so involved that they know how many rivets there are on the boiler plate of a K-37 locomotive. A yahoo is not as bad, but they can't have enough pictures of trains at particular cross-ings, tunnels and so on."

Abby made low train sounds blowing through her hand and rolled her eyes.

"Okay, okay," Bob said, "but you asked for this. We'll take a moonlight ride next summer on the Cumbres &Toltec. Have you ridden the train?" He pushed his empty plate to the side of the table.

"Once, several years ago. It was cold," Abby replied, faking a shiver.

"I can fix that," Bob said in a low tone. "I also play guitar and like easy jazz."

"You have me there; I like both," Abby said. "I seem to remember that you dated a woman who managed the inn a few years back." As soon as Abby said it she remembered the woman had died. "Oh gosh, I'm sorry. As you can see I'm a real dunce sometimes; mouth engages before brain's in gear."

"Not a problem," Bob said, reaching across to touch Abby's arm. "Diana Garcia. Lived in Cañones. We were friends and really just getting to know each other when she died . . . very suddenly. Tragic." Bob looked out the window and then back at Abby. "It was never going anywhere serious. She was older and had kids to look after. Each of us was a short-term diversion for the other. So how about some dessert?" Bob asked.

"Your place or mine?" Abby quipped instantly, surprising herself.

Bob hesitated, unaccustomed to that kind of invitation. "Well, since you asked, yours, he said pushing his chair back.

Over a frozen dessert and decaf coffee at the kitchen table they talked for another hour about each other's interests, each not wanting the evening to end — neither able to muster a move. Finally, Duster intervened by jumping on the table. Bob took the cue, got up laughing nervously, and slowly pulled on his coat while making polite end-of-the-evening remarks. He made an awkward move to kiss Abby goodnight, which she smoothed over with a hug and, in a promising voice said, "Let's do this again soon stranger."

Abby congratulated herself on not mentioning the shooting on Christmas eve, as it surely would have changed the tenor of the evening. Carmen had told her months ago to get back into dating, and damned if she wasn't enjoying the hidden agenda of it all. Abby and Duster looked out the kitchen window and watched Bob's taillights disappear down the road. Abby added several logs to the stove, snatched up Duster and headed for the bedroom.

In the early morning, Abby woke with a start, covered in sweat. The clock said four-ten and Duster was sitting wide-awake by her pillow. She let out a sigh and rubbed his head.

"That dream again, buster boy."

He edged closer and rubbed against her head. The reoccurring dream had gotten to the point that Abby thought she might need some professional help. At least a dozen times since the gun battle with Myron Galt in June of last summer, Abby dreamt of being in a showdown with a grinning skull-faced figure in a cloak daring Abby to shoot. Just as she was ready to pull the trigger on her pistol, she'd wake up in a sweat. Trying to fall back asleep was usually pointless after the dream, and this morning was no different.

3

In the pre-dawn darkness, Abby unrolled her yoga mat, put a soft music CD in the Bose and proceeded to lift her spirits despite the continuing dismal weather. Her usual morning routine consisted of warm-up stretches followed by three or four moving asanas, several balance positions and twists, and a few floor positions. She ended with a ten-minute rest or savasana, which was always energizing. Once a week she took a more demanding formal class that was good for making corrections in positions and learning something new. Like many practitioners of yoga, Abby was not interested in its underlying philosophy, but she considered the thirty-minute daily workout essential. She wished she could get Carmen and Nick to try it.

Since it was an extended holiday, and nothing but the big box stores were open, Abby reluctantly faced a few cleaning jobs around the house that she'd put off too long. She wished she had taken Carmen up on the skiing invitation, but with Nick in Albuquerque no one else was around to take care of Duster. Two days alone in the house was max for the cat. Thoughts of the NASA isolation experiment flooded back, and Abby admonished herself. Suck it up, she thought, you're not in a bell-jar now.

As Abby stared out the kitchen window at the gray color of nearly everything in sight, the image of the woman fleeing in the monk's robe came back. It haunted her like the ghost of some distant memory long forgotten or long repressed. Something about the fact that the killer was a woman was eating at her, something deep, personal and dark, something related to the damned dream.

Abby took out a yellow note pad from the cabinet, sat down at the kitchen table and began to scribble questions as fast as she could think. Why a woman? Why the monk's robe? Is she kin to the victim? Was this revenge? Was this a political assassination? Was it done for money? Is she local or from who-knows-where? Where is she now? Has she killed before? After a few more questions, Abby decided she needed some organization and wrote out several motive categories: love triangle/revenge, politics/business/criminal activity, and the question of gender. After more than an hour of writing she realized something sinister was pushing her and she stopped, stood up and walked outside for fresh air.

A light breeze rustled the few remaining dead leaves on the trees near the house. It reminded Abby of fall hunting with her father and Nick. Her father, now deceased eleven years, had told Abby she was a natural at hunting and had nicknamed her *cazadora,* the hunter. Perhaps that's what the killer was — a hunter. Perhaps, Abby thought slowly, she and the killer were alike in some fundamental way. On one hand, their similarities might make it easier to track her down. On the other, perhaps Abby would learn something about herself, something fundamental and perhaps unsettling. She wondered whether this was a variation on the Stockholm syndrome, taking on the characteristics of the adversary.

"First things first," Abby said out loud. Since she had no contract work at the moment, there was time for basic research and decided to start with the victim. Perhaps the Santa Fe and Albuquerque newspapers had some biographical information on Salazar. Both newspapers were now on-line, but the archives went back only one year. Tomorrow she'd need to visit the newspaper morgue at the central library in Santa Fe.

Abby began with the online Sunday edition of the Santa Fe paper. The story on Salazar had moved to inside pages, but it included of a half-page story on the life of the would-be political star. It covered the usual stuff about his family background complete with photos of his father, mother and siblings, action shots of him on the basketball court in high school, a description of academic honors at Highlands University, his meteoric rise in politics (without mentioning the political machine that produced his success) and his promising future; perhaps even presidential material. There were a few photos of him with women, but no mention of why he was still single at age forty.

Abby printed all the important material and placed it in a file. Then she wrote a few notes on topics to investigate, such as the women in his life, political connections and where he made his money. She'd tackle these ideas tomorrow. The Albuquerque paper ran much the same information, but mentioned several women in his life that lent an air of mystery and glamour. As Abby glanced at the photos of Alfonso with different women, one jumped out at her. She didn't look like the socialite type or even a trophy date. The woman's eyes were riveting, and Abby had the feeling she was looking at herself. She printed the photo as best she could and made a separate file labeled Mystery Woman. Tomorrow she'd combine the trip to the Santa Fe library with the biweekly grocery run.

Tuesday morning dawned crystal clear and cold, and after her morning yoga routine, yogurt and coffee, Abby was on the road in her '97 4Runner just shy of eight o'clock. The trip to Santa Fe took an hour, give or take three or four minutes, and Abby pulled into the nearly empty parking lot just before the library doors opened. This time of year with schools closed, Abby felt like she had a private research facility. Her boots echoed through the halls as she made her way to the newspaper archives. After an hour of tracing Alfonso's life in print, she felt she was looking at something scripted by a political boss or a grand paternal architect like Joe Kennedy. Alfonso was almost unreal: a cardboard puppet with pasted smile moving through one-dimensional cardboard scenery with Barbie-doll extras;

lots of fluff and glamour but little substance, at least none that came through the text.

Abby sat back and stared at the old tiled ceiling feeling she had been whitewashed. She knew that politics in northern New Mexico were largely a crudely orchestrated charade. Most people didn't care as long as their life and families were not threatened and jobs were handed out in a fairly equitable manner. Competence for jobs was seldom the issue simply because skills were not the issue. Alfonso was different: he had charisma, good looks and seemed more intelligent than most other politicians, probably because of the charisma. He definitely was larger than life, destined to become something big. But the stories lacked substance and depth, again probably the result of his charisma. Abby thought she wasn't learning much, or was she?

Abby quickly went back through all the stories on Salazar and discovered that over a period of ten years most of the stories in the Santa Fe paper had been written by one individual, Ramon Martinez. The name did not ring a bell as regular staff. Sure enough, he was not listed as a staff reporter or columnist. Before leaving the library, Abby called the newspaper office on her cell phone and learned that Ramon Martinez was a contract stringer and worked only sporadically. When she asked for a phone number they would give her only an email address. The library had Wi-Fi, so she emailed Mr. Martinez and asked for an interview under the guise that she was researching rising politicians for an out-of-state magazine. It was a long shot. Abby packed up and drove to her favorite stores for groceries and wine. She bought a salmon steak for dinner and left a message for Carmen to see if she was up for some company.

Driving home it occurred to Abby that Ramon Martinez just might be in one of the area phone books. Very few people in northern New Mexico bother with unlisted phone numbers, so it was just a matter of plodding through more than fifty numbers under R. Martinez in the various towns. As she passed the mortuary in Española she realized that Salazar's funeral had totally slipped her mind. More than likely it would have been held this morning at St Francis Cathedral in Santa Fe to accommodate the enormous crowd. Surely television news would cover it, and she had plenty of time to get home.

Duster greeted Abby with a tail brush as she came through the door, and she immediately turned on the television and filled his bowls. She pressed the record button for the six o'clock news and went about carrying in groceries and getting the salmon ready for the oven. Among the phone messages was one from Carmen.

"Hey, I'd love to come to dinner, but can't tonight as I'm getting back too late. How about tomorrow, or better yet, New Year's eve? I'm not up for partying this year, and if you're not either we could watch the ball drop on TV together. Call me. Hope you're enjoying the solitude. Skiing was a blast."

Abby made a note to call her about dinner. She popped the marinated salmon in the oven, set the timer for twenty minutes, made a small salad, opened a bottle of Sauvignon Blanc and sat down to watch the news. The slow holiday news period pushed the Salazar funeral to the lead story and gave it extra time. It began with a shot of people filing into St. Francis Cathedral, followed by an interior shot of the casket covered in flowers in front of the altar and a panorama of the overflow crowd. As the reporter described the scene and gave appropriate remarks about the deceased, b-roll film panned across the elegant architecture of the cathedral before zooming in on prominent politicians, celebrities and family. There were a few shots of the service, segments of eulogies, and guests leaving the church. Abby identified three of the mourners as persons of interest for her research.

First was Darien Roberts, the well-known gallery owner and developer of upscale resort properties. The camera showed Roberts getting into a BMW sports coupe with a well-dressed woman whom Abby assumed was his wife. Next, the camera and commentator identified the solitary, stocky figure of Alberto Ramirez, the most powerful political boss in northern New Mexico. It was common knowledge that Ramirez was the architect of Salazar's rise to prominence. In the crowd Abby recognized Silas Mendoza, who she remembered was at Taos Pueblo the night of the shooting. The narrator didn't mention his name, but Abby thought he made a gesture of some kind toward Ramirez. The mystery woman in the newspaper photo Abby had found at the library was nowhere in sight. To be certain, Abby watched the entire story again.

Abby found the roll of freezer paper she had stashed in the small pantry and set it on the kitchen table. On the yellow pad she made several preliminary sketches. She settled on two charts, one a geographic map of relevant activity, and the other intersections of principal characters, with Salazar at the center. She tacked them up next to the fridge. After printing all the names and places she had so far, she color-coded the information with push-tacks. Abby wasn't sure how she would use the charts, but they gave her visual data that appealed to her right-brained thought process. She had almost forgotten about Ramon Martinez and got out the phone book and made a list of names to call tomorrow.

As usual, Duster was asleep in front of the fireplace, which needed more wood. An hour later, looking for relief from the heat, Duster jumped up on his favorite chair at the kitchen table, looked over the mess of materials, and cocked his head toward Abby with big quizzical eyes. Abby started to laugh.

"Okay, buster Duster, I guess it's time for some play." She took the feathered stick off the top of the fridge and spent the next fifteen minutes tantalizing Duster into doing flips and twists. By nine-thirty both were zonked. Abby banked the stove and fireplace, turned out the lights and crawled under the large yellow comforter on her double bed. A light breeze rustled the wind chimes on the portal as she drifted off.

Wednesday morning came gray again, but the needle on the thermometer flirted with thirty. After a yoga routine, oatmeal, toast and coffee, Abby set to work on finding Ramon Martinez. After an hour and a half of calling numbers for the name R. Martinez, she found the right man in Truchas, a small mountain town forty minutes east of Española. After a brief introduction she wasted no time getting to the point.

"Mr. Martinez, I sent you an email about an interview on Alfonso Salazar and rising political stars. Could you spare me some time for a face-to-face conversation? I'm not working for anyone and have nothing in particular in mind other than as an investigator."

"Ms. Romero, I haven't had any contact with Salazar for a year, and while I hesitate to admit this, I got most of my information second hand."

Abby quickly interjected, "I was only ten feet away from him when he was shot, and I think the assailant was a woman, although the police don't think so." Abby paused. "Everything you'd tell me would be off the record. I think you might have information or insights about Salazar that would help me find his killer. We could meet at a neutral place of your choice, or I could come to Truchas."

"Off the record, huh. Remember, I'm a reporter and I know how slippery that phrase is."

Abby waited. She could sense he was vacillating.

"Okay. Come to my place tomorrow at ten. I assume you know Truchas. I'm out on the main road east of town, number 317 on a post on your right side, small adobe with a large yellow dog near the portal. My old green pickup will be in the driveway. Don't worry about the road, it's always bad. Please don't bring a recorder."

"Thanks Mr. Martinez, see you at ten. Do you like *bizcochitos?*"

"*Sí, me gustan,*" he said with a laugh.

Abby smiled. "*Bueno* bye *señor.*"

She jotted down a few questions to ask Martinez she hoped would get at Salazar's private life. She knew it would be tricky, but her interview skills were good. Show a real interest in the individual, smile and look the person in the eyes, pause at the right time, provide some leads, come back to important points when the subject was on a roll and so on. Abby understood she also had just the right amount of charisma to be fascinating to men without being threatening. She looked forward to meeting Ramon Martinez.

The phone jolted Abby out of her thoughts. Caller ID displayed D. Roberts.

"Hello, this is Abigail," she said in her business voice.

"Ms. Romero, my name is Darien Roberts. I'm a businessman and art dealer in Santa Fe."

"Yes, Mr. Roberts, I know who you are." Abby waited.

"You have a reputation of being a very successful investigator, and I'd like to hire you to find something taken from me recently. Are you available?" Roberts sounded serious, unhurried.

Abby listened.

"Would you consider coming to Santa Fe tomorrow morning? I know it's New Year's eve, but it won't take long."

"I have a previous appointment in the morning that might take several hours," Abby said.

"Okay, how about a late lunch at Santacafé as my guest?"

"Would one-thirty work for you, Mr. Roberts?"

"Yes, that would be fine. I'll have a carnation in my lapel," Roberts added.

Abby stifled a laugh. "Mr. Roberts, I'd know you anywhere. You were on the news last night at the Salazar funeral." Abby was curious how he would respond to that statement.

"Oh yes," Roberts said evenly. "Alfonso was a good friend of mine, tragic thing his death, struck down in the prime of life, and who knows why, terrible thing. I hope justice is done soon. Well, I look forward to meeting you. Till tomorrow then."

Abby put the phone down and stared out the window. Never assume things are as they seem, she thought. Her mind turned to the mystery woman, but was interrupted by the phone again. It was Nick Trujillo.

"*Nicolás*, how nice to hear your voice. How was the weekend with all the kids?"

"It was just right. No fights. We went to museums, did some small hikes, grilled steaks in the dark, and everyone wished you a happy new year and lots of hugs."

Abby smiled to herself. Nick's family was her surrogate extended family and she enjoyed the entire bunch.

"Were you able to get the Salazar affair out of your mind and enjoy the quiet?" Nick knew that Abby would not have been able to resist digging into the murder, but he teased her anyway.

"Oh sure, *amigo*, I just watched soaps and ate bonbons the whole time. Gained five pounds and look like a blimp. Who's Salazar, anyway?" Abby smiled over the phone.

"Okay, fair enough. Have your fun with an old man."

Nick was in his mid-sixties but didn't look or act like it, and Abby appreciated that he was her protector as well as a close friend.

"Listen," Abby paused a minute. "I've got an interview with a reporter tomorrow who wrote most of the copy on Salazar over the years. He lives in Truchas, name's Ramon Martinez. Can you give me any background on Salazar or Martinez?"

Nick was silent for a moment. "I don't know much about Martinez other than he supposedly owed Alberto Ramirez for fixing a problem in his past and repaid it by becoming Salazar's publicist of sorts. I would not bring this up in your interview. In fact, you don't want to get in Ramirez' headlights. A few people who did have disappeared, and I'm dead serious about that."

Abby made an appropriate noise to show she understood.

"As for Salazar, there are many stories and rumors, and probably all of them have some truth. One story you might want to keep in mind as you sift through this stuff is that Salazar had a connection with a powerful Mexican drug lord; one of those Guadalajara gangs or cartels supposedly. Apparently there was a woman involved, a real firebrand. I don't know details, but again, *amiga,* this stuff can get rough — *no?*"

"Nick," Abby interrupted. "Do you know this woman's name?"

"Let me think; I think it was Garcia, no, Garza."

Abby was silent.

"Did I press a button there?" Nick asked.

"No, never heard of her. It's just that I saw a photo of Salazar with a woman with piercing eyes, who might be this Garza woman."

"Abigail, be careful."

"Not to worry, *amigo.*"

"Yeah right. What are you doing for New Year's eve?" Nick asked.

"Carmen's coming over for a pajama party."

"Behave yourself and I'll check on you New Year's day."

"What are you doing, Nick?"

"I have an invitation from the Widow Montoya up the canyon, and don't say it."

"I won't expect a call. And . . ." Abby was laughing.

"Never mind, young lady."

They both said a quick smiling goodbye.

It was mid afternoon and Abby thought she ought to get something tangible done, but the phone rang again. "Jeez," Abby said to herself and then noticed it was Bob Janovich on caller ID.

"Bob, how's my favorite archeologist? Anything exciting going on at the ranch?"

"No, not since you were here last summer. I called to see if you are available for an evening of bringing in the New Year?"

"Well, I've made plans with Carmen for a quiet evening of girl talk and television. Sorry about that."

"Okay, what about a hike on New Year's day, weather permitting? Maybe Box Canyon or Kitchen Mesa, followed by my grandmother's goulash recipe?"

"Sounds wonderful. How about noon? I'll bring a bottle of red, and I love goulash."

"It's a date . . . uh, well . . . It's a plan," Bob responded with a laugh.

Abby smiled to herself, glad for a diversion from what she feared loomed on the horizon.

4

Just after dawn on Christmas day, Lupe Garza's companion left the spartan motel room on Cerrillos Road. There were no goodbye hugs, no exchange of money, no tomorrows, no last names. Both were in good spirits. Lupe took her time cleaning up and checked out of the motel by ten o'clock. At five-foot four with slim athletic build, high cheek-bones, shoulder-length black hair, and white gold studs in her nose and ears, she was accustomed to getting glances from both men and women. She had learned how to dress down to pass unnoticed or dress up to accentuate her finer attributes. Today she dressed to avoid undue attention: jeans, ankle boots, silver-gray blouse and denim jacket.

Lupe ate a large breakfast at the Spanish Pantry on Cerrillos Road and returned the borrowed vehicle to a parking lot near the plaza, where it would be picked up by pre-arrangement later in the day. From the parking lot she walked three blocks to an intersection where day workers and drug mules hung out, and traded the murder weapon to a young Hispanic male for drugs, which she dumped into a nearby trash barrel. Two blocks north, Lupe caught the noon shuttle to the Albuquerque airport.

By three o'clock Lupe was at gate three queued for an American Airlines flight to Puerto Vallarta through Phoenix. Nine hours later she rested comfortably in a rented condo several blocks off the southern stretch of a beach known as Playa de Los Muertos. As legend has it, local miners killed attacking pirates and stacked their bodies on the beach, or vice versa. Legends have a way of reaching extreme stretches of imagination, but tourists love them. Lupe enjoyed this section of PV as it was similar to the Castro district in San Francisco. Both were claimed by tourist brochures to be the number one gay destination in their respective countries.

Over the next few days, Lupe cut her hair short, dyed it brown and replaced the gold nose stud with one of fake turquoise. By design it made her look cheap, unlikely to get a second look from anyone except possibly another woman on the prowl. Her aim was to enjoy at least a month of anonymity, but her old digs in Guadalajara were just two hundred kilometers to the east, and word could travel fast.

She had been in on the ground floor of the drug business eight years earlier, and had risen from a low street runner to one of the personal bodyguards of the drug *jefe* in the area. Her first kill had been in his defense. Her first contract had been in revenge for his death. Now known as *vengadora* (the avenger), Lupe was well respected and appropriately feared for her excellent martial arts skills.

From a storage locker in Puerto Vallarta that she rented by the year and paid through Western Union, Lupe retrieved several weapons, clothing, a laptop and cash. Via the internet, she watched the media in New Mexico and took satisfaction in what she assumed was a clean getaway. She smiled in reaction to the perplexed responses of police to the lack of progress in finding Salazar's killer. But, as one detective put it, the fact that there were no clues suggested that it was an assassination. The word alone sent chills through locals in northern New Mexico. Families in the rural confines of a highly traditional culture eventually take revenge in their own way and all in good time. Assassination is an outsider term and didn't fit their framework for how disputes are settled.

As Lupe thought about the murder of Salazar being identified as an assassination, she became concerned that a trail leading to her could be found by someone more curious and resourceful than Santa Fe detectives who were jaded by the preponderance of murders committed by family circle or gang members. These were slam-dunk investigations that rarely took more than a few days. Suddenly Lupe wondered about the woman who followed her out of the Taos Pueblo Plaza that night. Was she more than the average onlooker?

Lupe checked all the newspaper stories she could find about the murder, but there was no mention of a witness. Then she remembered that Taos had a newspaper. She found a web site and, sure enough, a short story written by Mali Reznick mentioned an unidentified woman who gave information to the police. Lupe toyed with several ideas on how to contact Ms. Reznick. She decided to email her through a Yahoo account, disguising herself as a novelist doing research on the increase of assassinations worldwide. Several days later she got a short reply that was no help other than to identify the on-site investigator as Sergeant Duran with the New Mexico State Police. Lupe would follow up on that later.

This was supposed to be a rest period for her, enjoying the warm days and cool nights, the vibrant beach culture this time of year, the influx of tourists with money to burn and fresh seafood. But it was tinged with a nagging feeling that something was amiss; the trail was not as clean as she thought it would be. Reluctantly, she sat down and put pencil to paper, just like Abigail Romero was doing unbeknownst to Lupe, a thousand miles to the North.

With Salazar at the center of a chart, Lupe drew lines through the names of any important person she had met since first meeting Salazar ten years earlier when she was a hostess at the Gila Vista resort in Silver City, New Mexico. Salazar had been a special assistant to Darien Roberts, an art dealer and developer. Initially, Lupe was attracted to Roberts whom she thought was a ticket to a better life, until she discovered that Roberts was married and she turned to the charms of Alfonso who was ready and willing. They kept the romance under wraps as best they could for more than a year, and Lupe was hopeful that something more permanent would develop. She was naive, and it cost her.

When Alberto Ramirez discovered the relationship he sent one of his minions to pay her off and warn her to disappear. Anger still rose when Lupe thought about how quickly Alfonso dumped her to save his political career. He never even tried to contact her to apologize. Lupe reluctantly went back to Mexico to her home in Guadalajara and fell in with an emerging drug cartel.

Lupe entered the third name, Silas Mendoza, to the chart. Her drug cartel had "loaned" Lupe to Mendoza in anticipation of establishing a place to launder money in a casino Mendoza was trying to develop near Chama, New Mexico. Lupe served as a decoration for his wheeling and dealing forays in polite company. Periodically, those forays involved Darien Roberts and Alfonso Salazar, both of whom were still attracted to Lupe, but kept their distance. Lupe enjoyed the sexual and political tension of three powerful men in her circle, plus one or more drug lords that did business with Mendoza and others in New Mexico. At the time it was exciting but relatively safe for Lupe, as the drug cartel had her back. Now it was an unstable powder keg. Too many chefs in the kitchen, she thought.

The word 'kitchen' triggered a hunger pang and Lupe went to the small refrigerator. Nothing looked appealing except the *camarones* she bought on the fishing wharf yesterday afternoon. Three limes, an onion and a pepper on the counter begged for use, and in ten minutes she had a shrimp cocktail marinating. By the time the corn tortillas were done the shrimp would be ready.

By American standards, the condo was small and offered only the bare essentials for comfort: three-quarter bed, small dresser and table in a tiny bedroom, a sage green couch and stuffed chair in the living room with a window that opened to the street, an acceptable television and a pint-sized kitchen with a small table and door to a back patio. Cheap wall hangings of beach scenes and posters of a dancer and a toreador added some color, but it was not a place to entertain or draw creative inspiration. Lupe often wished she had taken up writing and she certainly had enough experience in her young life to fuel writing projects that would carry her through the Mexican winter.

Lupe put the *camarone* cocktail and tortillas on a tray and carried them out to the patio. It was *siesta* time. The neighborhood was quiet. A few small birds darted in and out of the walled patio, and Lupe flicked a few tortilla crumbs on the broken tiles that passed for a patio floor. The cocktail had just the right amount of zing, and Lupe started to relax. Then she remembered the woman who chased her out of the pueblo on Christmas eve.

Lupe had never seen her before that night, at least not that she could remember. She thought back to the procession and from her observation it seemed that no one accompanied Salazar that night. Lupe saw both Mendoza and Roberts in the crowd before the procession began, but she had not noticed the woman. But perhaps the woman was an aide or companion that was meant to be hidden or at least unobtrusive. Hopefully, Sergeant Duran would have the information she needed.

Tuesday evening there was a knock at the door. A woman with strong, attractive features, older than Lupe by ten years, wondered if Lupe would like to take advantage of the beautiful night and go for a walk on the beach? Lupe looked the woman over, smiled and accepted. Lupe's luck with women had always been good and she felt a sixth sense about who was legitimate and who wasn't. A light ocean breeze greeted the two as they reached the beach. They strolled to the far north of the wide stretch of warm sand, weaving through tourists who gave them no special notice, stopping several times at vendor stands selling sweets and talking easily about nothing in particular. The next morning they had breakfast together on Lupe's patio and talked about the old days of Puerto Vallarta before the filming of "Night of the Iguana." Lupe felt normal for the first time since returning to Mexico.

Later that day while looking aimlessly at the slow-paced street scene in front of her condo, she reflected on when she had started to feel okay about being bisexual. It was after returning to Mexico following the abortive relationship with Alfonso. She was bitter, but discovered that being lesbian was the best way to insure her physical safety in the drug world. Being a bodyguard to the *jefe* and sexually gay was like being a eunuch in the Vatican. Besides, she thought, she enjoyed it both ways, and she could always have it either way for any period of time. There was a feeling of freedom to it all.

The weather was clear, warm and calm, and the distant low booming blast from a tourist liner beckoned Lupe for a walk on the beach. Tourists would be returning to the pampered service and overly comfortable accommodations of the ship. They were a source of comic relief for Lupe: men in small straw hats, wide white belts on beige Bermuda shorts with dark knee-length socks and white walking shoes; women in flowery sundresses, wide floppy hats, large sunglasses and big purses easy for thieves in crowded streets to pilfer. A slight over-caricature she knew, but close.

Lupe took off her sandals and enjoyed warm sand sifting between her toes. A red beach ball bounced toward her, pursued by a small Mexican boy. Instantly, Lupe looked beyond the boy for a sign of danger. A quick glance to her right away from the beach and a full turn to her back revealed nothing unusual. The boy grabbed the ball and turned back without saying anything to Lupe. She felt embarrassed and angry at the same time. This was what her job had done to her, she thought, and kicked at a broken seashell in the sand. Thoughts of Salazar came flooding back.

The Salazar contract was bittersweet in her mind: part justice and part revenge — not simply business. In fact, Lupe had never killed simply for business. She wondered if anyone actually killed simply for the money. Killing involves hunting for prey as well as becoming the prey who escapes. The hidden agenda for the killer, or perhaps even the primary motive, was the juice or elixir that the assassin thrived on. At least it was partially true for her. Still, she had only taken jobs that, according to her morality, seemed worthy, or justified. She wondered if that caveat would eventually be her downfall?

The days leading up to the New Year celebration were bustling for Puerto Vallarta. Tourists were everywhere, and a cruise ship was docked in the harbor every day. Lupe usually ventured out late in the evening when the beach scene was familiar. Fortunately, she had avoided getting into drugs, although she could spot the traffic easily and sometimes made small talk just to know what the current action was in order to assess the problems that could occur. So far, the scene was calm, which didn't mean the police were in control.

By New Year's Eve, Lupe had cabin fever and decided the streets were predictable enough to do some trolling for an evening of pleasure. She had dinner at a beachside café, but drank only one glass of wine. The evening was young and could be long. The beach was the usual mixture of locals on both sides of the law, tourists both naive and savvy, a few police and a large number of families looking to stake out a spot to watch the fireworks that would begin in an hour.

A slim attractive woman in her twenties with long hair approached Lupe from the street side of the beach holding a cigarette between her fingers and asked for a light. Clumsy beginning, Lupe thought. Lupe shook her head no, but smiled anyway and held her gaze longer than normal. The woman smiled back and proceeded to walk with Lupe. The air was still and heavy with humidity. Lupe found the young woman's cheap perfume annoying, but tolerated it for the sake of anticipated pleasure.

After a few minutes the young woman said she knew of a sweet shop that had really good chocolate and asked if they could go there together. Lupe nodded and protruded her lower lip, suggesting the woman lead on. They crossed the main boulevard, walked past several resorts with the aroma of grilled fish wafting over the streets. After another block, street lights disappeared, and they made their way through an alley toward a street with a few dimly lit shops. Lupe suddenly was on alert and wrapped her left hand around the Cobra 22 magnum in her jacket pocket. She was an accurate shot with either hand. Lupe knew she should turn around and go back to the crowded beach, but the adrenaline rose like a fountain and she could not resist.

The young woman was two steps in front of Lupe when an arm reached out of the darkness and pulled the girl away. Lupe heard a muffled scream before a man's bare arm clamped on her throat, but he was an instant too slow. In one swift motion, Lupe spun around to her left, ducked down and threw her right fist into his crotch. Simultaneously she pulled the pistol from her jacket pocket, thrust it into the assailant's ear and pulled the trigger. There was a crack like a light bulb exploding and the body went limp. Instantly, Lupe turned to see a knife flashing toward her. She kicked high and back to the second assailant's throat. The knife flew, and a young man barely out of his teens turned and ran. Lupe whirled to take on additional attackers, but she was alone on the street with nothing but darkness and sounds of voices and laughter in the distance.

Lupe was breathless and her heart raced. The young woman was gone. She gathered herself and walked rapidly but calmly back toward the beach. She doubled back once to see if she was being followed, before taking a roundabout way to her rented condo. She arrived just before the fireworks on the beach started. Standing against the inside wall next to the front door, Lupe realized that fireworks could mask a bomb thrown through her window. Quickly she went to the back door, opened it a crack, saw nothing and slipped into the shadows of the patio. She stayed there quietly until the fireworks stopped thirty minutes later.

Lupe spent the first five hours of the new year wide awake thinking about the attack. It could have been a mugging, but it appeared more like a hit. Several sources came to mind, but the most important thing now was to stay alive. If it was a hit, they probably knew where she lived. On the other hand, the young man who fled probably did not report back to his boss, fearing for his own life, and the dead body would not be missed for hours. Lupe figured she had a cushion of a half day. Her best chance of getting answers involved calling in a favor with an old friend, which she'd do in a few hours. Meanwhile, she needed to pack for a trip, but her muscles would not move, and sleep overtook her as she slid down into the green stuffed chair.

The first light of the day through the kitchen window hit Lupe's chair and she was awake in an instant, but groggy and sore. After a few stretches she put water on to boil for coffee and turned on the laptop. Her alias among friends was Wanda James, and she checked the yahoo email account for wandaj99@yahoo. There was one message sent two days ago: *New venture, window open. Meet in Albuquerque usual place afternoon of January 5. Will book air ticket if?* It was signed SM and the return address was familiar. Lupe stared at the message for a minute before the shrill whistle of the kettle jolted her from her thoughts.

After the first cup of coffee and a warmed tortilla, she emailed the one person who could tell her if she was in immediate danger. Surprisingly, since this was a holiday, this person sent a return message an hour later saying there had been an inquiry about her location, but it had come from New Mexico, not Guadalajara. It also said *no intense local heat.* Lupe wrote down what she knew to sort things out and keep her head clear. The attack could have been a simple mugging. The attackers were most likely from PV and not very experienced. This seemed to rule out a high-level cartel operation. Lupe decided it was a clumsy attempt at a robbery, perhaps aimed at someone the attackers thought was an easy mark. But was the message from Silas Mendoza simply a coincidence? Why would he offer her a business opportunity now after several years of silence? Perhaps there was something she failed to consider when she took the Salazar job. Regardless, it was best to take no chances.

Since her informant had replied so quickly, Lupe decided to ask for more information. She wrote back, *Identity of New Mexico inquiry?*

Within minutes she got a short but very meaningful reply. *SM. Via Z.*

Lupe's concerns were confirmed. Silas Mendoza had made contact with Z cartel, her rival gang. Z had arranged for the hit on her, and deliberately made it look clumsy to confuse her. The Z people were in no hurry to bring her down, but she was on their list, and Mendoza was involved. No honor among most thieves, Lupe thought.

Lupe decided to accept the offer of an air ticket and to do it immediately. The safe bet was to exit Puerto Vallarta for a few weeks. Lupe packed light, took cash, mailed two months' rent to the landlord, called a taxi and dropped her weapons in the storage locker on the way to the airport. At the airport she paid cash for a one-way ticket and texted Mendoza to wire the same amount to her bank. Two hours later she was on American 262 to Phoenix, hopeful she'd be able to return to Puerto Vallarta soon.

5

Abby spent the rest of Wednesday afternoon putzing around the house, toying with ideas about the Salazar murder and wondering why Darien Roberts wanted to see her. A dark feeling tugged at a far corner of her mind. The last time she had such a feeling and ignored it, she had paid dearly. Whatever was gnawing at her in that gray area needed daylight and a reality check from Nick, Carmen or both. Tomorrow night after seeing Martinez and Roberts would be the perfect time.

At five o'clock, with the dying sun setting behind snow clouds, she put a container of frozen green chile stew in the microwave oven to thaw, took care of Duster's needs and went for a jog down the Barranca road in fading light. Two miles from the house, while she ran at a comfortable pace, a tan Subaru that did not belong in the neighborhood passed her going in the opposite direction. A lone driver wearing a woman's hat stared straight ahead without acknowledging Abby, something locals never violated. A shiver ran down Abby's spine. She stopped, turned and ran hard back to her house.

She arrived at her kitchen door ten minutes later sweating and out of breath. Duster was at the kitchen window making noises. There were tire tracks in the gravel showing a vehicle had turned around, but no Subaru had come back her way. Despite near darkness, Abby decided to jog up the hill toward other houses, but found nothing. Standing near the top of the hill she saw headlights from a vehicle that could have been the Subaru heading back toward Abiquiu on the main road. She returned home slowly, cooling down from the run. Abby's antenna was up, but all was quiet, too quiet she thought. She stood by the kitchen door for a moment and looked into the darkness, feeling the hunter's perception, sharpening the senses, unhurried.

Abby stood in the shadow of the tall ponderosa surveying the valley below for the lone bull elk she knew controlled this territory. Every hunter has had the experience of sensing the quarry was nearby, but had blended into the background, cloaked like an optical illusion in tree branches, leaves, bushes and shadows. Abby's father had taught her to relax her mind and let the image emerge. Suddenly, as if by magic, the bull materialized clearly forty yards away in a thicket with nose held high, smelling the danger. Time and place froze until one of them made a mistake.

Abby knew it was time to talk, to a woman, the woman she trusted with the thoughts that were running through her mind. She dialed Carmen's number.

"Hey *hermana*, I was just thinking about you. When do we get together for dinner?" Carmen asked in her ever-present cheerful voice.

"Your idea about New Year's eve sounds great," Abby said.

"The usual time?" Carmen asked.

"*Sí señorita.*"

"I'll bring that fizzy stuff, and we'll get silly," Carmen replied.

They went on for another fifteen minutes talking about Carmen's skiing trip and a guy she met in the bar after the lift closed. Both Carmen and Abby understood that the aprés ski scene at any resort is one of the more sexually charged situations, given the rush of excitement flying down the slopes all day. As if on cue, they ended the conversation both knowing they'd pick up easily the next evening. At nine-thirty with the wind kicking up and the threat of snow, Abby headed for the bedroom with Duster two leaps ahead of her.

Thursday morning under clear skies, a moderate temperature, but a falling barometer, Abby left for Truchas with enough time to stop for *bizcohitos* in Española. The road to Truchas was a throwback to the days when ox carts, buckboards and mules labored slowly up and down narrow dirt roads carrying people and freight between mountain villages. The road ambled through twisting turns up the windward side of the Sangre de Cristo mountains that run a third of the length of New Mexico from the Colorado border past Santa Fe. Today the road is part of the scenic route called "the high road to Taos" and a favorite for observing fall color when the aspens change. The road passes through Chimayo, home to the Santuario Chapel, famous for the healing powers of earth beneath the chapel, and the end point for the Penitente-inspired pilgrimage every year on Good Friday. Just past Chimayo, the road rises steeply past Cordova toward Truchas, which is perched precariously on the edge of a ridge that continues on toward the 13,000-foot snowcapped Truchas peaks.

While still picturesque with narrow roads dissecting alpine pastures, Truchas is colorful mainly in the sense of what its well-worn and largely abandoned buildings suggest about its importance a hundred years ago to subsistence farmers and small ranchers. Today, the village is a small art colony and has a post office for locals who have hung on despite major changes in economic life. It's a barely living example of what once was the standard life in northern New Mexico.

Abby arrived at the Martinez home promptly at ten with her offering. As advertised, the yellow dog was on the portal of the modest house to greet visitors with a lazy bark, slowly wagging tail and a baleful face. Martinez came to the door in a traditional red flannel shirt, well-worn jeans, cowboy boots nearly as old as Abby, and a large gray mustache matched by speckled black hair. A well creased round face fit well in a medium frame and his eyes twinkled like everyone's favorite uncle.

"I didn't expect such a lovely *señorita*," he said in a whiskey-tempered voice and pointed to a dark green overstuffed chair.

"*Gracias, señor*," Abby bowed slightly and sat on the edge of the chair afraid she would disappear if she sat back. "Great dog," Abby smiled.

"King Tut. Former wife named him. Good company for an old reprobate like me. Coffee?"

"*Sí*, black."

While he poured a dark brown stream into a mug chipped and stained from years of use, Martinez asked, "What do you want to know about Alfonso Salazar? I assume you didn't come all this way for the usual polite conversation and Sunday supplement stuff?" Martinez put the cup on a small coffee table in front of Abby and took a seat opposite her in a well-worn leather chair.

"I appreciate your candor," Abby said and took a tentative sip of coffee. "I'll get to the point. Can you tell me why someone would want him dead?" Abby asked in a normal tone without expression.

"Should I start with politics or sex?" Martinez asked raising his brow.

"Politics first." Abby cocked an eyebrow.

"I assume you know who Alberto Ramirez is?" Martinez watched to see Abby's reaction.

Abby put her cup on the table and looked up at Martinez. "I was born and raised in Española," she said. "My father was Carlos Romero who had a quarter horse . . ."

Martinez raised a hand to stop her.

"You probably know as much about Ramirez as I do," he said slurping his coffee.

"I figure he hand-picked you, Mr. Martinez, to write the stories on Salazar." Abby leaned forward and picked up her cup.

Martinez leaned back in the leather chair and crossed his legs. "You're as smart as you look young lady. Perhaps I should be careful — *que no?*" He raised his cup in a salute to Abby.

"Nothing spoken between us today will ever get in print, *señor.* This conversation about Alberto Salazar is between us." Abby held out her right hand with her little finger pointing at Martinez and her thumb toward her.

He took in a deep breath and continued. "On the politics side there are always deals, especially involving projects that need governmental approval. I won't go into particulars, but look into any developments or issues where Salazar could possibly be involved, and you'll find someone who was disappointed, perhaps seriously disappointed." He stopped and coughed to the side, one of those deep bronchial coughs, no doubt from a life of smoking, Abby thought. With a slightly reddened face he continued. "I'll give you three names: Darien Roberts, Alberto Ramirez and Silas Mendoza. Each has had designs on a resort/gaming project near Lake Heron, and each worked in competition with the others. Salazar was in the middle. Salazar took the safe route and threw his weight toward the Jicarilla tribe. This is public knowledge, and there is nothing to suggest foul play, but then you know how politics is played in *el norte.*" He sat back and cleared his throat.

Abby cocked her head slightly. "And the sex?"

"Ah, there are volumes," Martinez said grinning and leaning forward. "Salazar was in the same mold as the Kennedy brothers, and it had been going on since he was a teenager. And," Martinez paused for emphasis expanding his chest, "he was not terribly careful trying to hide his dalliances with married women, even the wives of powerful men. Rumor has it that women made a game of seeing who could get him into bed. I'd say he was lucky to live as long as he did. Thing is, he always had Alberto to bail him out, or cover up the mess." With that, Martinez sat back to assess Abby's reaction.

Abby dug into her bag and pulled out the file with the photo of the mystery woman with Salazar, handed it to Martinez and pointed to the woman. "Can you tell me who this is?"

Martinez looked for a moment and whistled low. "That's Lupe Garza." He looked up into Abby's eyes and hunched his shoulders forward. "They had a torrid romance that lasted well over a year and then she disappeared. Three or four years later she reappeared in connection with Silas Mendoza, but that seemed to be all business. Might be tough to follow her trail, but it could be worth it." Martinez stood and walked over to the counter to refilled his cup.

Abby stared into space for a moment and said nothing. Something inside her shifted; like a ghostly hand placed on her shoulder.

Martinez turned and asked "Did that hit a nerve? The two of you look alike, if you don't mind my saying." He turned back realizing the comment might have been too personal. "More coffee?" he said over his shoulder.

"No," Abby said bringing her focus back to Martinez. "This has been a big help Mr. Martinez." Abby pulled a business card out of her purse. "I'd like to stay in touch and get your feedback and advice if need be. May I?" Abby looked with anticipation at Martinez.

"I'll be here. Got nothing going except a few small stories and the novel that never gets finished." He smiled and they both stood and moved toward the weather-beaten front door. They shook hands while King Tut rose unsteadily and moved arthritically out of the way.

A warm breeze greeted Abby as she walked toward her vehicle. A lock of black hair blew across her cheek as she turned and waved to Martinez, who stood in the door admiring his departing guest. She hoped the afternoon appointment would go half as well as this one, but she knew better.

Abby sat in the 4Runner a few moments, transfixed by the rugged snow-covered peaks that seemed close enough to touch, and thoughts of Lupe Garza. The mystery woman was taking shape, and she intrigued Abby as much as the murder itself. But the feeling inside Abby about this person was more than curiosity. Something about the woman haunted Abby, like the shadow that disappears before it can be identified.

At one-twenty, Abby parked in the long narrow lot behind the restaurant located several blocks north of the plaza. Snow was melting rapidly and Abby hopscotched over puddles in the blacktopped parking lot. As she neared the door, a blue sports coupe zipped into the lot and parked in the back row as if it were a private space. Abby waited by the front door. Roberts climbed out of the low car with ease, swung the door shut as he turned toward the building and pressed the lock button on his key all in one fluid motion. He approached head erect looking straight ahead and expressionless without acknowledging Abby even though she was clearly in view. Dressed in a camel-hair coat flung open and European-style driving cap, his polished wingtip shoes carried him in the easy confident manner of a man who has everything and expects it to continue; a confidence that could easily be seductive. Three steps from the door he smiled wide and said, "Good of you to come, Abigail. May I call you Abigail?" Without waiting for a reply he ushered Abby in front of him through the open doorway with his right hand lightly touching her back. Abby suppressed a chuckle.

"And how shall I call you?" Abby asked, cocking her head a quarter turn back .

"Darien, please," Roberts said in an even pleasant tone.

Without asking, a young male host led them to a table in one of the back rooms. Roberts apparently was a regular, and the host knew by the guest's status, gender and age where to seat Roberts. He placed an unpretentious menu on the table without interrupting the flow of the scene. Abby was impressed.

Like many locals, she had been to Santacafé on special occasions, but could not afford its fare on a regular basis. Roberts could and did.

Abby noticed a Hollywood figure who lived in Taos at one of the larger tables, as did Roberts. Nothing was said, and Abby did not want to look like a gawking tourist, so she passed the table without a glance. Roberts did not offer to hold Abby's chair, which she appreciated. Fortunately, Santa Fe's dress style varies widely, and Abby did not feel underdressed in her dress jeans, white blouse and black leather jacket. On the other hand, Roberts' blue blazer, mauve shirt, rolex and grey slacks was appropriate for any smart restaurant in the world, including Santacafé.

Without looking at the menu Roberts said, "I've known about you for some time. Your track record as an investigator is becoming the stuff of legend." His practiced smile and good manners were meant to get the upper hand immediately. "May we order? They have an excellent club and their *quesadillas* are famous. I don't drink, but please have a glass of wine."

"I drink, but not during business," Abby said as she looked over the menu. "Hot tea, when he comes back, please."

The waiter appeared on cue and they ordered. Roberts asked for fried calamari, the house specialty, and a Caesar salad. Abby selected a Cobb salad. Might as well fill up on his dime, Abby thought. Through her business face she looked across at Roberts and waited.

Roberts began with small talk about the weather and asked if she had lived in northern New Mexico all her life. Abby said she had gown up on a nearby ranch and left it at that.

"Are you still a Lobos fan?" Roberts asked. Realizing a potential *faux* pas he quickly said that perhaps they should get on with business. With that segue, Abby knew he had done a background check on her and already had most of the answers to his questions, such as her degree in anthropology and sociology from the University of New Mexico.

"I lost something, or rather something was taken from me that is very important," he began. "A Mimbres pot, medium size, that has been in my collection for more than twenty years. I can't even put a price on it."

Abby remained silent looking closely at Roberts for tell-tales. He sat erect with shoulders square, hands folded on the table and looked earnest.

"I first noticed that it was not in its usual place two days ago," he continued and relaxed slightly. "I have not reported it and do not intend to. My insurance is already too high. Besides, you know police work around here." Roberts shifted in his chair and his eyebrows narrowed just a tinge. "They will assume that it's an inside job, and I'm sure it isn't. But that would mean a lot of snooping around, and my life is more public than I care for," he said through a brief nervous laugh.

"Was it in your home or gallery?" Abby asked.

"Actually, it was in my private office in the gallery and it was not protected. Frankly, almost anyone could have walked out with it. My first wife died of cancer in her twenties and I had a small vial containing some of her ashes in the bowl. Both are gone." Roberts stared into space for a moment, took out a linen kerchief and blotted both eyes briefly.

Abby looked away briefly to acknowledge his privacy before continuing. "You said two days ago. That would be Monday. Could the pot have been taken earlier?"

"Possibly." Roberts looked past Abby. She wondered if he was momentarily distracted or trying to appear thoughtful about his recall.

"Before Monday, the last time I was in the office was Thursday morning, Christmas eve, and I'm sure I would have noticed if was gone. Yes, in fact I remember touching it before leaving for Taos." Roberts cleared his throat and looked down.

Abby hesitated, and then asked, "Were you at the procession at the pueblo?"

"Why yes, were you there?"

"I was with several friends." Abby didn't offer anything else.

"Did you see the tragic shooting of Alfonso Salazar?"

"Yes, did you?" Abby asked quickly.

"I didn't see it up close, but with all the commotion I knew something terrible had happened. I found out soon enough. Salazar was a close acquaintance and associate. In fact, he worked for me about ten years ago."

Abby waited without speaking. She began eating. Roberts took a few bites and then said, "I hope they catch the killer. He's a big loss for the state; destined for bigger things." He looked off again with an expression of sadness.

"By chance do you have a photo of the pot?" Abby asked.

"Yes." Roberts reached inside his jacket and pulled out a folded color copy of the pot and another showing its interior. It was a standard Mimbres of black images on a gray background, with an animal symbol inside: this one was a fish. There seemed to be a stone or perhaps a flaw in the bottom of the pot. There was no vial. Abby took the photocopy.

"Do you suspect anyone?"

"No, I can't say that I do." Roberts had returned to his business mode. "Amanda has been with me for years and I trust her without question. There may have been some new cleaning people in the building over the weekend. You might start there." The room had emptied out and their voices began to carry.

Abby looked around the room and for the first time noticed there was no art on the walls. Apparently, the clientele was the attraction. "Mr. Roberts, I haven't agreed to do this yet, and I'm sure you realize that recovery is unlikely unless you have a culprit in mind." Abby looked serious and opened her hands with a "what-can-you-expect-me-to-do" gesture.

"Will you at least give it a few days? I'll pay your going rate for as long as we both think it is worthwhile."

Abby thought for a moment, shifted her chair back an inch and sat up straighter. "I'll give it a few days. It's possible you may get a ransom call or note. Also, I need to know if you know of anyone carrying a grudge against you, or if someone resents you over the death of your wife. Make a list with specifics and I'll stop by your gallery Monday if that is convenient. In the meantime I'll call the local pawn shops and alert them. Will you notify any galleries that might accept the pot for sale?" Abby looked at Roberts for his response as she placed her card on the table in front of him.

"Yes, I'll alert them. I should be in the office Monday by ten. If that doesn't work out, I'll call you. I do appreciate this very much." Roberts pushed his chair back and signaled the waiter for the check.

"Thanks very much for lunch. It was nice to meet you finally." Abby smiled, slung her purse over her shoulder and started for the door. She turned slightly and said, "See you Monday. Have a nice weekend."

Abby did not go directly to her truck. Instead, she went across the street and walked four blocks to the New Mexico Natural History museum to talk with a curator she had known since she worked in the state anthropology museum. She showed the photocopy to Maria Gonzales and asked if she could tell from the photo if the pot was an original.

Maria took out a magnifying glass and looked carefully. "I can't tell for sure, but as you know, when a pot looks this good it's probably a copy. And there is something in the bottom of the pot that looks strange." Maria looked up at Abby. "Why do you ask?"

"Darien Roberts said it was stolen and hired me to find it. He claimed it was in his gallery office. By chance have you ever seen this pot?"

"I was in his office once," Maria said, "but I can't recall seeing it. I usually notice objects if they look like originals."

They both looked at each other a moment without speaking. Finally, Abby picked up the photo and said, "Thanks much, Maria. How are Frank and the kids?"

"Everyone is doing very well. You wouldn't know them now." Maria raised her hands to show how tall they were. "Frank's still on the hill at his lab job. We're both looking forward to retirement."

The hill, as locals refer to Los Alamos is the major employer in the area, and Abby thought more than once about the security it could provide her if she ever lost the zeal for independence.

Abby gave Maria a polite hug, exited through the large wooden doors of the museum and headed back up the street to the Santacafé parking lot.

As Abby pulled out of the lot she mulled over the conversation with Roberts. Clouds had gathered and as she left Santa Fe light snow began to fall. Proceeding down Opera Hill Abby slowed the 4Runner to forty-five, fully aware of the dangers of this part of the highway in rain and snow. Still, a few vehicles flew by, tempting fate. Seconds later one of them was up against the hill-side retaining wall on the right facing uphill. The driver was getting out and had his cell phone to his ear. Three miles farther down the snow turned to drizzle, and the highway seemed less treacherous, but Abby stayed below the speed limit.

Abby relaxed a bit and turned her thoughts back to Darien Roberts. The so-called stolen pot looked bogus. He would have already called galleries and pawn shops if the pot was an original. And why not make a report and call the insurance company?

If Roberts saw the shooting, it was unlikely he missed seeing her chase the shooter. Finally, Roberts' demeanor did not look or sound like a person in distress. He was one slick dude, Abby thought. Suddenly she remembered that Carmen was due for dinner at six and punched her number on the cell phone.

"I'm just leaving Santa Fe and do not have anything for dinner."

"Not to worry. Mom made posole last night and loaded me up. I'll pick up fresh tortillas and I have some red sauce in the freezer. See you at six."

"*Bueno.*" Carmen had already disconnected.

For the next five miles Abby kept a sharp eye out for the Tesuque tribal police, who patrolled this stretch of highway with vigilance, an annoyance to locals, but a good safety measure nonetheless. As Abby passed the last of three casinos operated by the Tesuque and Pojoaque pueblos, she thought of Salazar again, and wondered why Roberts would be concerned about a pot at a time like this. And why would he go all the way to Abiquiu to hire a private investigator? Abby had many questions and no answers.

6

Abby pulled the 4Runner close to the shed so Carmen could park next to the kitchen door. An inch of snow had fallen and dark gray skies promised more tonight. The thermometer was falling. Abby brought in extra wood for the evening and let Duster hunt through the woodpile for mice, which were no longer plentiful. After the stove was full and the kiva blazing, she put some background music on the Bose, and pulled the cork on an Italian red wine. Carmen, as always, was on time.

In lightly falling snow, Carmen brought in containers of posole, red sauce, tortillas and a bottle of champaign all in one trip and deposited her cargo on the counter. She flung her arms wide for a big hug and they stood there a second and beamed at each other. Their friendship was cherished and they always showed it. Carmen stuffed her wool cap and gloves in one of the jacket sleeves and tossed the jacket over a chair.

"I'm all ears, kiddo, but before we start let's get that bottle of fizz in the fridge. I see you already have a red open."

Abby poured two glasses half full and put a bowl of salsa and some blue corn chips on the small kitchen table.

"First, let me bring you up to date," Abby said, sitting down and motioning Carmen to do the same. Carmen liked to pace, which Abby found distracting. Abby seldom wasted physical effort. "I've done a little research on Salazar and came up with a reporter who did nearly all of the promotion and news stories on him. Guy's name is Ramon Martinez and lives in Truchas. I was up there this morning and got some good stuff."

Carmen looked attentive and nibbled on the chips. "Was he the only one who wrote about Salazar?" Carmen asked.

"Pretty much. I figured him for being hand-picked by Alberto Ramirez, and Martinez confirmed it without saying why. Anyway, turns out that Salazar is a wheeler-dealer and a major-league womanizer. Bottom line is there could be a long line of people who had history with him."

Carmen leaned forward and asked, "Anyone we know?"

"Apparently he didn't restrict his flings to single women, so take your pick. I'm betting many of the go-getter women in Santa Fe were notches on his belt, although Martinez suggested it could have been the other way around — must have been a real stud. But there was one woman who intrigues me. Martinez gave her name as Lupe Garza."

Carmen shook her head indicating the name was a blank to her.

"So far I haven't run across any info on her, but I've just started."

Abby got up and put the posole on the stove, put two bowls in the toaster oven to warm along with the tortillas, already wrapped in foil. She topped off the wine glasses, sat down and continued.

"After Martinez, I met with Darien Roberts at Santacafé."

Carmen moved her shoulders from side to side and said, "Uptown, girl — all right."

"He wanted to hire me to find a missing Mimbres pot and I agreed, although I think it's a ruse. I get the feeling he is up to something else. He did a background check on me."

"Really," Carmen interjected.

"Yeah, although I didn't confront him on it. Have you ever seen him?" Abby asked.

"Sure, at least I think so," Carmen said. "Dresses like the east and drives a hot car; flashy and arrogant. Occasionally he's in the society pages and one of the girls in my office was a behind-the-scenes fling for a while. She used to brag about it."

"Did you see him at the pueblo Christmas eve?" Abby asked.

"Yes, he was on the same side of the plaza we were on; was not too far from where we were standing, but closer to the church. Dressed for the theater with one of those Russian hats. You didn't see him?" Carmen looked surprised.

"No, I guess I was preoccupied."

"Well, I didn't see him after the shooting, but then with all the commotion I wasn't looking for him either," Carmen said.

"Hmm." Abby thought for a moment. "He said he was there, but acted like he did not see me. If he was that close to you he must have seen me." Abby got up to check the posole and turned the burner off. "*Comida?*"

They clinked wine glasses and after tearing a tortilla into pieces they started in on the posole laced with red sauce. Eating sounds replaced conversation for a minute. "Your mom sure gets this right," Abby said. "She must slow-roast the pork."

"Oh yeah. Nothing fast about the way *mi madre* cooks — the old way."

"*Como mi abuela,*" Abby said, nodding her head.

"How is she?" Carmen asked. "She's over in Las Vegas in a home, *que no?*"

"*Sí, con demencia,*" Abby replied holding her thumb and forefinger slightly apart to show that the dementia was mild. "My aunt looks after her. Unfortunately, I don't see her often enough." Abby looked away, slightly embarrassed. After a few minutes they both pushed their chairs back a few inches.

"Carm," Abby looked down before looking at Carmen. "The big reason I wanted to talk to you, and I really need your advice, is that something is bothering me about all this. I don't know where to start. It's scary. In fact it's very scary." Abby looked down at her clenched hands.

"Hey, I'm listening. I'm with you," Carmen said calmly and reached toward Abby.

Abby started slowly. "You know my father always called me *cazadora,*" Abby looked out the window. "Well, I can't get this woman who shot Salazar out of my head. I need to find out why she would kill? Not just why she killed Salazar, but why would she would kill period?" She looked at Carmen and paused, shifting in her chair uncomfortably. Carmen let out a short breath.

"Okay, I think I know where you're going with this and I'm not really surprised. Go on." Carmen put her chin in cupped hands with elbows on the table and waited. Duster came over from his spot by the fireplace, sat on the floor next to the table and looked up intently.

Abby took a drink and swallowed slowly. "I've tossed this around in my mind a number of ways, and this is how I make sense of what's got me so obsessed with finding this woman." Abby sat up straighter, looked at Carmen and then away again. "I understand the hunt and all that goes into it, the tracking, the commitment, the focus, the excitement when the prey is in sight, and the split-second pause before pulling the trigger when you know you and only you are the cause of what happens next." Carmen drew her eyes close together and tightened her lips.

Abby took in a deep breath and continued. "I've never thought about shooting at another human being until Galt last summer. I had him in my sights, at least I thought I did, and I wanted to take him down — like a hunted animal." Abby stood up and walked over to the kitchen sink. She looked through the window that Myron shot out last summer aiming for the dummy Abigail had propped up at the table. Carmen followed her with her eyes.

"But everything happened so fast, and the hail, and Clay and . . . anyway, I didn't think about Galt much until I realized the shooter at the pueblo was a woman. And then there is this damned recurring dream." Abby described the dream of starting to shoot at the grinning skull-faced figure and waking up before pulling the trigger.

"I'm not sure if the dream is saying that I don't have what it takes to pull the trigger, or the opposite, that I can't wait to do it. That maybe . . ."

"You're afraid you could do it" Carmen said softly, completing her thought.

"Yes," Abby said, and looked back at Carmen. "At least I'm worried that perhaps it's in me. Why do I love the hunt? I've always loved the hunt, ever since I can remember. But now with this thing, perhaps . . . perhaps there is more to it?"

"Wait. Wait." Carmen stood up and walked over to the sink and leaned against it beside Abby. She tossed her head back and folded her arms. "Think about it. There's a big difference between hunting for animals and . . . and people. Even the trap you set for Galt is different. In fact, the Galt thing was supposed to be a capture, wasn't it." Carmen reached over and put a hand on Abby's shoulder. "Galt was battle, not murder."

"I know, I know." Abby turned, leaned toward Carmen and clenched her fists. "Perhaps there is a line that is crossed, a turning point of sorts. For my own sake I need to find out what turned that woman into an assassin. For my own peace of mind, I need to understand her, and that means I need to find her." Abby sat down and took another drink.

"*Hermana*, you know this is dangerous. You're looking in Pandora's box. A lot of people wonder if they could ever kill someone, but most of us dismiss it fast. It's too terrible to think about." Carmen stopped.

"This is different. What am I doing in this line of work? Who am I really?" She looked up into Carmen's eyes.

"Look, I know who you really are. But I can see you're worried." Carmen sat down and leaned back. "Who you are is what you've always been. If there is something hidden, it will stay that way. You're solid, kiddo."

"I guess I am worried. I may need to get out of this line of work. Stop being *cazadora*. But I can't stop until I find out what turned that woman into a cold-blooded killer. If she's a sociopath that's one thing, like Galt. But my gut tells me she's not. My gut tells me there is something going on that I need to understand for my own survival." Abby's voice was hard.

Carmen let out another sigh and leaned forward in her chair. "I know you better than anyone does, even Nick. So I know you won't let go of this thing. But you're going to need to talk to me. You can't hold all this in. Promise me you'll talk to me . . . often." Carmen reached over and took hold of Abby's wrist. "Promise me. Right now," she said firmly.

"I promise. I promise. And . . . thanks for listening."

Carmen pursed her lips. "Lets go back to square one."

Abby got out her files and spread them on the table while Carmen put the dishes in the sink to soak. Carmen sat down opposite Abby and put her hands under her chin.

"Here's what I've got so far," Abby started. "Salazar was shot by someone posing as a monk. I think it was a woman by the way she moved when I chased her. The getaway car was a dark SUV which was found in Alcalde the next day along with a burned monk's robe stuffed in a trash barrel. The clues end there. *Nada*, zip, nothing more since then." Carmen continued to look at Abby without speaking.

"Then we have the info from Ramon Martinez, and Darien Roberts running a background check on me and hiring me to find a fake pot. And, there was a non-local Subaru in the neighborhood the other day that came up to my house and turned around while I was out running. So, we have the pot, the Subaru and the background check all within a few days following the murder of Salazar. Too many odd events in that time period, even for northern New Mexico, *que no?*"

"So, *hermana*, let me work with you?" Carmen asked. "This sounds like a lot of work and you're not getting paid, except for the so-called pot."

Abby thought a moment. "Okay. I could use the help and we'd see more of each other. I think we should start with three people: Roberts, Salazar, and the woman shooter. I'll take the woman. Would you be willing to dig into Salazar and we both work on Roberts?"

"Sure, sounds like fun. My family loves gossip — hey we're *norteña* — so there should be lots of stories. And I know people who know Roberts. What say we get together in a week?"

"Good, and this time I really will cook something," Abby said.

"How about that fish baked in paper with all the peppers and stuff?"

"Perfect, and a good white wine. Oh," Abby said. "Bailey's has a new wine put out by Hatch Chiles. There's green and red."

"No," Carmen said, laughing. "You're kidding. I don't believe it."

"Seriously?" Abby stood with arms wide apart. "Would I kid about a thing like that?"

"Of course you would," Carmen said, still laughing. "I'll believe it when I see it."

They spent the rest of the evening going through a ritual they established when Carmen went through her divorce five years ago, making new year's resolutions, tallying the score from last year's, which often resulted in a tie at zero, and lots of laughing. One resolution involved Abby learning to dance salsa, which had ended in rage, tears, and laughter. Another involved Carmen taking a watercolor painting course, which ended the same way. Just before eleven they watched a repeat of the ball dropping at Times Square in New York. They toasted each other's health and happiness with the cold champagne, noticed that the snow had stopped with very little accumulation, and Carmen left for home to beat the highway drivers who over-celebrated.

7

Abby was dreaming about something when she heard gunshots. Duster was immediately alert; she saw the numbers on the clock reading 12:00 and remembered the local custom for New Year's.

"Shit," she said to Duster, "what a dumb tradition." One of these years someone is going to get seriously hurt.

She didn't know how long she laid awake before drifting into dreamless sleep. Slowly she became aware of a soft paw resting on her cheek. Duster's day had begun, and so had hers.

Abby looked out the kitchen window to check the weather for the hike with Bob. Sunlight flooded through the window and the temperature already registered thirty. She did a full yoga routine before the Rose Parade and made a breakfast with enough protein to get her through the hike with Bob. He was no wimp when it came to any outdoor activity, and she'd be pressed to keep up, but she would.

Abby arrived at the Paleontology Museum at Ghost Ranch at noon and found it locked as expected. Bob heard her park and came round the building from the back as she looked through the window.

"Leave your car there and we'll take mine to the trailhead. If it's okay with you I thought we'd do the trail toward upper camp and then boulder down the arroyo into the box and come back down the creek."

"Sounds good. I'll get my hat and water."

Shadows from puffy clouds danced their way across the steep sandstone cliffs that bordered the beginning of the trail, giving movement to the landscape, propelling the eager hikers on through patchy snow. Bob and Abigail walked easily together as they crisscrossed the partially iced-over creek before ascending through scrub juniper toward the upper snow-covered mesa. The trail varied from narrow rocky ledges requiring a sure foot to steep up-and-down sections through thick spruce and ponderosa pine. Evidence of bird life was abundant; at one point they stopped to check on an eagle's nest for new activity, but there was none. After an hour they rested at lower camp and took in the grand vista toward Pedernal mountain and Abiquiu Reservoir.

They spoke little, appreciating the topography and the stewardship of Ghost Ranch in protecting one of the most beautiful and fragile areas of northern New Mexico. After exactly the right amount of rest time, Bob stood and they started down the steep boulder-strewn arroyo toward the box, which formed the head of the creek that once supplied water to the original ranchers during the 1800s and still supplies irrigation water to the ranch.

Bob showed Abby several pictographs she had never seen that were tucked behind a large boulder located above the box-end of the canyon. A local legend told of the Archuleta brothers — the early settlers — driving stolen horses and cattle up the box to hide them. As the story goes, the Archuleta boys also took advantage of passing travelers, some of whom were never seen again. Soon locals began calling the area ghost ranch.

By late afternoon Abby and Bob had ambled slowly back down the creek to a natural pond formed from springs and creek run-off.

"My plan was to heat up the goulash here by the pond and relax until sunset, or until we get too cold."

"I like your plan," Abby said. "Wait, I'll walk back to the truck and help carry."

Thirty minutes later, goulash bubbled on the camp stove and tortillas had almost warmed in a small solar oven. Bob twisted off the cap on a bottle of red and they toasted the new year and themselves. Bob leaned over and planted a kiss on Abby's lips, which she returned with a sweet one of her own. They stood there wrapped in each other's arms for a long moment.

Conversation the rest of the evening moved from the climate center that Bob hoped to establish, to some new anthropology digs, to the joys and sorrows of living alone, which they both had done all of their adult lives. Abby mentioned a new study that showed married couples live longer than people living alone. Bob agreed it made sense, but brought up the old saying about old dogs and new tricks. He did acknowledge that while living alone had benefits, it would be nice to know someone else was there, someone to count on.

"Do you ever feel lonely?" Bob asked softly.

"If I'm honest, the answer is yes, but not often. I really treasure my privacy, and so far I haven't met anyone I'd give up that privacy for. But then I'm still young." Abby smiled weakly, and noticed that Bob's body stiffened slightly at her comment, possibly because of the ten-year age difference between them, which, she thought, could become an issue at some point.

As the sun hit the horizon, red and yellow waves of light fanned out behind the Pedernal forming a memorable sunset. The light faded to a steel-blue curtain, and Bob took a small blanket from the large picnic bag and wrapped it around Abby's shoulders. She snuggled into his chest and they remained silent until the chill off the cliffs ended the serenity of a perfect day. Abby said she had a chocolate torte in a cooler in her truck and perhaps they could brew up something hot at the museum or his quarters. The evening ended with the promise of more to come.

Lupe found the customs line short in Phoenix on New Year's day, which meant the agents were spending extra time with foreign nationals coming back into the country. The international annex of Sky Harbor Airport was no improvement on the typical customs facilities in most international airports; a featureless tomb with poor acoustics, drab colors and expressionless personnel that tried the patience of a weary traveler.

Lupe's status was secure, as she was fortunate enough to have established residency prior to 9/11. Still, anyone coming in from Mexico these days was given close examination, and a large German shepherd sniffed around her legs while she waited. Lupe had become quite good at surveying her surroundings while standing in a crowd, and so far she did not see anyone who could be a threat.

She took a shuttle to a blue and gray airport motel modeled for business people in a hurry. During a mediocre meal in the coffee shop, Lupe checked the Arizona Republic newspaper for any information on the Salazar case and drug activity on the border, and found nothing.

Saturday morning Lupe obtained a car from a rent-a-clunker firm with a cute name, paid cash for a month and drove the well-traveled freeways east toward Mesa, passing the large campus of Arizona State University, now bordered by an artificial lake in the once dry riverbed of the Salt River. Urban desert-dweller transplants from the midwest go to great lengths to pretend they do not live in a desert, she thought.

After thirty minutes of driving she approached the city of Mesa, a once quiet suburb of Phoenix, but now over a million strong. The Superstition Mountains formed the eastern horizon and she saw that a rare snowfall graced a formation called Four Peaks to the northeast. Lupe turned south on Mesa Drive, and in the shadow of the Mormon temple entered an old barrio that friends had told her about several years ago. After a few calls to places listed in a free tabloid she picked up at a gas station, Lupe found a cheap rental of a worn-out house, vintage early 1950s, that probably had housed a meth lab and couldn't pass a health inspection. Lupe knew that a decade ago the neighborhood had been a respectable Chicano *barrio* inhabited by industrious people on the rise in the land of opportunity. Most of those people were gone, having made it economically and socially, if not legally. Slum landlords now controlled the housing market and none of them was interested in beautification or safety. Lupe would make do.

Sunday afternoon, under sunny warm skies, Lupe strolled the large well-manicured grounds of the Mormon temple and smiled to passers-by for most of the afternoon. She declined an invitation from two well-scrubbed young lads in dark suits and white shirts to accompany them to the visitors center, and they left her to wander undisturbed the remainder of the afternoon. It all felt strange, but safe.

There were no businesses open within walking distance of the temple, so she snacked on junk food purchased from a gas station convenience store the day before. Monday she'd stock up on wholesome food and get a weapon or two from a gun shop she had noticed on the drive into town. She would not appear out of place in the shop because many women now packed heat, as they used to say sixty years ago in Hollywood movies.

She spent most of Monday catching up on sleep, consuming good calories, reading a paperback she had picked up at the airport and watching the street for people who didn't fit in. The television remained mute.

Tuesday, January 5th: Mendoza expected Lupe in Albuquerque. Lupe paced the small living room with her cell phone in hand. If she didn't show up in Albuquerque, Mendoza would know that she suspected something, which, of course, she did. She needed to run a story by him that would buy more time, but she couldn't take a chance on the cell phone's location being traced. Lupe grabbed the laptop and drove to Sky Harbor to use the free WiFi. If Mendoza's people traced her email, the internet provider address would be the airport, and that could mean she could be anywhere by the time he received the email.

Using the Wanda James Yahoo account, she typed "travel" in the subject line and wrote: *Will not arrive in Albuquerque today due to complications. Hope the window remains open. Thanks for thinking of me. Will contact you later*, and signed it L.

With that done, she had breakfast at a high-traffic café and went to a movie for distraction. Two hours later Lupe left the theater still in a defensive frame of mind, something she was unaccustomed to, didn't like and would rectify soon. She stopped at a market for fish and vegetables to sustain the diet she would need to keep her sharp. Tonight she'd start running along the irrigation canal banks that cut through the city, and, in the morning, add a Pilates routine and weights. In a week's time Lupe would be near top form.

That evening, after a run in pleasant sixty-degree weather, Lupe put pen to paper to review potential enemies and outline a strategy, although at this point she could not identify who was the most dangerous. There was Silas Mendoza, the crafty and powerful developer she had worked with as part of a deal between him and her drug cartel. That was four years ago, and being realistic, Lupe realized Mendoza did nothing that would not benefit himself. He would be a formidable adversary, particularly due to his connections with Mexican drug people.

Despite Lupe's on-and-off working relationship with Darien Roberts, and a brief sexual relationship with him ten years ago that she broke off, she knew Roberts harbored resentment against her. Roberts was not the kind of person who got over rejection, and he was connected on both sides of the law. Roberts could smile at you while sticking a knife in your back.

Lupe added three other people to her list. The political manipulator Alberto Ramirez could be very angry over losing Salazar, his prize political puppet whom he had painstakingly groomed for ten years. The same was true for Roberts' wife, Candace, who had invested large chunks of her own money in Salazar's political future. Finally, Ignacio Garcia, the Mexican drug boss might want Lupe dead in retribution for her part in killing Garcia's hit man, who had killed Lupe's boss.

Five powerful opponents, each with sufficient reason for wanting Lupe out of the picture permanently, and each with the resources to get it done. Lupe realized now that she had accepted the Salazar contract without giving sufficient thought to the repercussions. She had a little too much emotion in the job, too much resentment for being used by Salazar. Perhaps her alias — *vengadora* — had become a curse; vengeance had been turned against her.

Lupe leaned back in the chair and looked at her notes. Something was missing. Then she remembered the woman who chased her out of the Taos pueblo. Why would she fly in the face of danger? Lupe thought for a moment, but the only image that came to her was that the woman was very much like herself in appearance. She had only a fleeting view of this person, so she could be mistaken about the appearance. Still, Lupe wondered, why would the woman chase her? Was she also a hunter? Was there something about the chase that was compulsion, perhaps instinctual? Lupe decided she needed to take this person seriously, because if this person was a hunter like herself, she would be driven to act. Lupe sent an email to Sergeant Duran, the name she got from Mali Reznick. It was a long shot, but it was all Lupe had.

Saturday morning dawned gray but mild. Abby stumbled sleepily out of the bedroom. She could not remember if her mother was due back from the Caribbean cruise with Raoul today or tomorrow. Either way, Abby would wait for her mother to call. It would mean dinner or high tea at her mother's condo in Española. Abby knew her brother would have cleared out, as he didn't want to see Abby any more than she wanted to see him. No sooner had Abby opened the kitchen door to get a breath of fresh air than the phone rang.

"Mother, you're back. How was the trip?"

"Hi Kitten, the trip was wonderful. Your brother took lots of pictures and he promised to send them in a few days. The Caribbean is everything everyone says it is, and the ship . . . well, they just do everything for you. It was a bit embarrassing. Of course they always have their hand out, so I spent way more than I intended. And I think I put on a few pounds. I'll have to watch my diet for a few weeks. But how are you? How was your holiday?"

"It was quiet. I went to Taos on Christmas eve with Carmen and Nick, and Carmen came over New Year's eve. We had a great time together. I'm starting a small job for an art dealer in Santa Fe on Monday." Abby ran her fingers through her hair with her left hand and started to pace around the kitchen.

"Oh good. I was worried that you would be lonely."

"Mother, I'm never lonely. Besides, I always have Duster."

"When I get the pictures, I want you to come over for dinner. Perhaps Raoul . . ."

Abby interrupted. "Mother . . ." Abby stopped pacing, neck muscles tightening.

"Yes, I know, dear. But if he agrees to come, would you please come too?" Mary's voice rose and sounded frail.

"Yes, Mother," Abby's voice rising in concert with her mother. "I'll come, but only if . . . Oh never mind. Yes, I'll come."

"All right. I'll call you sometime next week. It's good to hear your voice, and I'm glad you're working."

"Good to hear yours also, Mother. Talk to you soon. Glad you're back safe."

Abby put the phone down and and let out a long sigh. Sensing the distress, Duster jumped on the table, turned his large eyes on Abby and started to purr. He turned and swiped her gently with his large, feathery plume-like tail. Abby smiled.

"And I always have you buster boy." She gathered his long body in her arms and deposited him on the floor, where he proudly walked off with his tail straight as a flagstaff.

Abby heard the wind chimes and looked out to see light snow gusting past the kitchen window. She wondered what Bob was doing and decided to give him a call. She wasn't surprised to find him in the lab at the ranch.

"Abby, what a nice surprise. Your voice brightens up a drab winter day."

"I was hoping you'd say that. Are you chained to the lab today?"

"Well, I need to catch up on cataloging stuff that's piled high in the chaos room. How about joining me in this dust bin of antiquity? Your presence would make this tedious job a lot more enjoyable, at least for me."

"On one condition. Any action at the ranch tonight?"

"Actually there is. There's an Elderhostel group that just happens to be studying folk dance and archaic Spanish customs. I think they are having a week-ending dance tonight. Music will probably be terrible, but what the heck. Oh, and the dining hall will be open. Am I whetting your interest?"

"No, but as you said, what the heck. I'll stop at Bailey's for takeout burgers and beer, if you'll spring for dinner."

"You're on."

"See you in an hour or so." Abby paused as she put the phone back in its cradle and thought, this thing with Bob was beginning to take on a life of its own, and perhaps it was about time.

After managing to munch down the giant green-chile cheeseburgers Bailey's is famous for, Abby and Bob spent the rest of the afternoon putting bones, clay shards and various tool-like fragments in plastic sleeves identified by code numbers with a magic marker. By five o'clock they were both weary, and Bob wondered aloud about a short nap before dinner.

"You can have the old couch in the back room of the museum and I'll take the cot over in the corner," Bob said.

Abby nodded in agreement. The meticulous job of cataloging had worn her out and folk dancing was beginning to sound even less enjoyable than it had earlier in the day.

After their *siesta* they had a filling dinner of chicken and dumplings similar to the same dish served by a popular interstate chain, which Abby hated, along with a Jello salad and yellow cake. Abby made the best of it and they managed to get through about an hour of folk dancing and talk from ever-energetic seniors before Abby begged off and asked Bob if they could call it a day. Bob promised a more appropriate evening next time and thanked Abby for being such a good sport.

On the way home, Abby realized she had never felt this comfortable with any man other than Nick or her father. Abby liked where this was going.

Abby looked out her bedroom window early Sunday morning to more gray skies and a single-digit temperature. She wanted to call Nick and fill him in on Bob; tell him Bob was becoming more than a friend.

"Hey *amiga*, nice to hear your voice." Nick answered cheerfully as she expected.

"I'm lookin' for some pleasant conversation and maybe some advice," Abby said. "You up for breakfast at the inn or Bailey's?"

"Sure, I was planning on Mass in El Rito at nine. Come to think of it, we could make early Mass at San Tomas in your parish at eight-thirty and join the crowd at Bailey's afterward. I haven't seen those folks in some time." Nick felt it was his duty as a surrogate uncle/father to get Abby to church every so often.

"Okay," Abby said hesitating, "I'll meet you in the plaza at eight-twenty."

"*Bueno* bye," Nick said and hung up.

San Tomas in Abiquiu was a majestic and classic adobe church constructed before WWII on the north side of the Abiquiu plaza, when the plaza still was a social hub for the Abiquiu pueblo. Today it presided over a small, dusty open square with a large gym on the west side that hosted the occasional dance and wedding or funeral reception, a small struggling library on the south side, and residences, including Georgia O'Keeffe's house, on the east. The existence of the plaza dated to early American colonial times; a dirt square that harbored mules, donkeys, traders, natives, and everything else that made this small corner of the world a primitive semblance of civilization. What remains today is the well-trodden ground of its history.

Abby parked the 4Runner next to a car of an elderly neighbor couple who she knew attended Mass regularly. They greeted Abby politely, without making comment on what a rare event it was for Abby to appear at church. The wind blew small clouds of dust through the plaza, and dogs raced excitedly around the arriving cars and trucks.

Nick arrived precisely at eight-twenty.

People greeted Nick as though he were a special guest. Identity in northern New Mexico is formed less by one's surname than by the place where a person was born and raised. Although Abby had lived in Barranca for five years, she was considered an outsider to Abiquiu natives, because she was from Española, twenty-five miles to the south. Nick being from El Rito, fifteen miles to the north, was also an outsider, but a welcome one as would be demonstrated in Bailey's after Mass.

Nick and Abby took seats in the rear of the church. She was always impressed by the wood carving on pews and the corbels holding up the massive *vigas* for the roof. Supposedly, each corbel was designed by a different family in Abiquiu. The priest was young and not Hispanic, and consequently was accommodated but not considered a parish leader. Leadership in the eyes of the parishioners was reserved for the Penitente Brotherhood, a lay organization that dated back several centuries.

In the early days of the Spanish migration north from Mexico, clerics were scarce. As a result, local men took matters into their own hands and formed this organization committed to preserving the true teachings of Christ. Today, *moradas*, or windowless places of worship, dotted the landscape of northern New Mexico. Some were still used for various rituals, particularly on Good Friday. Abby could identify three Penitente *hermanos* in the congregation this morning.

After the solemn proceedings of the Mass, a small group of locals descended on Bailey's, as they did most Sunday mornings, for spirited conversation and Bailey's famous breakfast burrito. Nick and Abby joined in and were greeted like regulars. Conversation ranged from the weather to water politics and what the spring lamb crop might bring. Everyone was looking forward to at least a half a lamb by Easter, which was late this year. No one mentioned the Salazar murder.

Later, in Abby's kitchen, after they reviewed a rough sketch of a new shed that Nick had agreed to build, he said, "You mentioned advice when you called this morning."

"Yes." Abby leaned forward. "I've been seeing Bob Janovich. And, I want to continue seeing him if he's interested, and I think he is."

Nick smiled broadly, came around the table, leaned over and hugged her. "I'm really glad. This is great news. You need someone like him in your life." He stepped back still smiling. "When can I have the two of you up to my place for dinner, or barbecue?"

"That might be rushing it, but soon I hope."

They spent another half hour talking without Nick pushing for details on Bob. He only asked if Abby's mother knew, and Abby was embarrassed to say that she did not. Nick frowned at that. Abby could see that if the relationship with Bob continued, it would push Nick into a more father-like role where Abby was concerned.

Early afternoon, as the sun's rays finally cut their way through the gray canopy that had gripped the sky all day, Nick said his goodbyes, gave Abby a big hug and drove back to El Rito. Abby thawed a container of lamb stew that showed signs of freezer burn, and spent the rest of the afternoon on the computer gathering information on female assassins in history and in clinical research. At five o'clock she decided time was better spent relaxing, so she mixed a rare margarita and eased into the evening. Tomorrow she'd get back to task.

8

Abby arrived in Santa Fe just after eight o'clock on a sunny Monday morning. She parked in the public lot across from the Lensic Theater and walked up the narrow snow-packed sidewalk to the Plaza Café for breakfast. The place bustled as it had for decades on a Monday morning, but Abby found a single seat at the counter and ordered the blue-corn pancake with maple syrup and applewood smoked bacon, a house specialty. A moment later an arm came around her shoulder and she heard the high-pitched friendly voice of Marci Lopez.

"What a nice surprise, Missy. You've been a stranger too long," Marci said.

Abby had known Marci Lopez since childhood when they were neighbors in Española and Abby rode horses with Marci's daughter, Marcella, who Abby called Cella. Marci always called Abby Missy, as she and Marcella would be missing for hours on their horses in the badland country near the Romero ranch. Marci was like a round ball in every respect: body, face, hair, eyes, and smile, which never quit.

"Do you still live in Abiquiu?" Marci asked.

"Yes, and loving it. How's Cella?"

"She and the kids are fine. They live in Taos, you know."

"No, I didn't. Do they like it?"

"Oh yes, and Cella even took up skiing. No horses though, too expensive."

"Marci, I have a question. I know you're busy, but has there been any talk on the street about a theft of a pot from the Roberts Gallery, or any talk about the Salazar murder?"

"No, *nada* about a pot. That Salazar thing is just awful, *no?* But you know the gossip. His affairs just caught up with him. People say it was an outsider, or maybe even a woman."

"Really. Why a woman?" Abby asked.

"Oh, you know the old joke about women being dumped in *El Norte*. Well honey, the list is long. Hey, I gotta get back to work. Good to see you, and come around more often." Marci hustled back to the kitchen and quickly reappeared with a large tray of plates that she balanced easily after years of practice. Abby thought about Marci's quip about local women being dumped by callous men. The women didn't take it lightly and didn't waste time feeling sorry for themselves. Martinez had been right about Salazar living on borrowed time.

Abby's breakfast order arrived just as her coffee needed a refill, and before she knew it, her plate was clean. While nursing the second cup of coffee, she looked around the room at happy well-lived faces, and felt glad she was in northern New Mexico this time of year. Winters ranged from windy and bitter cold one day to crystal clear, calm and warm the next. Businesses often built a fire in the small kiva fireplace and offered something warm to drink, and parking was not a problem after the holidays.

At nine forty-five she walked up the street past the plaza and down a block to the Roberts Gallery with a slight feeling of trepidation. In her gut she knew the hunt was on.

A tall, smartly dressed Hispanic woman smiled at Abby as she walked through the front door to the well-lit spacious gallery.

"You must be Ms. Romero," she said in a well-practiced friendly tone. "I'm Amanda Archuleta. Darien will be with you in a minute. Would you like coffee or tea?"

"No thanks, I just had breakfast at the Plaza."

"They always do breakfast well, don't they," Amanda said rhetorically.

Roberts appeared in the standard blue blazer and light blue shirt with no tie. His bright eyes, sandy hair, broad smile and casual manner oozed success. "Good morning, Abigail. Hope your weekend was pleasant. Do anything for fun?"

"No," Abby said, "just kept to myself and enjoyed the wintery weather."

"It is a nice time of year for us locals, isn't it?" he said cheerfully. "Let me show you where the pot was located."

He directed her to a small back room office. Several paintings were stacked against the wall next to a small utilitarian desk with a picture of his wife, phone, desk blotter and a small, gray stone object Abby guessed was a pre-Columbian fertility statue. A shelf held several pots, one of which Abby recognized as a Santa Claran sea serpent.

Tourists often asked why native people living in the high desert chose a sea serpent as an important spirit symbol. If they paid attention to the answer, they learned that native people consider water to be a living entity to honor and protect. Abby knew that the person who made that pot did not take water for granted.

As Abby looked at the shelf she realized it was designed for at least three pots. The asymmetry indicated a pot was missing.

"Tell me again when you last saw the pot?" Abby asked.

Robert leaned against the edge of the desk, stroked his chin and looked up at the ceiling. "I was in the office Thursday, Christmas eve, around noon, and I'm sure it was on the shelf then."

"Absolutely sure?"

"Yes, remember, I said I touched it before leaving? I'm fairly right-brained and I have patterns etched in my memory."

"Okay," Abby said. "I'm right brained also, so I get what you're saying. And when did you notice it was missing?" Abby continued to stand.

"I came in Saturday morning to pick up a file on a client and as I was leaving the office it hit me that something was wrong. I turned to look back and noticed the pot was gone."

"Was anyone working Friday or Saturday?"

"No, except possibly cleaning people, as I mentioned before, and I don't know their schedule. I have the name of the firm here." He handed Abby a card that read **Bird's Eye Cleaning: Top to Bottom**.

Abby put the card in her bag. "And you called other galleries?"

"Actually, no. I was embarrassed to tell them."

"Well," Abby said, "I've got to ask them, and pawn dealers as well. I've already called the ones listed in the phone book for Santa Fe and got nothing."

Roberts fidgeted with the wedding band on his ring finger and looked past Abby.

"I also need to talk to your employees." Abby gave up trying to maintain eye contact.

"I only have one full-time, Amanda Archuleta, whom you've met. She has been with me for ten years and I trust her without question."

"Good," Abby said. "One last thing, Mr. Roberts."

"Darien, please." Roberts said.

"All right. Are there any persons you suspect? Any grudges that would lead to this? Even any practical jokers who might do this for a 'gotcha' thing?" Abby shifted her weight to her right leg and tilted her head.

"I hadn't thought of that." Roberts looked pensive for a moment before he said, "If I come up with something I'll call you right away."

Roberts moved toward the door indicating he thought the interview was over. Abby followed and then asked him a question meant to catch him off guard.

"Why did you wait until Wednesday to call me?"

Roberts stopped and stood for a moment before turning slowly. "I was waiting to see if the pot would be returned," he said with a thin-lipped smile.

"Then you do suspect someone," Abby said flatly.

"I can't say at the moment. No, I'm sure there is no one." Roberts gave Abby an icy look. As an afterthought he said, "Frankly, I called several other detectives before calling you."

Abby returned the forced smile. Carmen was right, Abby thought, he doesn't take losing well. She knew that Roberts had underestimated her, but he wouldn't any longer.

Abby stopped and talked briefly with Amanda, but learned nothing new. Walking back to her car, Abby took a detour and walked a long block over to the museum to see Maria Gonzales again. When she asked Maria about illegal activity involving Mimbres pots, Maria said she had not heard of any illegal activity as long as she had been a curator. She explained that Mimbres pots in good condition are so rare that anyone who had one would have it under lock and key. Which, she added, suggested to her that whatever Roberts had, it was not an original.

As Abby walked back to her vehicle she theorized that Amanda knew the pot was a copy but covered for her boss out of the loyalty that is common among tenured assistants. Abby figured the pot was in cold storage somewhere to keep it out of sight. Just to be sure she called **Bird's Eye Cleaning** when she got home and got the answer she expected: the shelf was dusted and no pot.

So, Abby wondered, what was Roberts up to that he would be willing to pay her to find nothing? Was this somehow tied to the Salazar murder?

By late Monday afternoon Abby had added material to her files and a few more lines to her chart. Roberts was connected to Salazar with a dotted line, and to Abby with a solid line with a pot symbol in the middle. At first the diagram looked kind of silly, but perhaps it would give her a few ideas. She looked into space for a moment and then said out loud, "Robert's wife!" Abby decided to call her now under the guise that a woman's view would be valuable. She hoped Ms. Roberts would be more forthcoming than her slick husband. Duster began to run back and forth through the house, pausing at the kitchen door to chirp and paw at the door. Cats get cabin fever, so Abby opened the door and Duster dashed for the woodpile. Ten minutes later he was back at the door meowing for dinner. As Abby finished tending to His Highness' needs, the phone rang. It was Carmen.

"Hey, *hermana*, I've got some news. Sit down and take notes."

Abby pushed the files on the kitchen table out of the way and made ready. "Okay, shoot."

"First of all, Roberts seems to have a colorful and sordid past. Possibly present as well. My contacts say he takes trips without his wife for more than just art. You can fill in the blanks. None of this would be a big surprise given the way he sashays around town. But a juicier item is that his wife backed Salazar's political career big-time. She was very active in every fund raiser for Salazar's State senate races, and gossip was that she forked over a bundle herself. She comes from money, you know." Carmen took a breath.

"I heard that, and I intend to call her tomorrow for an interview," Abby said.

"Great! What happened with Roberts today?"

"I'm now sure the pot is a bogus hunt." Abby stood and walked around the kitchen while Duster sat and stared at her. "If the pot exists at all, it is probably a copy that he now has hidden away. He wants me for something else — I'm not sure for what — but he wants me close enough to keep an eye on me. I keep thinking that in some way this involves the Salazar murder. Maybe he is testing me out to see if I'm up to a bigger challenge, like finding the killer."

"Yeah," Carmen said. "The cops certainly seem at a dead end: surprise, surprise."

"I'll just have to wait and see," Abby responded.

"I've got some more digging to do," Carmen said, "so maybe we could get together at the end of the week. What do you say? I'm really enjoying this."

Abby always enjoyed seeing Carmen excited. "Sure, let's compare notes Friday. Maybe lunch at our usual place," Abby said.

"Call you Wednesday or Thursday to confirm," Carmen said. "Sorry I'll have to cut this short, but I've got company coming in a few minutes. *Bueno* bye." Carmen did not give Abby time to make a quip about her company.

Abby pushed her chair away from the table and looked at the ceiling. She was being drawn into a whirling vortex both ominous and exciting, and there was no backing away. She checked the Santa Fe phone directory and found a listing for Candace Roberts with her own phone number.

After three rings Candace Roberts answered with a husky "Hello."

"Ms. Roberts, glad I found you at home. My name is Abigail Romero and I'm investigating a theft for your husband and wondered if you could spare me thirty minutes of your time tomorrow?"

"Well, I doubt I could give you any information of value. In fact, I wasn't aware anything was stolen, but then I'm usually the last to know. What was taken?"

"A pot from the gallery," Abby said, "and I won't take much time. We could meet anywhere." She waited with anticipation.

"A pot. Hmmm. Well, all right. I'm due at the hairdresser for a cut at ten. How about lunch at Mucho Gusto at eleven-thirty? Do you know it?"

"Yes I do. See you then, and thanks very much." Candace said a curt goodbye. Abby put the phone down thinking Carmen was right, this is fun.

Abby spent the rest of Monday evening reading, interrupted by a short call from Bob seeking advice on a grant proposal he was writing for the Climate Study Center project that was consuming most of his time. While Bob was excited about the concept of a climate research center, it was becoming clear to Abby that organizing such an endeavor was not his long suit. She could sympathize. Night winds picked up and Abby and Duster made for the warmth of the double bed earlier than usual.

In the morning, Abby called galleries and pawn dealers from nine until ten-thirty before heading to Santa Fe and lunch with Candace Roberts. When Abby walked through the front door of Mucho Gusto, the host smiled and asked if she was meeting someone. She nodded and returned the smile while removing her jacket. The host asked if she was meeting Ms. Roberts, she nodded again and the host led the way. Candace Roberts was seated next to a window where she could see Abigail approach the restaurant from the parking lot. So, thought Abby, she wanted to size me up.

Candace did not get up, but smiled with straight thin lips and held out her hand. "I'm Candace Roberts. Nice to meet you Abigail." She did not ask permission to use Abby's first name, nor did she offer the familiarity of her own. Her hair was bleached blond with highlights, a well-styled medium-length cut. Large tortoiseshell amber-tinted glasses set off a square face that had been worked on, and her neck was masked by a colorful scarf tucked into an expensive wool jacket.

"Nice to meet you also, Ms. Roberts," Abby said politely while adjusting herself in the chair. "And thanks again for giving me time." Abby looked Candace in the eye. "Should we order first?"

"Yes, let's do. Everything they have here seems to have black beans, so I hope you like them."

"I do," Abby said. "I've eaten here before. I really like the *chalupas*."

"So do I," Candace said, sounding surprised. "It's times two then."

They made a little small talk and hot plates arrived sooner than expected.

"So tell me about this pot," Candace said, her voice rising slightly.

"It's a Mimbres that Mr. Roberts says is an original."

Candace interrupted and put her fork down. "The one in his office?" she almost shrieked.

"Yes, you know it then?" Abby asked.

"Oh my god, that thing," Candace said scornfully. "That's a copy that he got from one of his . . . well, let's say associates, ten years ago in Silver City." Candace coughed, cleared her throat and looked out the window for a moment. Her face reddened.

"Do you remember this associate?"

"Yes," she replied in a firm voice. "Her name was Lupe Garza and she worked for some resort down there. Darien and Alfonso, ah, that's the late Alfonso Salazar," Candace cleared her throat again, "were working in Silver City on some project connected with this resort. Mr. Salazar was his assistant then. That was before he got into politics."

Candace seemed upset by this conversation. Apparently a flood of memories were coming back to her, and Abby was intrigued. Candace continued.

"He said the pot was a gift from the resort, but it came from the Garza woman who had it made. There is a small piece of jasper embedded in the bottom, which you can ask him about. Can't say I'm sorry to see the pot gone, and I sure as hell can't give you any idea who would steal it. The only value is personal." Candace put her napkin on the table and suddenly didn't seem hungry.

Abby tried to smooth over the awkwardness of the moment and quickly suggested that perhaps the Garza woman retrieved the pot for some reason.

"I don't think she is even in the country," Candace said. "She disappeared years ago. I'll say one thing for her, she got around."

Abby took advantage of the opening. "Can you describe her?"

"Well, as you might expect, she . . ." Candace quickly recovered from the politically incorrect statement she was about to make, "She was from Mexico, classic beauty actually, dark skin and hair, engaging eyes, probably mid twenties then and about your height and build." Candace grew silent, her eyes in a blank stare. Abby's mind raced, wanting more. Candace looked at her watch. "I almost forgot, I've got an appointment and must get going." She hastily took a twenty from her purse and said, "Do you mind taking care of the bill?" and without waiting for a reply got up and hurried out.

Abby watched Candace Roberts walk rapidly toward a Lexus and drive out of the lot a bit too fast. The waiter came with the bill and Abby stopped him. "Does Ms. Roberts eat here often?"

"I can't say Miss. Is there anything else?"

"No, thanks, it was very good." Well, at least he didn't call me madam or ma'am, she thought.

Abby considered stopping at the gallery, but decided to wait for Roberts' call, which would come this evening after the caustic comments Candace would surely make to him during cocktail hour.

"The pot, so to speak, had been stirred good," Abby said to herself, and turned her attention to Lupe Garza on the drive home.

After sending the deceptive email to Mendoza on Tuesday, Lupe Garza returned home to find three new email messages. The first was from Mendoza.

"Disappointed you did not come. Opportunity slipping away. Where are you?" Signed SM.

Lupe thought for a moment. She had to assume that Mendoza knew that she was in Phoenix, but with over three million people occupying arguably the largest urban sprawl in the country, she could hide out indefinitely. Best places to hide were in large cities and wide-open country, she thought. Lupe figured Mendoza might have one of his aides do some checking with car rental firms, a few motels, and more calls and emails to her, but finding her would be pure luck on his part. Mendoza would have to lure her into a trap.

Lupe moved on to the other message. Sergeant Duran's message gave the name Abigail Romero along with an email address and phone number. In return, Duran asked Wanda James for her address and a phone number for future contact. Lupe now wondered if getting the name of Abigail Romero was worth the risk of placing Wanda James as a person of interest to the police, but she still had the gut feeling that the Romero woman was the greater danger and worth that risk. It was Tuesday evening and Lupe felt that the gap was closing between her and her enemies.

9

The phone rang just before six o'clock Abby looked at the caller ID screen and answered.

"Yes, Mr. Roberts, what can I do for you?" Abby asked, smiling to herself.

"You talked to my wife today. I didn't know you had planned to do that. She was quite upset." There was a hard clipped tone to his voice. Abby was not surprised.

Abby replied in kind. "When you hire me, I do the investigation my way or not at all, Mr. Roberts. I thought your wife might be able to give me more information on people who might have a grudge against you and might go to this extreme. I'm very sorry it upset your wife." Abby waited.

"Did she tell you where the pot came from?" Roberts' tone changed to inquisitive, but still edgy.

"Yes, she did."

"And . . .?"

Abby could feel his boiling point was near. "She said it was a gift from a resort in Silver City," Abby said calmly.

"Did she say anything else?"

"Yes, she did."

"Okay, this cat and mouse game is getting us nowhere," Roberts said, the boiling point reached.

Abby waited silently.

"All right, so the pot is a copy," Roberts barked. "But it still is very valuable to me and I want it back."

"What do you suggest I do, Mr. Roberts?" Abby loved getting the upper hand with men like Roberts.

Roberts was silent for a moment, cleared his throat and started again in a calmer tone. "Perhaps we should shift gears. Maybe you're right about its being a practical joke. Let's sit on it for a few days. In the meantime, the police are not getting anywhere on the murder of Alfonso and I want something done before it's too late. Would you be willing to continue on at your usual fee and see what you can find?"

Abby waited a moment. She had considered this offer as a possibility, albeit a remote one. But Abby certainly was interested, and why not get paid for doing something she had planned to do anyway? "Mr. Roberts, do you have any ideas that you would share with me? Without something to go on I could spend a lot of time spinning my wheels and wasting your money."

"Yes, well, we should talk, but not over the phone." Roberts sounded tentative.

Abby seized the opportunity. "I won't agree to this until after we talk. But I won't talk at all unless you understand that any investigation I do is my call regardless of where it leads. You must agree or I'll drop this right now."

Abby heard only silence for a few seconds.

"All right. Can we meet tomorrow at my office at ten?"

"I'll be there." Abby said goodbye, went to the cabinet for a bottle of wine, and with a half glass of red in hand, sat down to think and make notes while ideas were fresh. After an hour she made a salad and put a frozen pizza in the toaster oven. Duster was asleep in front of the stove, which needed more wood. By nine o'clock she had written all she could think of and went to bed.

An hour before dawn the dream came again, only this time Abby woke just after pulling the trigger. The skull-faced figured just laughed — maniacally.

Wednesday morning was clear, calm, twenty degrees, and Abby figured the drive into Santa Fe would be glorious, with sharp blue skies resting on the snow-capped peaks; a good opportunity to put the dream out of her mind. She picked up a breakfast burrito at Bailey's, chatted with Christine Bailey for a minute and was on the road before nine. Most winter holiday tourists had left the city and Abby was able to find a parking place on the street near the gallery. Just to be safe, she pumped two more quarters in the meter than she thought she'd need, as Santa Fe meter readers were vigilant.

Once again Darien Roberts was punctual and Abby sat across from his small functional desk promptly at ten o'clock. They both had their game faces on. "Beautiful morning, isn't it, Miss. Romero?"

So, Abby thought, we are going to be formal this morning. "Yes, indeed, Mr. Roberts. The mountains sparkled."

"I won't waste your time. But first, would you give me a bill for the time you spent on the vessel, and we'll start fresh this morning, that is if you decide to take the case."

"Fair enough." She handed an envelope to Roberts who laid it on the desk without opening it.

"To start, let me ask you what my wife told you about Lupe Garza." Roberts looked squarely at Abby without smiling.

"Very little," Abby said without registering surprise. "She said the woman worked for the resort, and I took it she was your contact on the business venture. She also mentioned that Mr. Salazar was your assistant at that time." Abby paused a moment. "And she did mention that the pot had a small piece of jasper embedded in the base, but she did not explain what that meant."

"What meaning did you make of all this?" Roberts asked flatly.

"To be honest, Mr. Roberts, I considered several options."

"Such as . . . ?" Roberts asked, his tone caustic.

"Look, I thought we were going to discuss the Salazar murder. I'm not interested in your personal life," Abby said politely. She folded her hands in her lap and raised her head slightly.

"Well, this might have some bearing on the murder," Roberts said with a wry smile while continuing to look at Abby straight on. "As I'm sure you thought, I had an affair with Ms. Garza — a very brief affair — because she fell under Alfonso's spell rather quickly. At the time I was upset, but in short order decided it was for the best." Roberts leaned back a little. "I can't say that my wife and I have an open marriage, but she has had her flings and so have I. Still, our marriage is more than a business arrangement and I care for her very much."

Abby put up both hands as if to say "your business is your business."

Roberts leaned forward and continued. "Alfonso's affair with Garza probably went on in a casual manner for more than a year. At the same time, Alberto Ramirez . . . do you know him?"

"Of course," Abby replied, still holding her hands in her lap.

"Ramirez was beginning to take an interest in Alfonso as a person with great political potential. When he found out that Alfonso was thick with a Mexican woman, which, as you well know, would not play well in northern New Mexico, he took steps to quash it, and Garza left Silver City, presumably for Mexico. As strong a woman as Garza is, Ramirez does not take no for an answer. I can imagine Garza was angry with Alfonso for caving in to Ramirez, but she disappeared so fast that I don't know any more than that. So there you have some background." Roberts pushed his chair back and his shoulders relaxed.

Abby leaned forward and put her hands on the edge of he desk. "Are you suggesting the Garza woman may have had a hand in killing Salazar?"

"No. Rather, I doubt it. Oh, I think she is capable, as are a number of women, but . . .

"Why do you say that about Garza?" Abby interrupted raising her eyebrows.

"Because I think she got mixed up with drug gangs in Mexico, and, as you read almost every day in the newspapers, they are a ruthless bunch of thugs."

Abby leaned back and looked at the floor a moment, thinking. This was the first she had heard about a link between Lupe Garza and drug activity. This could change things, Abby thought. "Do you know where she is now or where she has been recently?"

"No idea," Roberts said a bit too quickly.

"All right," Abby said slowly. "Do you have any more information or ideas about the murder?"

Roberts leaned forward and folded his hands on the desk. Abby thought he enjoyed looking earnest, like any salesman closing the deal on a product of dubious merit. "The Garza woman is not to be dismissed. From personal experience I can tell you she is very smart and I think rather amoral. Actually, I would hazard a guess that the police are on the right track."

"So you do think the killer was an assassin." Abby interrupted.

"Don't quote me on that. I know the police have suggested it, but that's partially media stuff. You know, suggesting that Alfonso was so loved that no one would want him dead, which is bullshit." Roberts had lost his slick veneer.

"So who?" Abby asked.

"I suggest you look into two areas: political rivals and business deals. I can't, or won't give you names, but they aren't that hard to find. In fact, one of them was at the Pueblo that night."

Abby looked at him and both were silent. Roberts blinked first. "Well," clearing his throat, "I think you have enough to go on. Give it your best shot and let's get together in a week or so, unless something big happens in the meantime. If there is no progress by then, I'll call it off and consider it a cold case."

Roberts looked at Abby with raised eyebrows anticipating an affirmative response.

"All right," Abby said, "but I have one question before I get started. Why do you want to solve this case? Why not just leave it to the police?"

Roberts was silent but his face gave nothing away. He didn't get where he is today by being an easy read, Abby thought.

"I could say that I want justice, but you wouldn't buy that. Let's just say I want it to be done right."

Abby didn't know what to make of that beyond inferring that Roberts thought the police might bungle it. But she filed his statement under "look at this again." They shook hands and Abby exited with a smile and nod to Amanda who returned in kind.

The parking meter had fifteen minutes left, so Abby decided to walk back to the plaza and look at the ice sculptures that chefs from various restaurants carved for the holidays. As usual, the plaza was filled with interesting looking people, dogs with scarves and colorful sweaters, and several vendors selling hot finger-food and cider. The plaza was always worth a detour for Abby and most locals. With one minute remaining on the meter, and the patrol at the end of the block, she pulled away from the curb and headed over to the library for a hour of research on Lupe Garza.

Today the library bustled and she had to wait for a reading machine. Abby found very little on Garza beyond the connection to the Silver City resort. There was a photo of Roberts, Garza and Salazar in connection with the proposed resort. Another article a few days later mentioned Silas Mendoza as a developer interested in the project. Abby added a mental vector between Mendoza and Salazar with Garza in the middle. Abby found one more article in a New Mexico travel magazine that mentioned the three names, confirming a triangle involving Mendoza, Garza and Salazar, which was what Roberts had been trying to sell. A profile for Garza was beginning to emerge, but Abby wanted to check some Mexican magazines before coming to any conclusions. Abby could finish that on the internet. She stopped for some fresh chicken and good bread on the way home.

Carmen called as Abby was putting dishes away.

"Hey, what's up?" Abby asked cheerfully.

"Got more news, boss. This is getting interesting."

"Fire away," Abby said.

"In more ways than one. Seems our Alfonso Salazar took frequent trips to Puerto Peñasco in Mexico. It's near the Arizona border."

"I know the place," Abby interrupted. "Anglos in Arizona call it Rocky Point. Was a small fishing village, but *turistas* took it over."

"Right. Anyway, the gossip is that Salazar could be seen on a yacht belonging to one of the Mexican drug bosses. You know, women, drugs and the high life."

"Any women in particular?" Abby asked. "I'm interested in Lupe Garza."

"I don't know, but I'll check," Carmen said.

"Have any of your sources said whether Salazar was into drugs?"

"Hey, who isn't, besides you and me and our parents? Well, Nick too."

"Okay, but I mean the possibility that Salazar might have been in the business. He always seemed to have more money than he should have. You know, expensive clothes, trips and cars."

"I doubt I can find anything out on that, but I'll try. Are we still on for lunch on Friday at the fish place, say one o'clock or so?"

"It's a date," Abby said, "or, shall I say I'll pencil you in?"

"You do that. Should I call your secretary and confirm?" Carmen's voice rose in sarcasm.

"Never mind," Abby said and laughed. They went on for another fifteen minutes about work, clothes, and men. Abby and Carmen knew just how long to talk with each other without it becoming tedious for either one; the mark of a very good friendship.

At nine o'clock, Abby made a cup of herbal tea, played with Duster and spent twenty minutes more researching Lupe Garza and updating the wall chart.

10

Lupe was accustomed to nights of loud music from neighbors when she lived in Guadalajara, but Tuesday night was too much even for her. She lost her patience and told off the offending neighbor, saying both he and his boom box would suffer an identical beating if it continued. The threat worked, although her low profile was no longer low. The next morning Lupe worked off her frustration with a long run on the canal banks and a good breakfast before settling down with the computer to find out more about Abigail Romero.

Lupe tried Facebook first and found nothing, which told her a lot. With LinkedIn she scored a hit. Abigail Romero was a business woman, specifically an investigator who specialized in missing persons, lost items, research on family members, and occasionally helped police with research beyond average police-work skill. In place of a photo there was a spear point and a quote that read "Seek and you shall find." Romero listed college degrees in sociology and anthropology from the University of New Mexico, work background that included NASA Ames, and hobbies of cooking, hunting and hiking. She displayed one photo of a mountain that Lupe knew was the Pedernal near Abiquiu, and a 4Runner parked in the foreground. She had posted another photo of a Mimbres pot and requested information on its recovery. Lupe instantly recognized the pot.

On the surface the LinkedIn site for Romero looked legitimate for a person in that business. The lack of a portrait photo could mean a number of things, but the spear point, the hobby of hunting and the business of investigation suggested to Lupe that this woman was a hunter, as she had suspected, and about the same age as Lupe, which she inferred from the dates of her college degrees. No mention of family, so Romero was also single. No cute pictures of pets, vacation shots or statements about politics or religion. This woman was a loner who was well focused and confident. This was someone to take seriously, very seriously.

The Mimbres pot on Romero's LinkedIn page piqued Lupe's curiosity. Roberts was up to something. One possibility was that he wanted to hire Romero to keep an eye on her. More important, Lupe thought, was that Lupe was connected to the pot and Roberts was putting Romero on a trail to find her. The big questions were why and would Romero take the bait?

The next question was to find out whether Romero was also investigating the Salazar murder? Lupe checked the Santa Fe and Albuquerque papers and found very little: no suspects and no mention of Romero. Lupe decided to use Wanda James. That ploy might help her find out if Romero was on to her, and if so, lure her into a trap. She sent a simple message to the email address listed on the LinkedIn site: *I have no information on the pot, but could you help me locate my twin sister? She's mid-thirties, last seen in Las Cruces, New Mexico and has been missing for a month.* signed Wanda James. Lupe smiled mischievously as she hit the send button.

Abby started Wednesday morning doing the same thing that Lupe Garza was doing five hundred miles to the southwest in Phoenix. Abby had established that Garza had moved from Silver City to Guadalajara about eight years ago, because her name appeared in a blog about drug activity seven years back. Like most people north of the border, Abby had ignored the extent of the drug wars in northern Mexico. She was surprised to discover the high number of blogs about drug cartels, far more than Abby would have guessed, and the blogs gave names and details about activities and casualties. This was war reporting that was even too graphic for an American media that feeds off fear.

Abby learned that, seven years ago, Lupe Garza had been mentioned in one of the blogs as a companion or bodyguard of one of the cartel bosses. A year later she was identified as being involved in a shooting between rival cartels. Shortly after that Lupe was identified as one of the most respected and feared enforcers for a top cartel in Guadalajara. A few months after the blog describing Garza as *vengadora*, several stories circulated about her cartel being overthrown by a rival gang. The top people in the deposed cartel had been killed, although there was no confirmation that Garza was among the dead. Garza disappeared from the blogs.

It was time for a brief call to Roberts. After a brief greeting from Amanda, Roberts came on the line.

"Morning Abigail, what can I do for you?"

"Good morning, Mr. Roberts, I have several quick questions. How old was Lupe Garza when you knew her in Silver City?"

"I believe mid-twenties. Why?"

"I'm just trying to build profiles on persons of interest."

"You said several questions."

"Yes. Do you think she is still alive?"

The pause lasted longer than normal. "Gosh, Abigail, I assume so, although I've . . . Wait, I think I saw her at some political function for Alfonso a year ago. That's the best I can do."

The political function sighting was pure bullshit, Abby thought. He wants me on her trail. With Salazar out of the picture, he wants her back. He's not paying me to solve a murder.

"That's fine," Abby said. "Thanks much." She hit the end button.

Abby crossed out the name Mystery Woman on the file folder and printed Lupe Garza on a new label in bold letters. She did not change the name on the wall chart as it added to the drama. She sat back for a moment and then quickly jotted down several questions. First, was Garza a sexual hunter? Second, did she have ambitions for power beyond being a sexual hunter? Was she amoral as Roberts had suggested? Or, was she none of these? Was Lupe a hunter and a loner, resourceful, smart and played by her own rules?

Abby decided to reject the innuendo from Roberts about Lupe being amoral and a sexual hunter. That was more bullshit from Roberts who was fast becoming a source of deception in Abby's mind. For some reason, Roberts wanted Abby to think that Lupe Garza was shallow, one-dimensional, someone not to be taken seriously, someone that might be easily trapped. That could be fatal for me, Abby thought.

As Abby put the Garza folder aside, she decided to check her email and found a message from a person she'd never heard of, a Wanda James, who requested Abby's help in locating a missing twin sister. A missing twin! Abby felt strange, that ghost again, tapping her on the shoulder. Abby shivered and glanced up at the wall chart. *Was the chart finally talking to her?*

Acting on impulse, Abby fired back a reply to Wanda saying she was working on a project that required her full attention, but she'd get back to her in several weeks. Next she looked up Wanda James on both Facebook and LinkedIn and found two older women living in the east, and a teenager in Alaska. Really, Abby thought, a person with a missing sister and she's not in any social network. She checked a few other local sources and Wanda James did not appear. Abby stared at the chart on the wall, her eyes focusing on the words mystery woman. After a timeless moment Duster trilled and snapped her back to the present.

Abby went back and reconstructed the night of the shooting. She made notes about how she felt when she saw Garza's photo in the newspaper, like she was looking at herself. Abby wrote 'missing twin sister' and circled it. She added all this to the profile folder and tried to put herself in Garza's shoes. Certainly, she thought, a careful assassin who had been followed would try to determine if the pursuer had simply acted on impulse, like a bystander chasing a purse-snatching thief, or, if the pursuer were a hunter and would not break off the chase.

Abby decided that Wanda James could be Lupe Garza. If that were true, it meant that Garza now knew a great deal about Abigail Romero. Furthermore, the email Abby sent would tell Garza, aka Wanda James, that Abby was working on the Salazar murder. The posting about the Mimbres pot on LinkedIn would also tell Lupe that Roberts was involved in the hunt. Abby quickly brought up her LinkedIn account and looked at everything. "Shit," she said out loud. Her 4Runner was in the photo. Well, the horse is out of the barn now, she thought.

Abby needed a plan. First she deleted the posting about the pot in the LinkedIn account and the photo with the 4Runner. Abby added a post that said she would be traveling for several weeks. The new post, along with the deletions, would tell Garza that something had changed. Abby hoped she was adding more ambiguity to the equation: two hunters, each hunter also a prey. The game was on in earnest and the juices were flowing.

At noon, Abby got a surprise call from Carmen who said she could not make lunch on Friday, but could they do dinner tonight? "I'll bring *chile verde, burritos and sopapillas* from *El Cantina*," she said without waiting for Abby.

"Can't say no to that. Come when you can. I've got some Monk's Ale."

"And I have some info on that Garza person," Carmen said. "Tell you tonight."

It was late afternoon on Wednesday. Lupe was working at the kitchen table sketching out plans when a shadow moved slowly past the west-facing living room window. She heard the low rumble of base notes from a large speaker in a car. Instantly, Lupe hit the floor and crawled rapidly to the corner of the window. A vintage white Cadillac low-rider moved from her right down the street and turned left at the corner. Lupe raced to the bedroom and grabbed the Colt-45 with the laser sight from her bag and strapped a 22 Cobra Magnum to her ankle. Quickly she moved beside a window that looked out on the back yard, stood against the wall with enough view to see the gate to the alley, and held the Colt in her right hand down along her leg. All houses in the neighborhood had back yards walled with sump block just high enough to make climbing difficult. She heard the Cadillac belching hip-hop verse in the alley.

The gate opened slowly and two Mexican-looking youths entered the yard without weapons in their hands. Lupe unlocked the kitchen door and stood behind a cabinet next to the door.

"Yo, Mr. Pioh, you home?" the youth in the lead called out. The leader was stocky, medium height, wearing long baggy pants, a Dallas Cowboys jacket and a bandana on his head. The other was shorter and dressed exactly the same.

They approached the back door and knocked loudly twice. "Joe, you in there?" The knob on the door turned slowly. Lupe waited until the two men were in the doorway, spun toward them, dropped to one knee, and aimed the laser beam directly on the first youth's crotch.

"Hands on your head. NOW!" Lupe commanded. "Drop to your knees."

"Hey, who the fuck are you? We're . . ."

"No talk punk. On your knees. NOW! Keep your hands up."

"What the fuck is . . ."

"Shut up!" The laser beam moved to the forehead of the apparent leader. "You *jefe*?" Lupe asked.

"*Sí*"

"Lie face down, both of you, slowly."

"What's this . . ."

"Be cool, bro, I'll ask the questions. First I want your weapons on the floor. All of them, and I know what you carry. You know with this beam I won't miss."

The two carefully removed two handguns and two knives.

"Now push back and do it slow." Lupe kicked the weapons into the far corner of the room. "Who's in the car?" Lupe asked.

"Miguel, and he probably can't hear," the leader said.

"Call him in here," Lupe demanded.

"I'll try, but . . ."

"Do it," Lupe said sharply.

A short minute later a younger youth slouched into the kitchen. When he saw his two companions on the floor he took off running, and in seconds Lupe heard the Caddy tearing down the alley.

"So much for that," Lupe said. "All right, bros, talk to me. What's your game?"

"The dude what lives here owes us," said the taller one.

"You're not up to speed, bros. I rented this place last week. He's gone. What's your gang, *banda?*"

"Fuck, you must be new here," the leader said. "This here's our turf. We decide what goes down." He spit on the floor.

"That's real cool, muthah," Lupe said and laughed. She ripped off a paper towel and tossed it in front of the one doing the talking. She knelt down on one knee and said calmly, "You see this tattoo on my neck?"

"Yeah, so what?"

"Do you know what it means?"

"Yeah."

"I don't think you do. Look at it and don't forget it. I'm not here for long, but neither you or any of the bros will bother me again. *Comprende?*" Lupe put the beam between his eyes. "*Comprende?*" she said again firmly.

They nodded slowly without looking at each other.

"Now wipe up your spit, throw the towel in the garbage in the alley and leave the way you came. You'll get the weapons back *mañana*. You boys just got real lucky."

They shuffled out the door without looking back. The smaller of the two said something on the way through the gate and the big one shoved him.

Kids, Lupe thought, as she watched them leave.

Carmen arrived at six-thirty with containers packed with the kind of food northern New Mexicans crave and consume with regularity. Locals talk of getting their *El Cantina* fix as though it were their drug of choice. With longnecks of ale, Abby and Carmen made only sounds of gastronomic pleasure for five minutes. Finally Carmen said, "One of the girls in the office used to work at a resort in Silver City and knew Lupe Garza."

"Great," Abby said and looked up eagerly at Carmen.

"Well, from the way she described this Garza, she is a lot like you: similar appearance, intense, smart and gets what she wants."

"Am I like that?" Abby said raising her hands and voice in jest.

Carmen gave Abby a are-you-kidding-me look. "Moving on," Carmen glared at Abby. "Garza seemed to be involved with that gallery owner for a time, but then moved over to Salazar, and the way my office mate told it, it was hot."

"I got some of this from Roberts himself," Abby said.

"But did you know that Roberts was seen with her again, recently?"

"No," Abby gasped excitedly. "He did not mention that. How did you learn that?"

"I have another friend who lives in Madrid, and when I mentioned the Garza thing to her, she said that Roberts met this woman who sounds like Garza at that funky bar in Madrid for a couple of late lunches about six months ago. She's a waitress there." Carmen stood up with beer in hand.

Abby pushed her chair back. "Yeah, I know the place. Did she say anything about how they acted or how many times they were there?"

"She said it was only twice that she knew of, and it did not seem like romance. She also said they always sat in a corner and tried to avoid being noticed. Oh, and they arrived separately. He usually was there first." Carmen waved her bottle at Abby for emphasis.

"How did she dress?"

"Damn, I didn't ask that." Carmen set the bottle down hard.

"Do you know if she's been there recently?"

"I did ask her that. No, she hasn't seen Garza for months."

Abby stood and walked over to the sink, leaned against it and looked back at Carmen. "What do you make of this? Ten years ago she was in bed with Roberts and then quickly switched to Salazar big time. Then she leaves and goes to Mexico where she becomes involved with a big drug cartel. I got this all from blogs on the internet. She surfaces again here and meets with Roberts, not Salazar."

"We don't know that she wasn't with Salazar," Carmen added quickly.

"True, we don't."

"Wait, I've got more," Carmen interrupted. "The waitress in Madrid swings both ways, not something I understand, but she does. Anyway, she said Garza also showed up at a gay bar in Santa Fe, and she thinks that Garza hooked up both times the waitress saw her."

"You're kidding! Garza is gay, or bi?" Abby started to pace.

"Looks like it," Carmen said. "I don't know what this means, but it might cancel the sex thing between Roberts and Garza."

"Maybe," Abby said. "But it might be one-sided. For some reason, men apparently find lesbians and bad women hot. But then why were the meetings between them in Madrid so businesslike? Abby leaned against the sink again and took a swallow from the longneck. "Have you come up with anything more on Roberts?" Abby asked.

"Only that he is known for being highly competitive, which you already knew, but perhaps competitive to the point of getting even when he loses, which apparently isn't often."

"Got an example?" Abby asked.

"Remember I said someone in my office admitted to having a relationship with him awhile back?"

"Yeah."

"Well, I asked her again about it and she said that when he broke it off she had the feeling she shouldn't push it. She wouldn't go into detail, she just drew a line across her throat and rolled up her eyes."

They both were silent for a minute.

"Man, Carm, we've got ourselves mixed up with a bunch of cold twisted people. Hey, let's let this rest and talk about some fun stuff. You've done great."

They spent the next half hour talking about diets, clothes and men, without Abby mentioning the dream. Duster romped in and out of the conversation. By eight-thirty Carmen's tail lights faded from view. Abby felt energized but unsettled. She'd tackle it all again tomorrow with a clear head.

11

The former tenant in Lupe Garza's barrio rental had left an old television in the house; the mark of a fast getaway. While cooking a lean dinner, Lupe turned on the local news in time to hear the anchor say *"Police in Santa Fe New Mexico have arrested a suspect in the murder of the popular politician Alfonso Salazar. For more on the story we go to Elena Alvarez in Santa Fe."*

The screen showed a young Hispanic woman standing outside a building she pointed to as housing the detention center.

"Police have arrested Joey Martinez of Santa Fe in the murder of Alfonso Salazar. Police found the weapon used to murder Salazar in Martinez' apartment when they investigated a burglary. Among items alleged to have been stolen was the Salazar murder weapon. Martinez denies shooting Salazar, but police say he cannot account for his whereabouts on the night of the shooting, although a family member said Martinez was in church in Taos on Christmas eve."

Background film showed a distant shot of the Taos Pueblo, a photo of Salazar, a mug shot of a defiant Martinez, and the usual yellow tape across the door to Martinez' apartment.

Lupe smiled to herself. She knew the case would not hold up, but the arrest got the police off the hook temporarily. Some young attorney would defend Martinez for the publicity, and a serial burglar would be off the streets for months. In the meantime, Lupe would have some elbow-room to maneuver, although she figured the Romero woman would not slow down her hunt. Tomorrow she'd make a decision about New Mexico.

After her yoga routine Thursday morning, Abby turned on public radio in time to catch local news and hear the report about the arrest of Joey Martinez. She went immediately to the online edition of the newspaper, read the story and put in a call to Darien Roberts. He called back an hour later.

"Yes, Mr. Roberts, I read the story," Abby told him, "and I'm sure they have the wrong person."

"Why do you think so?" Robert asked in a tone of indifference.

"I'm convinced the shooter was a woman."

"A woman! But it was a person in a monk's robe! The police have been saying all along that it was a man." Again, indifference in his tone.

"I know, and I told the investigating sergeant at the scene that I thought it was a woman, but he didn't buy it," Abby said flatly. There was a long pause.

"What do you want to do?" Roberts asked.

"Continue my investigation, regardless."

Another long pause. "All right. For now we'll continue our arrangement, but I need to be kept informed of what you have."

Before Roberts could hang up Abby said "Ahhh," and she dragged it out hoping to induce a bit of suspense and possibly catch him off guard, "A strange thing happened yesterday." I received an email from a woman named Wanda James." Abby strained to hear if there was even a flicker of recognition from Roberts.

Nothing.

"I think Wanda James may be Lupe Garza, and I believe Garza may be mixed up in this."

Roberts was silent. Abby thought she heard a muffled clearing of his throat. "This sounds like a stretch to me, but follow it up as you think best. I . . . , oh never mind. This turn of events is, well . . . Just keep me informed." Roberts sounded frustrated. The line went dead.

"Well, Duster," Abby said to a cat paying no attention, "I'm working for a puppeteer who is losing his grip."

Duster ambled away flicking his tail.

Abby went to the wall chart and wrote the name Wanda James with a question mark in parentheses next to the words mystery woman, and drew a line to Roberts and added Madrid also in parentheses.

Lupe rose early Thursday morning, launched into her morning running routine and mulled over her options while enjoying a soft breeze, sixty degrees and bright sunshine. Problem with the weather in the Valley of the Sun was that it was seductive. Easy to forget your problems when it feels balmy and everywhere else except Florida people are battling old man winter. Reluctantly, she decided to meet the problems head on and go back to New Mexico. She'd call Mendoza after a shower and light breakfast.

"Mr. Mendoza, sorry I missed the appointment, but I've been working."

"Thank you for calling back." Mendoza's voice was all business. "The proposition I spoke of is still open. Are you interested?"

"Can you tell me more over the phone?" Lupe tried to sound detached.

"I can tell you this: I have an opportunity to broker a deal for some merchandise south of the border. I could use your assistance."

Lupe paused a moment. According to her informant, Mendoza had been in contact with the Z cartel, her rival gang prior to the hit on her life in PV. She answered tentatively, "I've been out of touch and not sure I could accomplish what you need."

"We need to talk." Mendoza never took no for an answer.

Lupe knew she had to meet with him in order to have some control over how events would play out. "How about the small mall with the Apple store? I'll meet you out front tomorrow at ten o'clock. There are several restaurants in the area."

"Why not today? By the way, where are you?"

"Why, Mr. Mendoza, I'm sure you have already figured out where I am. Tomorrow, sir, at ten. If something comes up I'll call."

"All right, at ten." He didn't sound pleased.

Lupe hit the end button, wrote a note to the landlord saying if she wasn't back in ten days to rent the place. She left another note on the back gate that said *items you left here are in one of the trash barrels.* Lupe put the guns and knives in a grocery bag and dropped them in a large barrel. She packed, filled the gas tank at a nearby station, bought some trail mix and energy bars, and headed north through Payson toward I-40. Lupe estimated the trip to Albuquerque would be eight hours with a few short stops. She heard about a place called the Ranch Kitchen near Gallup that had great lamb stew, and she'd be there after the noon rush.

As Lupe drove, she mentally ran through several scripts about Mendoza. Salazar had reneged on a promise to smooth the way for Mendoza to open a casino in Rio Arriba County, and Mendoza was probably still angry. At the time there had been some talk that the deal might go to Roberts, who was one of Mendoza's primary competitors. That turned out to be false, as the deal eventually went to the Jicarilla Apache tribe. Mendoza could possibly fault Lupe for not being more proactive on his behalf with Salazar, but that wasn't her job, and Mendoza understood that. Mendoza could possibly be smarting over losing Lupe as a showpiece during his business deals, but that wasn't a capital offense either. Perhaps, Lupe thought, she was simply an expendable chip in his eyes.

And then there was Alberto Ramirez. Lupe was painfully aware Ramirez would like to even the score for the loss of Salazar, his prize political puppet. Of the two, Mendoza and Ramirez, it be Ramirez who would want her dead, but of the two, only Mendoza could profit financially. "They are working together," she said out loud. From here on, Lupe decided, she would need to be extremely careful.

After lunch, Abby decided to take another look at the Garza file. She knew something was missing. The information Abby had so far made it look like Lupe Garza jumped around from one place to another, from one man or woman to another, and in-between she worked as a paid killer. Was she a psychopath, a cold-blooded woman or someone in need of firm ground? Abby poured over the material again looking for some constant in this person's life. Exasperated at finding nothing, she decided to call Ramón Martinez in Truchas. She found him home.

"Mr. Martinez, this is Abigail Romero."

"*Señorita Romero,*" Martinez replied. "What can I do for you?"

"I'm fascinated with one of the women in Alfonso Salazar's life, the one you identified as Lupe Garza. What can you tell me about the personal or private side of this woman?" Abby rather enjoyed listening to Martinez' whiskey tempered tones. He was both articulate and lyrical, and could be professorial when moved.

"A pleasure to hear your voice, *señorita,* but I'm not sure I can be of much help. I never actually met the woman, but of course I heard stories."

"Can you give me some stories you think might help me understand her?"

Martinez began by describing a person who had a tough veneer, but he sensed something fragile or vulnerable about her, which he thought made her all the more attractive to powerful men like Salazar, Mendoza and Roberts. As far as something firm or constant in her life, he simply said, "Well, she's a woman, isn't she?" Abby knew it was a tongue-in-cheek remark, but she couldn't help but laugh.

"Anything else?" Abby asked still smiling.

Martinez was silent a moment. "There is one thing, well, maybe two. In fact there was a news story in the Española paper during the time she either worked for or was assigned to Silas Mendoza." Abby made a brief "uh huh" sound to keep him going. "Garza apparently saved a dog's life on the stretch of highway near Hernandez."

"I'm familiar with the reputation of that area for road kill," Abby said.

"Mendoza hit a dog with his car, and the paper ran a photo of Garza wrapping a bandage around the dog's leg. Seems a reporter just happened by and took a snapshot, one of those human interest type shots that gets readers' attention. The story with it said she insisted they drive the dog to a vet and miss some important meeting. Story headline was something like *couple misses meeting to save dog*. I remember it because I was working on a PR piece for Salazar and remembered he was once involved with Garza."

"You said two things." Abby said.

"Yes, the other was an allegation about Garza that came from an anonymous source. It was during that same period, when there was a lot of talk about a casino near Chama. The allegation was Mendoza was trying to influence the state for his own benefit, and Garza, his aide, was actually working for a Mexican drug cartel. The allegation had an impact, as Salazar eventually threw his weight toward the Jicarilla tribe and Mendoza lost out. Garza was furious and was quoted as saying 'I'd like to kick someone's righteous ass,' without naming names."

"Wow!" Abby said. "This has been very helpful Mr. Martinez." Abby felt elated.

"I wish you would be a little less formal *señorita*. And don't hesitate to stop by, even if you don't have *bizcochitos*."

Abby laughed and thanked him, saying, "I'll make it a point, *señor*."

Abby mulled over what Martinez said about Lupe. Garza was definitely a study in contrasts. She looked at Duster, who was staring at her intently. "Buster boy, maybe I'm making this more complicated than it needs to be."

Duster trilled and bounded to the windowsill to stare at whatever cats stare at. Abby threw on a ski jacket and walked down to the river to her private contemplation place to see if that would help. When she returned an hour later, after watching several eagles fish in the river, she crafted several emails and decided to run them by Carmen after work.

On Friday morning Lupe arrived forty-five minutes early for her appointment with Mendoza at the mall in Albuquerque and parked in a spot that afforded a quick getaway. She thought the Arizona license plate would not be conspicuous, as Arizona vehicles were common in New Mexico. Lupe took a circular route to an unobtrusive spot fifty yards from the Apple store, took out a newspaper and notebook and waited.

It was a breeze-driven chilly gray forty-five degrees and Lupe pulled her black wool coat around her neck and gray knit cap over her ears. Her short hair did not give her much warmth. Ten o'clock came and went with no movement around the Apple store except the inevitable Mac techies who arrived precisely at ten. At ten-fifteen a stocky man in a dark-gray coat and fedora walked with a slight limp up the mall, stopped at the Apple store and looked at his wristwatch. It was the man, and he appeared to be alone.

Lupe had no intention of taking Mendoza up on his offer but was willing to risk meeting him to determine just how lethal an opponent he was. As she approached him, Lupe kept a sharp eye out for anyone who might present a danger. She was sure Mendoza noted this too. He spoke first.

"I have not had my second cup of coffee. How about Starbucks?"

Lupe nodded and they walked back the way Lupe had come to the Starbucks on the corner. Mendoza made small talk about the weather and asked if Lupe had a good trip. Lupe smiled at that and nodded, confirming that Mendoza knew she had been in Phoenix, which he surely wanted her to know. Crafty bastard, she thought, but then so am I.

Lupe ordered a latte and Mendoza got a standard black coffee. No frills for this guy. They took a table in the corner where Lupe could see everyone and also watch the doorway.

"It's good to see you, Lupe. I've missed our conversations."

Lupe looked into Mendoza's flat eyes and gave him a thin-lipped smile. "You know the people who loaned me to you moved in another direction." Lupe cocked her head with no expression suggesting he get to the point.

"First, allow me to express my gratitude that . . ."

Lupe held up a hand.

"I was at the pueblo Christmas eve," Mendoza said despite her objection. "Very dramatic, I must say."

Lupe sat stone-faced and looked at Mendoza who looked a tad exasperated. She opened both hands several inches, indicating the ball was still in his court.

"Yes, well," Mendoza coughed slightly and looked intently at Lupe. He spoke quietly but clearly. "I could use your skills in setting up a safe meeting with a particular *jefe* in Guadalajara for the sale of a significant supply of arms. It would mean a five-figure commission for you, payable to a bank of your choice."

Lupe looked at Mendoza in a poker gaze; two steely-eyed black-hats in a showdown.

"I'm curious, Silas. You lost a very lucrative deal on the Chama casino, and I've heard the rumor that I could have been more helpful to you." Lupe held Mendoza's eyes — no mean feat.

"Yes," Mendoza blinked. "I also heard that rumor but paid it no mind. I also know that Roberts was seen as a beneficiary of Salazar's lack of effort on my behalf. However," he leaned forward and hissed, "Roberts also lost. Besides, revenge is a waste of time and energy. I'm a practical man and there is no profit in revenge." He tapped the table with his index finger twice.

Lupe's mind was working fast. True, Mendoza wasn't in this for revenge, but Ramirez was. Regardless, Lupe would be the loser if she bought into the deal. They were working together and she needed to be very careful. Her protection for the moment was that the Z people had the rights to her and she wouldn't be hit on this side of the border.

"You know, Silas, when the cartel loaned me to you, they were only interested in laundering money through that proposed casino. But they didn't put their eggs in one basket." Lupe let that statement hang, hoping it would put Mendoza's mind on something other than her. She needed him to keep thinking that she was in the dark. "Anyway, I'll need to think your proposal over. Your job would require shifting a prior commitment. How much time can I have?"

"I need to move quickly. I'd need you in Guadalajara by Monday." Mendoza was trying to look earnest, and Lupe was enjoying the charade.

"I'll let you know tonight." She stood, put her purse with the Cobra 22 inside on her shoulder, touched an index finger to her forehead, turned and walked out smartly. She walked to the other side of the street and rapidly toward her car, trying to catch any movement in her peripheral vision. She stopped short of her car and looked around. Nothing. Without wasting movement she unlocked the car and exited the parking lot.

Lupe made three turns and doubled back before feeling certain she was not followed.

Back at her motel room she quickly looked over the email, checked out and headed north to Santa Fe. Just before one o'clock she turned off at the Cerrillos exit and checked into the first motel that looked acceptable.

That afternoon Lupe cleaned the Cobra and Colt, prepared hollow-point shells, went through several scenarios of how Mendoza might try to deal with her and how to counter his moves, and sent a text to her contact in Guadalajara that said *Any news of big "A" deal? Who?* Two hours later she received a response: *Sí, Z, B-alert :-(* . Lupe stared without expression at the message for a moment, sighed and went back to making preparations. It confirmed her fear about Mendoza working with the Z people. While Lupe wanted to visit her favorite gay bar in Santa Fe, she couldn't take the chance. She bought gas-station food from across the street before calling Mendoza. He answered on the second ring.

"Silas, I've given your proposal a lot of thought and regrettably must decline."

"Well, I can't say I'm not disappointed, but I'm also not surprised." There was a short pause. "Could you do me a favor and meet me tomorrow morning just to get your advice on how I could proceed most effectively?"

Lupe had anticipated this move. "Where and when?"

"A flea market called Kachina in Santa Fe is having a starving artist and craft show tomorrow. We could blend in with the crowd and talk."

Lupe wondered if he or one of his people followed her to Santa Fe. He certainly knew she was here. He probably was staying in the apartment motel that he often used, which was a block from the flea market. "All right, say nine o'clock? I have a lot planned for tomorrow."

"That will be fine. Perfect, in fact. See you there." Mendoza's voice gave nothing away, even when he was planning to have someone killed.

Lupe put the phone down and looked cautiously out the window for anyone who might be a tail, although she knew she was safe — until tomorrow.

Silas Mendoza dialed a number he seldom used. After three rings a rough voice answered.

"Yes?"

"We have a problem."

12

Late Thursday afternoon, Abby toyed with the idea that she'd send Wanda James an email in an effort to flush her out. She was torn between wanting to capture her for the murder, and talking with her to simply understand how she might have moved from hunter to assassin. It was a dilemma that had been gnawing at her since the morning after the shooting. She jotted down several trial messages and dialed Carmen's number.

"What's up?" Carmen's voice was upbeat.

"I'm thinking of sending an email to Wanda James," Abby said slowly

"Why?"

"Well, I want to flush her out . . . to talk to her."

"Yeah, I was afraid of that. Look, this is really dangerous territory, and as your friend I'm against it. But I know you, and you'll do it anyway. Read it to me," she demanded.

"I'm assuming that Wanda is Lupe Garza."

"I know," Carmen said, exasperated.

"But I want her to know I'm not just hunting her, but I have a problem I want to talk about with her."

"Why would she care about your problems?" Carmen asked.

"In my gut I think we both are struggling with the same problem, and she can sense that."

"That's one hellava stretch, *hermana*."

"I know, but I want to try."

"Go head, read it to me."

"I have three. *Wanda, I'm not your enemy, but I want to talk. I think we could help each other.*

or

Wanda, I've been thinking about your problem and have a suggestion. Perhaps we are like sisters and could help each other.

or

Wanda, I have a dilemma and perhaps we could help each other. I have the feeling that we are like sisters."

After a few seconds Carmen responded. "Abby, I don't like the sisters thing. You and I are like sisters, not you and some killer." She grunted. "Let me think." Carmen was silent for a moment. "How about this? *Wanda, do you believe in a parallel universe? Let's talk"*

Abby mulled that over for a moment, and said, "That's perfect. Thanks, Carm."

They talked a few more minutes about plans for the weekend. Abby thought she'd ask Bob on a hike and cook dinner for him at her place. It was his birthday. Carmen said, "Now you're talk'n kid."

Friday morning Abby went for a longer-than-usual run, finished off with yoga, and played with Duster. During that time she came up with several good reasons why she should not send the email to Wanda James. After taking a shower she sent the email anyway, took a call from her mother and accepted her dinner invitation for early evening. She called Bob Janovich and invited him on a hike and dinner tomorrow at her house for his birthday. As Abby put the phone back, it rang in her hand.

"What are you doing this afternoon?" Carmen asked. "Reason I ask is there is a wellness fair, or whatever they called them, at a gallery in Abiquiu."

"Yes, at the Full Moon," Abby said. "It might be fun for a few hours. As long as I can get to my mother's for dinner."

"Meet you there at two," Carmen said.

Abby and Carmen arrived at the Full Moon gallery within minutes of each other. The parking lot was full and they had to park in the back and trudge through snow and broken ice.

"I'm up for a neck message, how about you?" Carmen asked.

"Sounds good," Abby said. "What else do they have?"

"The usual stuff for these things, but I think there is a psychic doing readings, which might be fun, if it's not too expensive." Carmen looked at Abby for a reaction.

"Go for it if you want, but I'm not into that stuff," Abby said head down.

After the neck massages and some herbal tea designed to cleanse and rejuvenate the immune system, Carmen went over to the table where several exotically dressed people were set up for various readings from Taro cards to reflexology to coaching. Carmen picked out a silver-haired native-looking woman who called herself White Raven, thinking she would appeal to Abby. Abby could hear Carmen asking if the woman would conduct readings for two people for the price of one. To Abby's surprise, White Raven agreed, and Abby was committed.

Carmen went first and the Taro cards told her she was a well-balanced person in spiritual and mental health but not in physical health. White Raven prescribed yoga, exercise and better eating habits, and gave her a pamphlet on foods to avoid. Abby shrugged and gave Carmen a told-you-so look.

When it was Abby's turn, White Raven's face grew more serious and she asked Abby to stand off to the side of the table away from everyone else. The woman walked slowly around Abby. She took Abby's hand in hers and after a minute put it down without a word, took a step back and seemed to study Abby. Abby stood stock still, but glanced over to Carmen pinching her eyebrows together. Next White Raven asked if she could touch Abby's body. Abby agreed and looked over at Carmen and shrugged. The woman remained silent and proceeded to touch Abby lightly on her head, back, and kidney area, none of which made any sense to Abby. Finally, White Raven looked intently into Abby's eyes and placed her hands gently on the sides of her head. For an instant Abby thought she detected fear in White Raven's eyes. Closing her eyes, the woman seemed to go into a trance.

Abby shot Carmen another look and rolled her eyes up.

After a long moment White Raven open her eyes and said, "Please sit down."

"What's the problem?" Abby asked impatiently.

White Raven reached in her bag and pulled out a small bundle of sage. She looked at Abby with a grave expression. In a hushed voice she said, "You are in great danger. There is evil near you."

"What do you mean?" Abby asked.

"All I know is that you are in danger," the woman said gravely.

Abby was not shocked. Wanda James was out there somewhere and Abby didn't dismiss the potential danger. "Do you see anything in particular?" Abby asked.

"I do not know," she said slowly, "but I see an old woman, and others; also a color: a shade of green. May I make a suggestion?"

Abby simply opened her hands. She was speechless and alarmed.

"You need a cleanse or a sweat. Possibly even a silent retreat. Do it soon, child."

Carmen began to write a check and the woman motioned it away and said, "I cannot accept money for this."

Abby and Carmen rose to leave feeling uneasy. When they got to the door, Abby turned back and saw White Raven waving a smoking sage bundle around her table and herself.

In the parking lot, Abby said, "What was that all about?"

"Sorry, kiddo, that sure was a downer." Carmen said. "How about a beer at Bailey's?"

"No, I think I'll just go home, take a nap and get ready for dinner at mother's tonight. Not to worry, I'll be fine," Abby said.

Friday afternoon, Mendoza emailed an old photograph of Lupe to his partner, and learned that the problem would be taken care of at the shopping mall where Mendoza and Lupe were scheduled to meet Saturday morning. From there Garza was to be taken to the border where a transfer would be made. Mendoza knew this could cost him financially at some future date, but business was business and he didn't give it a second thought.

Dinner at her mother's Friday night went very well for Abby, mainly because her brother did not show. Mary Jackson Romero liked to eat early now she was into her sixties, and Abby was home by nine o'clock. Bob had accepted her invitation even when she said the menu included rabbit. Early Saturday morning she put a butchered hare into a crockpot with onions, tomatoes and red wine, and turned the thermostat to two hundred for an all-day slow cook. Abby figured she could make a quick trip into Santa Fe for a birthday gift and be back to meet Bob at one o'clock at Ghost Ranch. She heard there was a starving artist and craft fair at Kachina Mall and thought she might find something interesting if she got there early.

Saturday morning before leaving the motel for an observation of the Kachina Mall, Lupe checked her email and found the cryptic message from Abigail Romero. She looked at it a full minute. Lupe was surprised this woman had figured out Lupe's identity so fast. But Lupe could not decide whether Romero was trying to flush her out for a capture, or if something else was at stake. While working with the drug gangs in Mexico, Lupe had learned not to over-think problems. Act and react was their motto.

"First things first," Lupe said. She packed a lunch, took her weapons along with binoculars, and left the motel early enough to find a concealed spot where she could see the entire parking lot of Kachina Mall. She was in place at eight-forty-five.

Lupe had no specific plan other than to take Mendoza down if an opportunity arose. But taking out Mendoza might be only half the problem, and the odds could be stacked against her. Knowing how careful Mendoza always was, Lupe figured it would be a surprise if he actually showed.

Two slightly overweight men with phones stood at opposite ends of the mall's parking lot watching cars that entered the lot. The usual array of Santa Fe locals began to arrive spending a Saturday morning doing nothing in particular and in no particular hurry.

Abby pulled into the lot, parked and hung the GPS pendant that Nick had given her several years ago on the rear-view mirror. Since she was in a hurry, she didn't want the pendant to stimulate extended conversations with artists, who were sure to notice it. She also left her handbag and took only a small wallet with a driver's license and one credit card.

As she climbed out of the 4Runner, one of the men said into his phone, "That's her in the 4Runner." They closed quickly on Abby and before she knew it two burly guys were on each side of her and a gun was shoved into her ribs.

"Scream, I shoot," one of them said with a heavy accent. They marched her to a large four-door sedan with the motor running, pushed her into the back seat with the men on either side, and accelerated out of the lot.

Lupe noticed the 4Runner pull into the parking lot and was able to see the woman hustled into a waiting car. Mendoza was nowhere in sight. Lupe jumped into her car and followed at a safe distance.

"**Sonofabitch**," Abby screamed trying to wriggle out of their tight grasp. "What the hell's going on?"

"You go back to Mexico," one of them barked. "No talk or get this." He produced a syringe with a long needle from the back pocket of the front seat. They sped north out of Santa Fe and turned west after the last casino in Pojoaque. Within minutes they were in an area called El Rancho, consisting of small ranches separated by arroyos, old cottonwoods, fields and lots of fences. The car pulled into a tree-lined dirt road and parked at the back door of a single-wide trailer. Abby was not blindfolded and she would remember it clearly. Apparently her abductors thought she would never see this place again.

They pulled her roughly from the car, pinned her arms to her sides with a belt, slapped a wide piece of duct tape across her mouth and pushed her stumbling into the house. To her surprise there was a short elderly Hispanic woman in the kitchen busy at the stove. Abby was led into a bedroom, pushed on the bed and the duct tape was taken off more gently than it was applied.

"What the hell's going on here?" Abby demanded loudly. "Who are you? Why am I here?"

The man who seemed to be in charge stood in the door-way legs wide and said "*Mañana*, you go to Mexico, all I know," and shut the door.

"My arms," Abby shouted.

The man came back, unhooked the belt, left and locked the door behind him.

"How the hell can I be back in a situation like this?" Abby screamed at herself. She breathed in deeply and blew out a loud breath of air. Fuming, she looked around the small room. Thankfully, there was a bathroom. The only window was too high to see out, and the handle to open it was gone. The only furniture in the room was a small table and the bed with a green blanket; no sheet.

The woman knocked lightly on the door and asked in Spanish if she could bring in some tea and a tortilla. "Sí," Abby said calmly. The man in charge opened the door and stood between Abby and the woman with arms folded across his chest looking defiant. She put a tray on the table, bowed slightly and backed out of the room. The man shut the door and Abby heard the lock. One or two good kicks would bring that door down, Abby thought.

Lupe parked part way down the dirt road from the single-wide and walked as far as she dared to get a view of the trailer. She saw no movement for five minutes. Then a short man came out, lit a cigarette, took a small bottle of something out of his pocket, drank it in one swallow and tossed it into the bushes. A mini of tequila, Lupe thought. She waited until the man finished his smoke before walking rapidly back to her car.

A light breeze blew small dust devils on the narrow road ahead of her. The landscape probably looked lush and homespun in summer but now it was bleak and uninviting. She knew the abduction had been meant for her, and Mendoza's men had mistakenly taken someone who looked like her: same build, similar features, same age. Only the hair was different, because Lupe had cut hers. As she walked, flashcards went off in her head: the email about a parallel universe, Romero's LinkedIn account and the photo of the 4Runner.

"My god," she whispered out loud. "They snatched the Romero woman!" She started to laugh. What an incredible stroke of good luck. She almost danced the remaining steps back to her car.

Abby raced through reasons for this rotten turn of events and came up with nothing that made any sense other than it must have something to do with the Salazar murder. But how? She had made virtually no progress on the case. And, sending her to Mexico didn't make sense. They had the wrong person. So who was the right person? Suddenly, she thought of Lupe Garza. Had they mistaken her for Garza? Was she here? But why would they send her back to Mexico? And then it made sense. Garza must be wanted in Mexico by a rival gang. Abby had to convince her captors they had the wrong person. Her wallet. She still had it.

"Hey," she hollered loudly and pounded on the door. "You've got the wrong person, I can prove it"

Only low voices came from the other room. Abby kept it up until she heard the lock turn. She stood back and held out her wallet as the man opened the door. *"Mira mi identificación."* The man shook his head.

"No, falso," the man said.

"Mira," Abby pleaded.

"No, you Wanda James."

"Mi no Wanda James dammit! Abby sighed deeply and went back to English. "I'm Abigail Romero and I've lived here all my life. Look at my driver's license!" Abby stopped. Wanda James? That confirms it, she thought. I must be a dead ringer for Lupe Garza.

She repeated, "I'm Abigail Romero from Abiquiu. Look in the wallet and you will see. *Mi no Wanda James."* Abby threw the wallet on the floor and backed away. The man kicked the wallet back and locked the door. Abby sat on the bed angry and defeated. Then without thinking she poured some tea and drank. Within a minute she began to feel drowsy, the room began to spin slowly. As Abby lost consciousness, she remembered sliding off the bed and hitting the floor hard as everything went blank.

Lupe got behind the wheel and drove slowly out of the cold dusty neighborhood without seeing anything except mangy dogs and a few crows. She thought about the Romero woman, and the more she thought, the more the stroke of good luck looked bad. When those clowns got to the border tomorrow and discovered the mistake, the Romero woman would probably be killed, most likely in Mexico. Lupe began to feel shame. To let an innocent person take the fall would bring dishonor on her reputation in Mexico, and word would spread fast; the Z people would see to it. Lupe would have to get Romero released or rescued and soon.

Lupe pulled off the highway into the empty parking lot of the Pojoaque high school. After thinking through several scenarios, she decided that rough stuff was too risky. A clean and easy ploy would be to get Mendoza thinking about a kidnapping charge. She dialed Mendoza's cell phone. He answered immediately, which meant he had either just heard about the capture or was waiting for news.

"Yes." His voice was tentative, as he knew the incoming number was coming from her phone.

"You got the wrong person Silas. I know the car and it would mean the FBI," and hit the end button.

At one o'clock Bob Janovich looked out the front door of the museum at Ghost Ranch expecting to see Abby's 4Runner either parking or approaching the museum. He was surprised to see only a boy on a bicycle and a dog running alongside. At one-thirty he called Abby and got her answering machine. He called her cell and got the same. At two o'clock Bob called Carmen Tafoya and got her answering machine. Finally, he found Nick Trujillo at home. They decided to meet at Abby's house right away.

Thirty minutes later Nick opened Abby's kitchen door to find Duster in his usual relaxed state. While he fired up his own laptop, Nick explained that he had given Abby a pendant several years ago with a GPS chip, but Bob stopped him mid sentence saying he knew all about it. After several minutes of punching in numbers and applying maps, Nick found Abby's GPS chip in a flea market mall in Santa Fe. An hour later Nick and Bob pulled Nick's truck into the Kachina parking lot. Almost at once they found the 4Runner, locked, with the pendant hanging from the rearview mirror and could see Abby's purse on the floor.

Nick looked at his watch, just past three-thirty. "Knowing Abby," Nick said, "she came here early this morning, probably about nine or nine-thirty; that's six hours. She could be anywhere."

Lupe drove back to the house where Abby was being held, parked at the end of the dusty road and walked toward the single-wide. Again, the neighborhood seemed deserted. A cat ran across the road in front of her and a dog barked in the distance. Bushes and trees that lined the road were devoid of leaves and Lupe could see the house clearly from thirty yards. She heard a noise from the back of the house. Men were talking in Spanish. A car engine started. Lupe ducked behind a large cottonwood and hunched down. Minutes later a car came by and Lupe thought she saw the Romero woman hunched over in the back seat between two men.

When the car was out of sight, Lupe looked carefully to see if anyone was near the house. No one. Lupe turned and walked rapidly back toward her car. As she drove out of the barrio she could see a dust trail ahead of her, but her view was blocked by a building as she approach the main road. She could not determine if the car turned left toward Pojoaque or right toward Los Alamos. Lupe guessed the captors would drop her at the nearest least conspicuous place. If it were her decision, Lupe thought, she'd drop her at the Pojoaque High School only minutes away. It was just past one o'clock.

The parking lot at the high school was no longer empty. A lone car in the middle of the lot moved forward slowly and stopped and then repeated it several times. Lupe realized it was someone learning to drive. Her next option was the casino on the north end of Pojoaque. She drove around the parking lot several times before giving up. An hour had gone by since the kidnappers had left the single-wide. As she drove out of the lot, Lupe saw the large tower for a gambling place called the Sports Bar a quarter mile to the south. There was a parking area behind the building with trees that might provide cover for the captors to release Abby without being noticed. Lupe stopped near the building where she could see the rear parking area. A woman sat next to a tree and her head was moving slowly side to side. Lupe watched as she got to her feet unsteadily and weaved toward the building. She must be drugged, Lupe thought. Despite the woman's disheveled appearance, Lupe understood immediately how Abigail Romero could have been mistaken for her.

Everything was blurry to Abigail and she felt sick to her stomach. She needed a bathroom. She had driven past the Sports Bar a thousand times but never had gone in. Any port in a storm, Abby thought. Her feet and legs would not behave, but she needed that bathroom. As she lurched through the front door, a uniformed man sitting on a high desk gave her one of those 'you're not coming in here like that,' looks and put up his hands and began to climb down from his perch.

"Please, I need a bathroom, I'm sick. I'm not drunk. Please."

A woman officer appeared from nowhere and led a doubled-over Abby to the nearest bathroom without comment.

Fortunately for Abby the crowd was still light, and all the stalls were vacant. After what seemed like an eternity, Abby felt good enough to venture out. She found a phone, borrowed enough change from a winner at the slot machines, and called Nick's cell phone number, which she knew by heart.

"*Amiga,* where are you?" Nick shouted into the phone.

"I'm in the Sports Bar in Pojoaque," she croaked. "I've been," and she covered her mouth with her hand and whispered, "kidnapped, but I'm okay now."

"Stay there. Bob and I are in Santa Fe by your truck," Nick said hurriedly.

Nick looked at Bob and pointed to the rear bumper of the 4Runner.

"Look under the rear bumper for a key taped to the underside."

Bob knelt down and ran his hand under the inside of the bumper.

"Got it," Bob said and stood up.

Nick returned to Abby. "I'll come to the bar now. Bob will bring your truck, and we'll meet you in fifteen minutes. Do you need anything?"

"Water." Abby hung up and went back into the bathroom. After fifteen minutes she still felt woozy but walked unsteadily into the lounge to wait for Nick and Bob.

Lupe watched Romero enter the building. When she didn't come out right away, Lupe assumed her unfortunate 'twin' would be okay. Lupe felt strange looking at a near mirror image of herself, and then she remembered the email about a parallel universe. Perhaps at some point, Lupe thought, they'd talk; perhaps they'd have to talk.

Lupe drove back to Santa Fe, pulled into the motel parking lot and looked for Silas' Mercedes. It was gone. She dialed the motel number and learned that Silas Mendoza had just checked out. Lupe knew of a house he rented in Santa Fe during the summer and decided to pay it a visit. She drove by slowly and did not see his black Mercedes. Although Mendoza was a very private man, Lupe had learned a lot about his habits during the period she worked with him. He was a man of rigid routine who liked kinky sex from professionals when he was troubled by a business deal. He hung out in movie theaters for the same reason.

She drove to the large movie complex at the south end of town, but after fifteen minutes did not find the Mercedes. She was tired and hungry and decided to give up the hunt for today and went back to her motel. After double-checking for Silas' Mercedes, she parked at the rear of the building and waited five minutes before entering.

13

The three of them sat in the lounge of the Sports Bar talking quietly while Abby recovered. The carnival sounds of slot machines and the occasional winner's whoop contributed to the surreal ambience, as none of them ever had ventured into this smoke-filled denizen for horse players and slot-machine addicts. Abby thought she probably looked like a down-and-out hooker, but did not convey that to her companions. After ten minutes, Abby felt she could walk straight and the three made their way through the maze of slot machines and curious looks from pre maturely aged regulars. Outside, Abby began to laugh and in seconds all of them were chuckling at their experience.

The advertising tower for the Sports Bar sent a long shadow across the parking lot. Abby buttoned her coat and hunched her bare head into the collar. It was not until then she realized her hat was gone. Perhaps the old woman had appropriated it. Bob offered to drive Abby in the 4Runner, and Nick nodded in agreement. Nick said he'd call tomorrow and headed back to El Rito in his well-kept pickup.

Abby smiled weakly to Bob as she climbed into the passenger seat. She put a hand on his arm. "Sorry I spoiled your birthday."

Bob looked at Abby solemnly and said, "Right now, there is no place I'd rather be."

Bob respected Abby's privacy, and they drove in silence until they reached the top of the hill near Santa Cruz. Finally Abby said, "You deserve to know what this is all about." She looked straight ahead through the windshield, ignoring used-up buildings and empty fields that lined the South approach into Española. Bob glanced in her direction to show that he was ready to listen.

Abby cleared her throat. "I witnessed the Salazar murder at the Taos Pueblo and tried to follow the shooter. We all thought the shooter was a man in a monk's robe, but later I figured out it was a woman."

"But they arrested a young man in Santa Fe," Bob said surprised.

"Yeah, right. They have the wrong person and they know it, but he probably is a suspect in a lot of minor felonies, so they are holding on to him." She cleared her throat again and blew her nose. "But the Martinez boy had the gun, so they're going with that for now."

Bob said nothing, and Abby paused trying to decide what to leave out.

"To make a long story short," Abby paused, but Bob jumped in.

"Abby, I'm a scientist, remember. The long story is good."

"Okay. But I'll start with the short one and fill in the details."

Bob nodded. "Good."

The traffic was heavy with people headed for the two casinos in Española, but Abby was oblivious to everything outside. They stopped for the last traffic light on the north side of town and Bob looked at the gas gauge. There was an easy in-and-out gas station and chicken shack across the road. "You want to top off the tank at the station?"

"No, I'll fill it at Bailey's," Abby said. The highway out of town was bleak any time of year but more so in winter. With daylight fading fast, the oncoming stream of headlights irritated her. She waited until they were at highway speed and continued.

"This thing today was mistaken identity. I was mistaken for a Mexican woman named Lupe Garza. I think she killed

Salazar, most probably for hire. There will be no way of proving that unless she confesses, which I doubt would ever happen."

Bob said, "Okay," just to show he was following and wouldn't interrupt, but this was a shock to him.

"I've been trying to find Lupe Garza, but not so much because she killed Salazar." Abby paused.

Bob looked over at Abby with an expression that she would not soon forget. She hadn't stopped to think that this was a side of her he did not know.

"Look out," Abby screamed. Two dogs darted out from the shoulder of the road on their left side and narrowly missed an approaching truck. Bob braked hard. One of the dogs cleared the 4Runner, but the other, much smaller dog was caught midway between the front tires. There was no thump and Abby quickly turned to see the dog, apparently unscathed, scampering to safety.

"Wow," Bob sighed. "That was close. We must have passed right over the little one."

"Well, they don't call this stretch around Hernandez 'dead-dog mile' for nothing," Abby said. "I've never hit one, but almost everyone I know has. It's probably just a matter of time."

"You'd think by now the dog population would be too low for it to be a problem," Bob said. "But then, locals don't want to neuter their animals."

"*Machismo* bullshit," Abby added and sighed. "Okay, where was I?"

Bob's curiosity was still high. "You were saying you weren't trying to find the Garza woman because . . ."

"Right, right. Well, to be honest I'm obsessed with why a woman would become a hired killer, and I don't think she is a psychopath."

"Why not?"

"I have this feeling that like me, she's a hunter, not a killer, but for some reason there was a turning point and she crossed the line." Bob glanced at Abby. "I need to know what that turning point was," Abby said with conviction.

"For curiosity or because . . . ?" Bob let the question hang.

"Not for curiosity. I need to know if I'm on the same path."

"Wait." Bob interjected looking at Abby. "You surely don't think you could become a killer . . . in cold blood?"

"No. . . I'm not afraid that would happen. But when Myron Galton went down last summer, I shot at him. I guess I never told you that. I guess the only people who know that are Carmen and the military guy who helped me. But I wonder if I would pull the trigger when I didn't have to. I wonder if that's what she did, and one thing led to another."

There was a long pause while Bob tried to think of how to phrase the next question. He tapped the steering wheel with his fingers.

"Abby, I'm on overload with all this, but let me play the neutral observer for a moment." Bob cleared his throat. "You probably have more social psychology training than I do, but if I could guess, I'd say your fear is not all that uncommon, especially for someone in your line of work. And every person who has ever served in the military has at least thought of pulling the trigger or has actually done it. And that action with Galton last summer was very much like a military action. Sounds like you're in post-traumatic-shock syndrome accentuated by the fact that you're smart enough to over-think this." He waited.

"I'll accept that." Abby's hands were folded together tightly. "But it doesn't change the fact that I want to find her. Now more than ever, because I think she saved my life today." She looked over at Bob with damp eyes.

"How?"

"I think she saw me abducted, and knowing what would happen to me, she didn't want my life on her conscience. Think about it. She probably knew that she was the target, and she knew who was doing it. She probably was hiding somewhere at the mall watching. Perhaps she was going to take out the kidnappers herself. When they grabbed me, she followed. She knew they would take me to Mexico, and when they discovered I was the wrong person they would kill me. What I can't figure is how she got them to dump me."

"Well, I'm sure as hell glad they did," Bob added quickly. "But . . ."

"Yeah, I know," Bob said, "she is still in danger." He let out a sigh.

"And . . . I feel an obligation to help, if I can." Abby looked out the window as they approached Bailey's General Store.

Bob turned into the lot and pulled up to the pump at the far end. Only one car was parked by the store at this late hour. Abby put her debit card in the machine, and Bob pumped the gas while Abby cleaned the windshield. No one came out of the store, and they left without needing to talk to anyone. Ten minutes later Abby unlocked her kitchen door and rushed over to turn off the crock pot. Duster pranced about, chirping a simultaneous welcome and demand for food and fresh water.

"Put me to work," Bob said cheerfully.

Abby showed him which plates to get from the cupboard and where she kept the flatware while she took care of Duster. She got a bottle of red wine from her stash under the sink, pulled the cork, poured two glasses and toasted his birthday. *"Feliz cumpleaños, señor."*

"Muchas gracias, señorita."

"I hate to delay dinner, but I really need to shower off the slime." Without waiting for a reply, Abby bolted for the bedroom. In fifteen minutes she was back in damp hair, work-out pants and a black tee-shirt that read, 'Bailey's General Store - Abiquiu New Mexico' in red letters.

"That was quick," Bob said. "I barely got a chance to get into your library."

Abby put the crock pot on the kitchen table with a large serving spoon and they each dished out portions of rabbit, potatoes and carrots on stoneware plates made by a local Abiquiu potter. Bob commented on how tasty and tender the rabbit was and told Abby she could fix it again anytime. "Did you buy *el or la conejos aqui?*" he asked.

"*Los conejos.*" Abby corrected, "and they're from El Rito, a relative of Nick's — Marianno. They're very lean. But Mariano taught me how to cook them slow to break down the protein. And the carrots are from Nick's garden, dug late in the fall so they are sweet." Abby smiled and they each took a sip of wine.

Bob finished before Abby, pushed his chair back an inch and waited for her to finish.

"My appetite is not very big tonight," she said and put her folded napkin on the table. "And, another apology," she said. "No birthday cake or present."

"Another time," he said and beamed at Abby.

"*Sí,* and soon," she said and winked.

"Clean up or talk first?" Bob asked.

"Clean up."

They put dishes in the sink to soak in soapy water and put leftovers in plastic containers in the fridge. Abby scrubbed out the pot and put the clean dishes on a rack to drain. They kept the wine glasses.

"Let's sit on the couch next to the stove," Abby suggested.

The small adobe house was laid out in an L shape east and west with windows facing south to capture the winter sun, and one north-facing window with a view of the river below. The wood stove was in the west corner and a kiva fireplace warmed the east corner between the living room/kitchen area and the single bedroom, which formed the end of the L shape. A portal stretched from the bedroom to the west end of the house on the north side — great in summer; unusable in winter. The house was functional rather than a masterpiece of design, which is what Abby's friend Nick and his friends were accustomed to building. Abby always thought of it as temporary quarters, but they seemed to have become permanent.

Bob sat at the end of the couch away from the stove and Abby sat close to him. She felt spent, but still angry.

"Talk as much as you want," Bob said. "Guys always want to fix things, and I'm no different. But I'll try to keep my mouth shut. Want music?"

"No. Let's just sit."

The silence went on for several minutes, and finally Abby let out a sigh. Bob put his arm around her. After a few minutes she grabbed for a tissue from a box on the coffee table, blew her nose and stood up.

"Okay," she said. "Let's look at this damn thing," and walked over to the chart on the wall.

Abby began. "The rule of thumb is always to follow the money. In this case the money most likely involves drugs or people involved in drugs." Abby blew her nose again. "Their plan, whoever they are, was to take Garza to Mexico. Which means someone local has a deal with Mexican drug people. If only Mexicans were involved, it would have been done by now, and someone would be dead. So, I think its safe to say that these particular drug people are not in northern New Mexico."

"So who?" Bob asked.

"Look at my chart and see what you make of it."

Bob stepped back with hands on hips to take in the chart's total picture. He was accustomed to looking at fine detail in excavations and making grids with precise locations of materials placed within the grid. But at some point, the archeologist or anthropologist stands back and takes a total view in their mind. They might call it a gestalt, or getting a sense of the whole, and often the whole is more than the sum of the parts. Abby knew exactly what Bob was doing.

She stood off to the side and kept quiet. She already had a theory but didn't want to interject an idea to distract his train of thought.

Finally, wagging a finger at the chart he said, "I think something is missing."

"I agree," she said. "What do you think it is?" She stepped closer to him standing by his side.

"This chart is set up to deal with the Salazar murder, and you have this mystery woman in the intersection of the connecting lines. I think you've correctly identified her as the killer, but not who was behind her or hired her, unless she acted alone, which I don't think you buy."

"Right," Abby said.

"So while the chart explains or rather describes the Salazar murder, and brings at least four people into the picture as culprits, it doesn't explain why Garza would be abducted and why a mistake would be made in her capture. That leads me to believe the abduction was probably done from a photograph."

"Bingo!" Abby said. "Go on."

"Tell me more about the details of the abduction."

They filled their wine glasses and went back to the couch. Abby described the three men in their forties who spoke in broken English, the old woman who brought her the drugged tea, the spartan bedroom, and the El Rancho location. "They could easily be Mexicans, but I think they live here. My guess is they are tied to Ramirez or Mendoza, or both. Have you ever been to some of the remote towns in northern New Mexico?"

"Yes. I know what you're getting at. English skills are poor at best. In fact, I've run into people in those villages who could not speak English at all, and they were fourth or fifth generation residents."

"Right." Abby nodded and shrugged.

Bob went back to the kitchen to look at the chart. "It shows here that Garza worked with Roberts and later with

Mendoza. She had been involved sexually with Salazar, but was tossed out of the picture by Ramirez. Does this mean that Ramirez knew what she looked like?"

"Not necessarily," Abby said. "Most likely he would have someone else do his dirty work."

"We're looking for someone who does not know what Garza looks like. And both Roberts and Mendoza definitely can identify her. That leaves Ramirez. The question is, who gave Ramirez a photo, one that could easily look like you? It has to be either Mendoza or Roberts."

Abby had been following Bob's train of thought step for step and jumped in. "My bet is Mendoza. Probably by email."

"Why him?" Bob asked.

"I can't be sure," Abby said, "but I think Roberts wants Garza back for personal reasons, not to ship her off to Mexico on some deal. That leaves Mendoza, who is, above all else, a wheeler-dealer."

"I would agree," Bob said. He turned to look at Abby. "Follow Ramirez or Mendoza and you find Garza. But, do you really want to get caught in the cross fire?" Bob put his glass down and took Abby by the shoulders. "Please promise me you'll give this a day or two. Really think this through."

Abby looked away, sat back against the couch and stared off in space for a moment, before turning toward Bob. "You're right, and I'm tired."

Abby was feeling the heat from the stove and her eyes were getting heavy. She went back to the couch and Bob followed. Within minutes, Abby was slumped against his shoulder at the end of the couch. Bob gently laid her head against the arm of the couch with a pillow underneath. He covered her with a large blanket, put another log in the stove, turned out the lights except for one above the sink, locked the kitchen door behind him and drove back to his home near Ghost Ranch running through the bizarre events of the day as he drove.

Abby woke up some time after midnight and hobbled off to her bedroom and a more comfortable sleep. She made a note in her head to thank Bob.

14

Sunday morning came much later for Abby than usual. She quickly realized why Duster had not bothered her earlier. Heavy snowflakes mesmerized the regal cat from his perch in the bedroom. Abby put on heavy wool socks and a sweater, joined his vigil and took in the magical scene.

"When did this start buster boy?" she asked softly. He trilled his usual response, jumped down and pranced out of the room to his empty bowls.

As Abby finished tending to Duster's needs, the phone rang. Predictably, it was Nick.

"I know you'd rather talk about the weather than fill me in on your misadventures," Nick said in a fatherly tone, "but I'd like to put my mind at ease, if that's possible. I mean, *Dios mio*, Abigail. It's only been six months and you're back in another life-threatening situation." He paused to take a breath. "I didn't press you on this yesterday, but today I'd like some answers."

"Is it snowing up there?" Abby said cheerfully. "Sure is beautiful here."

"Young lady, you are . . ."

"Nick, it was all a big mistake. It could have happened to anyone," she said knowing she could not convince him. "Yes, I've been working on the Salazar murder, but this had nothing to do with that. This was a drug deal and they were looking for someone who looked like me. When they realized their mistake they dumped me. Really, Nick, that's all there is to it."

There was silence for a long awkward moment. Finally Nick said, "I'm glad you are seeing Bob. He seems like a solid guy. But I'm family."

Abby interrupted again. "I know, I know, and that's the problem. I don't want to worry you," she said pleading. "Look, this thing is under control now. I'm no longer looking for Salazar's killer, and the drug thing was just a mistake, I'm sure of it. But I'm on alert and I'll keep you in the loop. I promise."

Nick was silent again. He respected Abby's independence, but ever since her father died, Nick had assumed the role of guardian out of a deep friendship with her father. He was family, and family is the most important bond in northern New Mexico. Abby clearly understood the power of family, and she appreciated that Nick was a protector and also a close friend. But the obsession with Lupe Garza was not something she could talk to Nick about now or ever.

Abby and Nick talked a bit more. They said goodbye both feeling uncomfortable. They both knew the awkwardness would heal.

Abby looked outside at the heavy falling snow. Shoveling the driveway could wait. Although she was sore from her ordeal, she decided to take a walk in the snow and enjoy the large flakes that would stick to her eyelids and melt on her tongue; best not to waste these all too infrequent snowfalls, especially on a Sunday morning when there was no need to drive anywhere.

An hour later Abby was back home with red cheeks and renewed vigor. After shoveling, stretching and eating a big breakfast, she called Carmen and brought her up to speed including the involvement of Nick and Bob.

"All right, so where does that leave us?" Carmen asked after hearing the details. "I take it you are not going to the police with this."

"No. That would be a waste of time, and I'm sure the publicity that would follow would make our investigation more difficult. Let me think this over and get back to you later today. If anything occurs to you, write it down or call."

"Are you sure you're okay?"

"Yes, really. There wasn't any rough stuff, and the drug they gave me, whatever it was, has worn off."

"Call me for sure. I don't want to drive if I can help it today, so I'll be home. But if you need me I'll be there in no time." Carmen was one of those friends who would come half way around the world if you needed her, and without asking for an explanation.

Abby put the phone back in the charging cradle and tuned the radio to the classical music station from Santa Fe. She spread out her charts on the kitchen table and began to make notes based on her conversation with Bob last night. With those items down on paper, Abby started rethinking the drug angle. Was it possible that either Mendoza or Ramirez had Salazar killed, and now one or both of them were trying to dispose of Garza? In fact, Abby thought, the person who hired Garza could be trying to get two things done for the price of one.

Following this line of thought, Abby developed a scenario in which a person or group wanted to make a drug deal and used Garza. No wait, she thought, there is no need for a sweetener in a drug deal. It's all money. You meet the price or not. But if the drug cartel was the buyer, then a sweetener makes sense. What would they want to buy? Guns. In that eureka moment, she slammed the pencil down on the table and broke the point.

It was mid afternoon and Abby was hungry. The snow had stopped and sunlight was flirting with the flocked trees outside her kitchen window. She swept the driveway free of an inch of new snow and gathered some wood for the stove and fireplace. She was thinking of Bob as she came through the kitchen door and the phone rang.

"Just called to see if you're enjoying this beautiful snow-fall." Bob's voice had a calming strength to it. "I'd offer to shovel your driveway but I'm temporarily snowed in."

"Already done, thanks to the good night's sleep I got, which I have you to thank for."

"When can I get that birthday cake?" Bob asked.

"For sure next weekend; maybe before that. This week looks busy for me, how about you?" Abby asked.

"Only the grant stuff, which I'm procrastinating on. How about I call you Tuesday evening and see where you are?"

"Sounds good," Abby said.

"Go easy on yourself," Bob said and hung up.

Abby hit the end button, looked over at Duster who was fixated on something out the window and said, "Yeah, I know, buster boy, this thing with Bob . . . Hmm."

Abby called Carmen. "Hey, I've been thinking, and have way more questions than answers. Nothing is going to make sense until I can get some information from Lupe Garza, and that may be impossible. But . . ."

Carmen interrupted. "You said you thought Lupe Garza was responsible for getting you released. And you think this Wanda James is her alias."

"Yes," Abby said anticipating Carmen's next statement.

"Then try an email."

"I was thinking the same thing. Great minds and all," Abby said.

"What do you think it would it take to get Garza to meet with you?" They both were silent for a moment. "How about the direct approach?" Carmen said. "Send an email saying *thanks for the help* and *how can I help you?*"

"I like it. Short and to the point," Abby said. "I'll do it now."

"Good, and call me if you get a reply," Carmen said.

Lupe sat in her motel room in Santa Fe in absolute silence. She thought best with nothing to distract her, much like a hunter in the forest on full alert. She was sure Mendoza would get help in trying to track her down. First she needed some information. With the free internet activated, she emailed her friend in Guadalajara and asked two favors. Find out if the heat on her from Z was intense or simply an on-going debt on the books to be squared someday. And, send the following message to Mendoza: *LG still has friends in Mexico and can stay in here indefinitely in comfort.*

As Lupe clicked the send button she noticed a new email message in her inbox. It was from Abigail Romero: *Thanks for the help. How can I help you?"*

Lupe thought about the message for a long time. It was clear Romero knew that Lupe had helped her. Perhaps that meant Romero was not trying to capture her. But Lupe knew that kind of thinking could be disastrous. She wrote back under her Wanda James account:

You can't. Don't try. Careful who you trust.

It was late Sunday afternoon. Lupe knew that the cartel people would know by now that she had not been delivered to the border. Mendoza may have tried to accomplish damage control, but even he knew that would be useless. Arms sales had become a buyer's market and the Z people would move quickly to another seller. Mendoza would be angry, but so was she, and her skills at eliminating an adversary by force were at least as good as his, if not better.

Two hours later she received an email from Guadalajara neither comforting, nor unexpected.

Abby called Carmen and read her the message.

"She's warning you off," Carmen said. "Probably wants you out of the way."

"Yeah, but also, I think she's wary. She doesn't know if I'm still in the hunt for her. Makes me all the more intrigued," Abby said. "I think what I suggested earlier is probably true."

"What?" Carmen asked.

"That Mendoza used Garza as a bargaining chip in making some kind of business deal, probably selling guns to a drug cartel. Garza is probably on a wanted list by some gang, and Mendoza thought he could deliver her. I'll bet Ramirez is involved."

"How?" Carmen asked.

"Possibly as a partner. I think I'll go by that house in El Rancho tomorrow."

"You be careful!" Carmen said. "You're using up your nine lives."

"Hah, perhaps you're right," Abby said. "I won't be foolish."

A high pressure system moved into New Mexico overnight and Monday morning dawned clear and bright. Abby called Darien Roberts early and left a message for him to call her regarding new developments. Just past nine o'clock, Abby's phone rang.

"Morning, Abigail, what are the new developments?" Once again Roberts' tone was all business.

"I want to discuss them with you in person, Mr. Roberts. Can we meet this morning in your office?"

"I have a few important matters to attend to, but how about lunch?" Roberts did not sound curious.

"Lunch would be too public," Abby said forcefully. "Either your office or a park bench by the river."

"Well, you certainly have my attention now. I'll make time in my office as soon as you arrive."

"I'll be there in an hour." Abby was out the door five minutes later. Traffic was light in Santa Fe and street parking was available a half block from the gallery. Amanda Archuleta went through her usual pleasantries with Abby and said Darien would be with her shortly. Abby looked at some acquisitions that apparently had been hung over the weekend and wondered who on earth would buy them. Minutes later Roberts emerged from his office in shirtsleeves and chinos, a departure from his more dressy weekday attire. Abby wasn't sure what to make of this.

"I'm all ears, Abigail," Roberts said smiling. He motioned her to the chair opposite his desk.

"I'll get right to the point," Abby said, leaning forward from the edge of her chair. "I was kidnapped last . . ."

"What!" Roberts shouted.

Abby held up both hands. "It was at the Kachina Mall early Saturday morning." Roberts leaned forward looking serious. "Three armed men speaking in broken English. They took me to a house in El Rancho, drugged me and said they were taking me to back to Mexico the next day. Five hours later I was released near a Pojoaque casino."

"Christ, I'm shocked." Roberts shook his head in disbelief. "Do you think this had anything to do with your investigation? Wait a minute. Why do you suppose you were released?" Roberts seemed genuinely surprised.

"I'm sure they thought I was Lupe Garza," Abby said without emotion.

"Lupe? I didn't know she was here. Why her, for God's sake?" Roberts shook his head again. "This doesn't make sense. You're sure you were mistaken for Lupe? I can see some similarity, but obviously the people who snatched you had never seen Garza." Roberts stared at Abigail.

"I'm sure. I also think she observed the abduction and somehow had the dogs called off." Abby watched Roberts for a response. He either was very good at not tipping his hand or he genuinely didn't know anything about the kidnapping or Garza.

"I don't know if this had anything to do with my investigation, but I'm prepared to resign and leave this up to the police." Abby looked intently at Roberts.

"Have you reported the kidnapping?"

"No, and I don't intend to."

"Why not? Well, come to think of it, what good would it do." Roberts' tone had changed to one of frustration. Whatever his plans were, this clearly was a complication, Abby thought. "I certainly see why you would not want to continue, and I certainly do not want to place you in harm's way. But, I really want you to continue." Roberts leaned back. His voice was not outright pleading, but close.

"Well, I will continue, but entirely on my terms. Pay me for my time to this point, and I'll expect nothing from here on. I'll keep you informed as I see fit. Neither of us will be obligated to the other again."

Roberts slouched in his chair, looked at the ceiling and sighed lightly. "All right, that sounds fair. But do me one favor. If you find Lupe Garza, let me know. If she saved your life, I want to thank her." For the first time in the conversation Abby felt he was being disingenuous.

Abby walked back to the 4Runner and thought about Lupe's warning: *Careful who you trust.* Abby suddenly felt exposed. There were too many unknowns and she had no protection. As *cazadora,* Abby usually operated from cover and now there was none.

Driving home Abby went over what she had learned from Roberts. He was not involved in the kidnapping. He seemed surprised about Garza, and, he wanted to find her, although Abby was not sure why. She shifted her focus to Mendoza. As she approached Pojoaque she remembered the trailer in El Rancho, and took the exit toward Los Alamos.

Abby parked at the end of the dirt road and walked cautiously toward the single-wide. There were no vehicles and no signs of life. She stopped twenty yards short of the building, stood next to a large cottonwood and listened for a few minutes. The only sounds were birds and the meow of a cat. A horse whinnied in the distance. Suddenly she heard the back door open and an elderly man walked toward a trash bin with a plastic bag. Abby approached and waved to the man calling a greeting in Spanish. He smiled and said *bien, bien,* and continued toward the back door. Abby continued past the house for another thirty yards and then turned back. It appeared none of her captors were anywhere nearby.

Abby knocked at the back door and when the man appeared Abby said *"Por favor señor. Habla Inglés?"*

"Sí," he said and motioned with his hand that his English was limited.

"Do you own this house?" Abby asked and smiled.

"No, *señorita.* I take care of the house for someone." The man had a kind face and motioned for Abby to come in. Abby put up a hand to say she was in a hurry, but thanked him.

"Can you tell me who owns the house? I'm looking to rent and wondered if this house might be available?"

"Lives in Chama. Big rancher. He's a *patron.* Takes care of my wife and me. Good man." The man said nodding his head.

"Señor Ramirez?" Abby asked.

"Sí," the man said and bowed slightly in respect.

"Gracias," Abby said. "I know him." Abby backed out of the house and walked rapidly back to her car. She could hear Nick's caution: *Stay out of his headlights.*

Abby arrived home feeling tired and anxious. One of her unknowns had been clarified, and she noted it on the wall chart. Mendoza and Ramirez had worked together to capture Garza, and it was unlikely they would stop. They wanted her dead, each for a different reason. Abby thought of another warning, Bob's: *Don't get caught in the crossfire.*

15

Abby heated up leftover soup for dinner Monday night and turned on the television to take her mind off the Salazar case. After a half hour of mindless drivel she turned it off, put an easy jazz CD in the Bose and picked up the phone to call Carmen. It rang in her hand. "Hey, I was just dialing your number."

"I always beat you to it and I work at a desk all day. You go first, as my stuff is long and real juicy."

"Okay, but mine is also a heart stopper. I stopped by the house in El Rancho this afternoon, and it is owned by Alberto Ramirez."

"Holy shit, how did you find that out?" Carmen asked surprised. "That sure adds to the confusion, doesn't it? Also the danger. So, go on."

"None of the kidnappers were at the house, but there was this old man who said he was a caretaker. I pretended to be looking for a house to rent and we went on from there. Funny thing was that it was all so normal. But there was no car or truck, and the old woman was nowhere to be seen. So, what do you have?"

"One of my informants in the office told me she was talking to a friend over the weekend and this person knew that Candace Roberts used to go to Rocky Point in Baja for long weekends with Salazar. She said that her husband didn't know, but that's doubtful."

"When was this?"

"Not sure, but I think it was within the last year or two."

"Any other details?" Abby asked.

"She mentioned they were on a yacht owned by some drug *jefe*."

"How reliable is this person? I mean Candace doesn't seem to fit with that kind of crowd."

"I think the info is good. Think about it. There were lots of rumors about how much Alfonso screwed around. Why wouldn't he hook up with Candace Roberts? With her connections she was bound to fall in with him sooner or later. And didn't you tell me Roberts had an affair with Lupe Garza and Candace found out about it? Turnabout is fair play, kid."

"Yes, I agree, it makes sense," Abby said. "So what's your theory? Did one of them kill Salazar?"

"Definite maybe," Carmen said being facetious. "Either Roberts found out and was jealous, or Candace did it herself when Alfonso dumped her. I mean he dumped everyone after the novelty wore off. In fact," Carmen took a breath, "it makes more sense that she did it because of her vanity. Knowing what Alfonso was like, Roberts knew he could just wait for the affair to run its course."

"I need a glass of water," Abby said. "Keep talking."

Carmen went on about how the yachting parties were pretty raunchy with sex and drugs, the kind of stuff you read about in airport novels. "I mean Candace Roberts is no spring chicken," Carmen added, "but I'll bet she got off on it as long as Alfonso was treating her as *numero uno*."

"Okay, I've got my water. I think I'll talk to Candace again and see if I can pry out more about Salazar."

"Good idea," Carmen said.

Abby continued, "All we have on Salazar so far is that he was a fair-haired boy in politics who couldn't keep his pants zipped. It's worth knowing if there was any real substance to the guy. Either he was killed for his many affairs, or drugs were involved and he didn't pay his bills. Or," Abby paused, "he fucked up some business deal and the big boys took him out."

"Or," Carmen added, "all three."

"Yeah, could be. I'll call Candace in the morning after I'm sure that Roberts has left for the gallery."

"So what else is new in your life," Abby asked.

They talked for another ten minutes about family matters bugging Carmen. Several of her young cousins were talking about dropping out of high school, and Carmen was butting heads with adults in the extended family that did not see the value of education, an all too familiar problem in northern New Mexico.

Lupe spent Monday trying to track down Mendoza without success. She knew how good he was at staying out of sight, but the black Mercedes he drove was conspicuous in Santa Fe, a city in which pretension gives way to what locals refer to as a less upscale 'Santa Fe' style. Lupe considered that Mendoza may have gone back to Albuquerque, in which case a search would be futile. She had one more option, requiring night work.

The Golden Fleece massage parlor was located in a narrow strip of politically contested land just barely flanking a broad arroyo southwest of Santa Fe. For years it could not be decided which political entity had jurisdiction over the land, so the Golden Fleece went merrily on its way providing a service with a steady clientele and few complaints. Periodically, a sheriff's cruiser would be seen in the vicinity, supposedly to keep the peace.

Lupe drove past the Fleece's dirt parking lot and saw the black Mercedes parked at the end of the single-wide trailer building in a shadow not exposed to the blinking lights. She continued on for another mile without seeing any headlights in the rearview mirror. Lupe's plan was to take him as he entered his car, hoping that none of the burley Fleece bouncers would accompany Mendoza outside. The Colt 45 was on the seat beside her. Mendoza had faced his car out so he would not need to back up. Lupe could pull alongside and fire several shots before he started the car, pull around back of the building, and be out on the road before anyone could follow.

A large cottonwood tree at the lot's edge provided the only cover. Lupe waited and thought about the absurdity of the situation. It had become survival. Once she had respect for Mendoza's cunning and pragmatism in his business dealings. He was a master of closing the deal before the other party really understood the terms. She never thought about his intrinsic amoral character until she realized he was selling her life to make a business deal. In the end she was just another poker chip in his game of money and power. She rested her hand on the Colt and narrowed her eyes toward the irritating blinking lights.

During the next half hour, two vehicles with single middle-aged males parked and entered the building. No one came out. The car was cold and a breeze blew dust in swirls across the lot. Flashing bursts of dirty gold light made the scene look cheap, and muffled nondescript music leaked from behind wind-battered walls. Lupe shivered and was about to doze off when the front door opened and the stocky figure of Mendoza framed in pink light filled the doorway. Mendoza turned sideways and allowed a much younger man nearly twice as large to pass. The large man stopped and surveyed the parking lot. He spotted Lupe's car and began to walk toward it while reaching around his back with his right hand. Silhouetted against the flashing lights he appeared even larger than when he came through the door.

"Shit," Lupe barked. She started the car and roared out of the lot raising a dust cloud that blocked her rearview vision and masked her escape. She drove about a mile and pulled off on a side road to wait for the Mercedes. An hour went by and it never appeared. Lupe drove back to the Fleece. The Mercedes was gone. She had lost the element of surprise.

Tuesday morning Abby was up early. After twenty minutes of the stretching routine, a shower and breakfast, it was time to tackle Candace Roberts. Abby used her cell phone in the hope of avoiding caller ID. It worked.

"Good morning Ms. Roberts, this is Abigail Romero again. I hope you can help me out?"

"Ms. Romero, I think we've had quite enough talk. The last time was not a pleasant experience."

"And I apologize for upsetting you," Abby interjected without waiting for Candace to continue. "I'm still investigating the murder of Alfonso Salazar and I really need your help. By the way, I should clarify that I'm not working for your husband. This is all on my own."

"Yes, well I really . . ."

"Please, Ms. Roberts, only an hour of your time at the most, and whatever you say will stay between us."

"I don't see that I . . ."

"But you can, Ms. Roberts. I need to understand this man in order to . . ."

"But I really didn't know him all that well."

Abby said nothing for a moment, hoping the pause would pay off. It did.

"Well, all right. The man deserves . . ." And Candace trailed off.

"Thank you very much, Ms. Roberts. Could we meet today? Somewhere at your convenience?"

"Why don't you come to the house after lunch, say one-thirty?" Candace Roberts gave directions to a house located in the maze of old adobe houses known as the *Acequia Madre* neighborhood east of the capital complex. Abby would have preferred a more neutral setting, but she'd take what she could get.

Abby arrived five minutes early and parked in the narrow driveway. A large dog barked from a neighbor's yard as she approached the door. Abby hit the iron door-knocker twice and Candace opened it seconds later.

Candace was not dressed for show today. "May I take your coat?" she said pleasantly. "Let's go into the garden room," and she led the way. A large pot of hot water for tea sat on a small, old, carved pine table. Abby took a straight-backed chair and Candace sat in what Abby thought was an antique Spanish-colonial chair with a large cushion. It reminded Abby of her family ranch home. They made tea and small talk for a few moments before Abby asked if Candace would mind describing Mr. Salazar. "I'm trying to get a sense of his personality and what made him tick." Abby thought an innocuous opening would be the most productive. After several minutes of review material, Abby hit her from left field.

"Can you tell me if there is any truth to the rumors about drug use?"

Candace looked surprised. "Well, how would I . . ."

"His trips to Rocky Point for instance," Abby interrupted.

Candace Roberts looked out the window in silence, then back at Abby with a sad and exasperated expression.

"Nothing goes beyond this room, Ms. Roberts." Abby leaned forward and waited. Candace dabbed her eyes with a small blue handkerchief.

"I should have expected this," she said in a tone of resignation. "Alfonso was a very charismatic and very charming man. Few women would be able to resist him. Have you seen the play "Phantom of the Opera," Ms. Romero?"

"Yes, I know what you're getting at." Abby's eyes gave that look that only an adult woman can make when talking about sexual attraction.

"Well, women would have stood in line for an evening or more with Alfonso." Candace glanced at Abby and then looked off into space. "And he was the party animal people said he was. He made life vibrant to the point you didn't want it to end and you didn't think about tomorrow or the consequences." She looked down at the floor.

"I've been there, Ms. Roberts. I understand it very well," Abby said, still leaning forward on the edge of her chair. "And it took me a long time to get back to normal." They sat in silence.

"Do you think Mr. Salazar got in too deep with the drug people?" Abby asked. "In debt I mean?"

"Yes, I'm sure of it." Candace had snapped back to reality. "But his political influence could have paid it off, and Alberto . . . do you know who Alberto Ramirez is?"

"Yes, and I know *Señor* Ramirez was Salazar's patron."

"Anyway, Alberto would somehow fix problems. I sometimes wonder if Alberto got sick of babysitting Alfonso." She frowned.

"Do you think Alfonso would have made an affective senator for New Mexico?" Abby had a good idea what she would say, but she wanted to see Candace's expressions and body language.

"Yes," she said, hesitating. Candace looked down briefly and shifted in her chair. "Like others from this state, he would have grown into the job. He was smart and a quick study when he needed to be. And, he was a shoe-in to be elected. Alberto would have made deals with the Republicans down south." Candace sat back and relaxed. "I worked on his campaigns myself. I will say this, Alfonso needed to develop more humility and he tended to be careless in his personal life. He was like gifted athletes who are pampered throughout school and feel the rules that apply to most of us don't apply to them." She raised and lowered her brow quickly in a *ces't la vie* manner.

It was clear to Abby that Candace Roberts had not overestimated her lover. Abby asked a few more questions about politics and Salazar's personality, again to see how Candace would respond and also to put her at ease. At the appropriate pause in the conversation, Abby said she had plenty of information, stood, thanked Candace for her cooperation and hospitality, and moved toward the door.

Candace opened the door and partially blocked Abby's path. "The answer to the question that you were polite enough not to ask is yes," she said to Abby looking her straight in the eye. "But, unfortunately, one woman at a time was never enough for him."

With sad eyes, Candace stepped back and slowly closed the door. Abby bowed slightly and exited without adding to Candace's embarrassment.

Tough woman, Abby thought, and wondered if Candace Roberts could have killed Salazar for being the bastard he was. On the other hand, bad boys have their attractions, as Abby knew full well.

16

Lupe slept in Tuesday morning and missed the continental breakfast at the motel. Concerned she was losing her edge, she drove over to the community athletic complex, purchased a day pass and spent the next six hours running, swimming, pumping iron and consuming energy drinks. By five o'clock she was tired, but felt invigorated. After a shower, Lupe decided to stop at her favorite bar. She failed to see a black Mercedes well hidden in the mix of other cars in the parking lot.

Lupe entered through a back door from the ally. Despite the lack of an attractive costume for trolling, Lupe hooked up with an attractive woman who called herself Celeste. "Escaping the Chicago winter," she said in a low pleasant voice. Celeste was taller than Lupe, slender but not athletic, possibly older and not the hard-edge type that usually frequented this particular bar. Celeste suggested they go to her apartment for dinner and fun; Lupe was just mellow enough that her antenna was down.

Lupe followed Celeste as she weaved a rented red Mustang with Florida tags through traffic to a south-side condo with a For Sale sign on the small front lawn. Celeste told Lupe she was renting for a month of R&R and Santa Fe charm. Soft jazz played in the background, and Lupe guessed it came on with the hall light switch. They made small talk about 'the city different' as Celeste showed her through the condo, and then excused herself to make a phone call in the bedroom. Lupe looked at magazines placed strategically on a glass coffee table in the front room.

Celeste returned in a revealing lavender jumpsuit with two glasses of white wine, and placed them on the glass coffee table in the manner of a well-practiced hostess. She went back in the kitchen for a small tray of cheese and crackers, put the tray on the table, sat down gracefully in a large white armchair opposite Lupe and crossed her legs with a flair.

"Please excuse the plastic glasses, but the owners locked up their crystal." They sipped their wine and talked for ten minutes about living in Santa Fe in winter before Celeste excused herself again, presumably to do something about dinner. Lupe began to feel drowsy and sick to her stomach. She tried to stand, bumped into the coffee table knocking over the wine glasses, lost control of her legs, hit the carpet hard and watched the ceiling slowly spin around and out of sight.

Lupe dreamt she was floating or being carried and then fell through space, landing on a hard cushion that began to move. For a long time she rocked back and forth on a boat that made her more sick. Grotesque faces grinned from shadows and said things that didn't make sense. Finally the rocking stopped and she floated again and dropped, but this time with a softer landing that didn't move. The faces disappeared and Lupe sank to the bottom of a pit with heavy weight on top of her.

Lupe woke in darkness. She felt a rough blanket on top of her and a musty mattress underneath clothing that was pinching her armpits and crotch. She could move, and nothing hurt except her head, but her throat and mouth were parched. A strange grinding noise came from somewhere in the distance. Lupe rolled over, put her feet on the floor and tried to stand. She fell back on the bed and noticed a faint light coming from the ceiling behind her. Must be a window, she thought. She tried standing again and this time she stayed upright. As she felt her way around the room she found a light switch. The room gradually came into focus from a lamp on the floor in one corner. Besides the bed, there was a small table, but nothing else except a door that led to a bathroom. The grinding noise now sputtered, and she realized someone was snoring in another room.

After using the bathroom and getting a much-needed drink from cupped hands, she sat on the edge of the bed and tried to make sense of what had happened. Someone, probably Mendoza, had successfully kidnapped the right person this time, and tomorrow she'd be on her way to Mexico. She was confident that when she recovered from the drug, she could find a way to take out the guys in the other room. She had a small knife sewn into the bottom of one of the pockets in her cargo pants, and with her martial arts skills, these bozos would be no match when the time came. Suddenly, she felt the cell phone in her pants cargo pocket. In their haste, the captors had not searched her. Lupe considered her options.

She remembered Abigail Romero. Lupe had found Romero's phone number in the Yellow Pages and entered it in her contact list, figuring at some point it would come in handy. Now was the time to find out what Ms. Romero was up to and what she was made of. The screen on the phone said three-ten a.m.

Duster heard the phone first. He vaulted from the foot of the bed and stood looking wide-eyed from the doorway. Abby stumbled into the kitchen and picked up the phone. Caller ID read unknown caller. "Shit," she said out loud. "Must be an obscene call." She opened the line and listened for the telltale heavy breathing and the inevitable stupid question.

"Ms. Romero, is that you?" a soft voice whispered. "This is Lupe Garza. I've been kidnapped."

Abby was dumbstruck. "Yes, this is me," she said also in a whisper.

"Can you help me? I think I'm in the same house where you were. They'll probably take me to Mexico in the . . ."

Abby heard a loud voice in the background speaking Spanish and suddenly it was muffled. Abby thought she could hear Lupe saying she had been dreaming. She must have put the phone under the blanket, Abby thought. Abby listened for a long time and thought she heard a door close. Very softly Abby heard "Can you help me?"

"I'll be there at dawn," Abby said and hung up.

Abby thought for a moment. Her instinct was to call Carmen and ask for help. But if Carmen came along it could complicate things, put Carmen in jeopardy, and besides, this wasn't Carmen's problem. Best to beg forgiveness later, Abby decided. And Nick and Bob, well, they'd both insist on the police. It was time to repay a debt, and play out the obsession she had begun two weeks ago. As she dressed in camouflage hunting clothing, she thought over how to get Lupe out of the house. Abby needed a diversion, and decided a fire was her best bet. Timing was crucial. If she got there too late, Lupe would be gone; too early and she risked detection from barking dogs. She decided to set the fire at first light, which would be just after six-thirty.

Abby put on her camouflage parka, wool gloves and a stocking hat, and went out to the shed to check her spare two-gallon gas can: it was nearly full. The cold night air amplified the noise of gravel and ice crunching under her boots, and she felt the same excitement of pre-dawn preparations for a late fall elk hunt. Duster looked out the kitchen window, his eyes shining like two reflectors in the light of Abby's flashlight.

Although the drive was forty-five minutes, Abby left early in order to find a vantage point near the main highway where she could intercept the kidnapper's car — which she knew well — in case they left early. Abby checked her equipment: Kel-Tec with a full clip in its usual place beneath the front seat, full spare clip in the console, binoculars, more than enough matches and a few energy bars in case of a chase. She'd top off the tank at the all-night quick-stop in Española and fill the thermos with coffee. After a wave to Duster, she locked the kitchen door at exactly five o'clock.

Abby parked the 4Runner near a derelict trailer just off Highway 502 at six o'clock. The temperature on the thermometer glued to the windshield said twenty-eight. Orion and Sirius were poised above the western horizon in the crystal clear night sky and the moon was new. Houses were dark, and there were no headlights. Abby tried to stay warm, but by six-thirty she was cold and needed to move. She crept the 4Runner without headlights down the dirt road until she could just make out the trailer through the trees. There were no lights in the house and she could faintly see the front end of the large sedan in the driveway.

Abby drove slowly past the house and continued for a quarter mile before she turned around, headed back toward the house, and parked twenty yards short of the driveway. Through the trees a steel-blue ribbon of light appeared on the eastern horizon. The house was still dark as Abby walked slowly along the edge of the road hugging the tree line. Just before the driveway, she stopped to survey the scene. A lone dog barked twice in the distance and a cat scooted under some bushes next to the house. She hoped the cat would make a safe getaway.

Abby swiftly moved to the far side of the shed and began to empty the plastic can. Fortunately, large tumbleweeds — which become incendiary torches when ignited — had blown against the shed and were wedged into the bushes. She poured gas on tumbleweeds and bushes. As she screwed the gas cap back on she heard a voice in the house. She tossed a match, watched the ground erupt immediately, ran back to the truck, tossed the can behind the front seat and started the engine. Shouting came from the trailer and two men stumbled out the back door while pulling on jackets. Like hapless Keystone Cops, they jumped into the car, barreled out of the driveway throwing dirt and gravel in their wake and disappeared down the road.

17

Within minutes the fire had completely engulfed the large shed. Abby drove to the edge of the driveway just as a woman, dressed like a boy, bolted from the back door of the house. Abby shouted "get in," and without waiting for Lupe to slam the door, raced down the road. Before they reached the end of the road a huge flash of light was followed by a loud explosion. Abby slowed to get a look at the house, but saw nothing but a ball of red flame shoot skyward.

"Go slow," Lupe snapped, "they could be in one of these arroyos."

The fire raged behind them and lights came on like flashbulbs in houses through the trees.

"There," Lupe said in a loud whisper. "Two o'clock. Stop."

Abby stopped and strained to look for movement. Nothing. Voices crackled in the distance as dazed people emerged from unseen houses not knowing what to make of the giant red glow and boiling black smoke a quarter mile to their rear.

"We need to move, now," Abby said frantically. The 4Runner shot forward. The vehicle that Lupe spotted at two o'clock did not move. It was a sedan much like the one that chauffeured Abby and Lupe to the now smoldering hulk of rubble, but it had no wheels and the windshield was gone. "Just another junked car," Abby said relieved.

When they reached the highway Lupe said, "Go left."

"No," Abby snapped. "Police and fire will come from that direction. They may come from both directions, but it's safer to go right." Without waiting for an answer, she turned right sharply and headed west. Abby hunched over the steering wheel, knuckles white and jaw tight. Frantically, she ran through options in her head. She had not thought about how she was going to handle a dangerous assassin in her truck. Naively she hoped, this double of hers would be grateful and agreeable, and then she realized how stupid that sounded.

Abby threw rapid glances at Lupe, who was staring ahead pretending not to notice Abby's nervousness. As hunters, both were like-minded and drawn to the other by that reason, but each was wary the other was an adversary and possibly an enemy. Within minutes they crossed the Rio Grande at Otowi, and Abby had a decision to make; head for Los Alamos or turn right for the San Ildefonso and Santa Clara reservations and Española. Abby turned right.

Finally, Lupe spoke in a questioning tone. "Thanks, but why?"

"I owe you," Abby fired back, "and I pay my debts."

"Sure, good words," Lupe said sharply. "Look, you wouldn't have been in that jam if it hadn't been for me. We both know that." Lupe sounded on edge and Abby suddenly realized how tightly she was gripping the steering wheel. Abby stared straight ahead and said nothing, realizing that Lupe wondered whether this was a rescue or a capture.

"I guess you could say we're even," Lupe finally said. "No, that's bullshit. We both want something." Lupe looked intently at Abby.

"You're right," Abby said, a bit more relaxed. "You didn't ask for help because you needed it. You need to find out about me."

Lupe made an affirming noise in her throat.

Abby knew she would be outclassed by this woman in close quarters combat, but she sensed nothing would happen until Lupe got the answer she was looking for. At that point, Abby thought, Lupe could be dangerous. Abby decided to play her hole card. She shifted in her seat and turned her head a quarter turn toward Lupe. In a lowered tone Abby said, "I need to talk to you about a problem, and you're the only one who can help."

"Hey, I'm no therapist and I've got some heavy shit on my plate, including you." Lupe turned and looked out the window at the brightening day. She turned back looking straight ahead. "Yeah, I could have handled those two bros, and you're right about needing to see you. Where are we going anyway?"

Morning commuter traffic to Los Alamos was increasing and they were headed against the grain as they drove into Española. This provided Abby with some safety, as both reservation and highway police were thick this time of day. Abby knew Lupe was watching carefully.

"I'm hungry and you must be too," Abby said calmly.

"I'm not up for girl talk over coffee and croissants," Lupe said wryly.

Abby ignored the comment and thought food would reduce the tension between them.

"There's a northern New Mexico café just past the first light in Española. It's a no-frills mom and pop place. Opens in five minutes. We can satisfy each other's curiosity in a half hour and be on our way." Abby didn't look at Lupe for her approval.

"What about cops or Mendoza's boys?" Lupe asked.

"There is only one place to park, and we'll check it out," Abby said trying to sound calm.

The café was empty except for two elderly men who probably came every morning for breakfast and small talk with the waitress. Lupe marched directly to a back booth and positioned herself so as to see the front door and the windows facing the street. A middle-aged thin waitress dressed in a tan uniform, with long hair in a net, and a nametag that said Matilda came over with two menus and asked if they wanted coffee. They both nodded and Matilda left without saying anything more. Lupe sat ram-rod straight on the edge of the bench with both elbows on the table, chin in her hands and looked over Abby's shoulder toward the door.

Abby assessed the appearance of the situation. The two of them looked like a gay couple the morning after some crazy night of drugs and who-knows-what. Abby in camouflage clothing and a stocking cap to cover unwashed hair, and Lupe, looking like a boy in tight denim jeans and jacket, were both out of place in a blue collar restaurant that served the basics. Surely Matilda had said, "get a load of those two," to the cook as she passed by his window to deliver coffee.

They both ordered *huevos rancheros* with green sauce. While Lupe used the rest room, Abby waited by the rest room door to make sure Lupe didn't make a move to leave. Lupe noted Abby's caution when she came out.

"Are you worried?" Lupe asked with a sarcastic grin as she eased back into the booth.

"Yes," Abby said, "Wouldn't you be in my shoes?" and then added, "But I'm a pretty good judge of character and I think I'm safe until you find out what I'm up to. I also think you know that something other than this trouble brought us together, and it isn't sex. I know you're 'bi.' I'm not." They sat down

Lupe laughed, sat back and put her hands up palms out. "How could I have sex with my twin?"

Abby chuckled and looked up at the ceiling. She knew the remainder of the encounter would be okay.

Lupe tilted her head the way Abby often did and looked at her with a puzzled expression. This intriguing woman who looked part Hispanic and part Anglo was beginning to grow on Lupe.

"Was it your father or mother who was Anglo?" Lupe asked.

"Mother, and I don't take offense at the term coyote. It's not used much any more."

"You shouldn't. I'm proud of being *Mexicana*," Lupe said with spirit.

A fire truck with siren blasting wheeled down the road adjacent to the café.

"So, where is this going?" Lupe asked flipping her fork back and forth.

"If you're worried I'm going to turn you in, forget it," Abby said and looked earnestly at Lupe. "I'm not working for anyone. I'm in this only for myself."

Matilda brought two plates and set them on the table with the standard caution about the plates being hot.

After several bites Lupe said, "Not bad, but too much cheese."

Abby nodded. "Place has been here forever. My father used to bring me here on Saturday mornings during the winter when things were slow at the ranch."

"You ride?" Lupe asked.

"We raised cutting horses, and I raced barrels at local rodeos," Abby said.

Lupe nodded approval.

They ate at a ravenous pace, heads down, without talk, neither paying attention to the other for several minutes.

Simultaneously they pushed their empty plates to the side. Lupe looked at Abby with steady eyes and said, "Ball's in your court."

"I think you and I have something in common." Abby cleared her throat. *"Mi padre me llamó cazadora."* Abby waited and watched Lupe's face.

"Sí, yo soy una cazadora también" Lupe pointed her thumb to her chest and sat up straighter. "After seeing your web-site, I suspected we had this in common," Lupe said.

Abby heard voices and realized more people had entered the restaurant. She noticed Lupe keeping an eye on the crowd.

"I'll get to the point," Abby said hunching forward. "I think there may be a fine line between hunting and taking a life. No, that's not exactly what I mean."

Lupe waited and looked at Abby, intrigued. Abby fidgeted momentarily and put her hands under the table so Lupe would not see them shaking. Abby leaned forward, looked Lupe in the eye and spoke quietly.

"Last summer I was in a gunfight with a man who tried to kill me, and it was the first time I shot at another human being. It all happened very fast and I didn't think about it until later. And then it bothered me. It bothered me a lot, and it still does. I guess I wonder if I've changed." Abby was aware that she was tapping her right foot rapidly.

Lupe pressed in toward Abby. "You want to know if you could kill another human being." Lupe said it as a statement rather than a question. She no longer looked like a boy. She was hard but confident, not an arrogant or brash bully.

Abby nodded her head once, her lips pursed, her eyes sad. The background noise had faded and Abby's sole focus was what Lupe Garza would say or do next.

Lupe shifted slightly, leaned even closer, and in a hushed tone said, "I can't answer that for you. But I can tell you that I have, and probably will again." Lupe tapped her fingers lightly on the table, leaned back slightly and continued. "I've never done it strictly for money. I've been paid, and paid well. Am I a hired killer?" The gesture with her hands said yes and no. "Right now I need to survive and I'll do whatever." Lupe sat back and narrowed her eyes. "What you really want to know is what does it take?" Lupe held her gaze, like a poker player sorting through the possibilities.

Abby swallowed.

Lupe let out a long breath and pursed her lips together at the corner of her mouth in a gesture of uncertainty. "I'm not sure I want to continue with this," Lupe said and looked hard at Abby.

Abby decided the best strategy was to say nothing. Silence can be an uncomfortable void that the other person might fill.

Finally, Lupe continued. "The truth is that I've never thought about it." Lupe looked past Abby to the front door. Her eyes widened.

"What is it?" Abby asked and turned to look. Two sheriff's deputies had just come in and sat at an open table. They seemed oblivious to Abby and Lupe and talked casually to Matilda, who apparently knew them.

"Why aren't they at the fire?" Lupe asked.

"Probably a shift change." She gestured for Lupe to continue.

Lupe turned her gaze back to Abby. Her eyes were dark and haunting. "As you already know, it's like being a hunter." Lupe said. "You start out with an enemy or a target and lock on. Feelings are buried. You focus. It's no different for any soldier." Again she tapped her fingers on the table. "The target is an object in your sight. You pull the trigger without thinking about anything except hitting the target. What happens later is another matter."

Abby's eyes bored in on Lupe and in a low voice asked, "What was the turning point? How did you go from hunter to . . .?"

Lupe looked away, her shoulders dropped an inch and she sighed. "No particular reason, only explanations. One is that I fell into a gang culture. Those people were my support group. They were honest and stood by me. There was no bullshit, like there was with Alfonso." The pitch of her voice rose. "I'm sure by now you know about that. The bastard just walked away. So doing the gang's dirty work became a job. In Mexico I did what I needed to do for my family, my fellow gang members." Lupe looked off into space, her face more relaxed. Abby remained silent, hoping to get more.

Matilda came over with the coffee pot. They both covered their cups with their hands.

"There's also something you know but may not want to hear." Lupe put her hands on the table, palms down, and looked at Abby with eyes tinged in delight. "There's the juice, the rush of the hunt, the stalk, the kill and getting away. I won't deny it, it's there," and Lupe' lips parted just enough to send a shiver down Abby's spine.

There was a long silence. In that moment, Abby knew the difference between her hunting experience and what Lupe did as *vengadora*. But Abby did not know if she could resist being seduced by it — by the juice.

Finally Abby broke the silence and asked, "How did they get you last night?"

Lupe sighed, tossed her head and said sheepishly, "I fucked up. I picked up a woman at a bar and we went back to her place. I should have known better, but . . . Anyway, she drugged me with something in the wine. I'm sure it was Mendoza and Ramirez. Mendoza promised my ass as a sweetener for an arms deal in Mexico: to a rival gang. It's big money."

Not knowing what to say next, Abby asked, "Where do we go from here?"

"Depends on whether you're satisfied. Is your hunt over?" Lupe asked tilting her head and raising her eyebrows.

"Yes . . . Yes, it is." Abby pursed her lips, crossed her arms and let out a sigh, feeling ambivalent.

Matilda brought the check and Abby paid with a credit card. As they walked out, one of the deputies said, "Morn'n' boys." Lupe shot a tight-lipped smirk in their direction. Abby ignored them.

They both got in the 4Runner without comment. Abby eased into traffic and said, "I'll take you to Santa Fe." Lupe was silent.

After a few blocks Lupe said, "I'll bet they had my car towed. I'll need to see if the cops are watching."

Abby took the main highway instead of the way they had come. She scanned the dial for news and found an Albuquerque station that had a story. In addition to describing the drama of the fire and several accounts from neighbors, the commentator said the severity of the blaze was due to an explosion of munitions stored in a shed near the house. One fireman said that the cache of munitions was much greater than any hunter would have, and speculated it looked like it was meant for drug gangs, probably on the border. There was no confirmation of who owned the house, which was a total loss. "Fortunately," the commentator said, "there was no loss of life and no indication of how the blaze started."

Near the top of Opera Hill above Santa Fe, Lupe said, "Do me a favor and stay the hell away from this. Mendoza or Ramirez might have figured out you were involved in the fire. Still," Lupe took a breath, "they might think I have friends here. They may not know about you. When I saw you snatched at the shopping mall, I called Mendoza and told him, 'you got the wrong person and you don't want the FBI,' and hung up. They were worried enough that they dumped you fast. I was sure they would. At the time I was surprised at how much we looked alike." After a pause, Lupe said, "This is really going to piss Ramirez and Mendoza off."

"Who do you think they'll suspect?" Abby asked.

"The gangs," Lupe said a bit too quickly. Abby didn't comment.

Abby only knew of one towing yard, and it proved to be the right one. They scanned the street and lot for a police car, but saw nothing. Lupe had cash sewn into a secret pants pocket and paid the towing fee. Abby was impressed. This person knows how to live on the edge, and does it constantly, Abby thought. Lupe came over to Abby's vehicle and stopped a few feet short. She stood tall, cocked her head slightly and smiled with her eyes. "Think I'll go to Argentina and learn to tango," she said, and turned back toward her vehicle making a small hand gesture waving goodbye.

For the first time Abby noticed Lupe moved like a dancer with a slight graceful spring in her step.

Abby headed north feeling uneasy.

18

As she drove down Opera Hill out of Santa Fe, Abby could see a brightly colored helicopter circling off in the distance near Pojoaque. Must be a news chopper at the fire she thought. At Pojoaque, she took the exit to El Rancho on Highway 502 to see what was going on. Multiple flashing lights lined the dirt road leading to the vicinity of the fire. Good time to rob a bank Abby thought. Every cop in northern New Mexico must be here. Without warning a black SUV with government plates whipped around her from behind and turned into the El Rancho area. Abby followed, but a Pojoaque tribal police officer blocked her path holding out both hands. As she rolled down the window and leaned out, the cop made a circle in the air with his hand telling her to turn around and leave. No comment, no information, no nothing for civilians: just leave.

The chopper made cracking noises with its rotors as it banked around a sharp turn, and from force of habit Abby craned her neck to see it. Abby thought of trying to make an end run around back to get a better look, but then asked herself what the hell was she doing. "You're stuck, girl, " she said out loud. Go home and call Bob or Nick. Better yet, she thought, stop at Bailey's for wine or beer, or both, and take the rest of the day off.

Then she saw it. A sedan identical to the one used by the men at the trailer was slowly moving up a hill to an old chapel ruin overlooking the El Rancho valley. Abby pulled over and grabbed the binoculars from the tray under the glove box. It had to be the same car, she thought; there couldn't be two like it in this neighborhood. The large sedan parked on the north side of the ruin away from Abby's view. It would be in a shadow on that side and have a good view of the remains of the burnt trailer. "All right, Abigail, something to work on," she whispered to herself.

Abby drove a mile back toward Pojoaque on 502 and turned left into a very small village that bordered El Rancho on the east. After several false turns and dead-end driveways she found herself at the base of the hill. She worried that the men in the sedan had spotted her by now, but they might not remember her 4Runner. A closer view of the chapel ruin revealed that it was an old Penitente *morada* that would still be used for special events, despite no roof and crumbling walls. A classic Penitente cross stood at the front and east end of the ruin. A rough wagon-path road led up the hill from the east, curving several times to ease the climb.

Abby was still in camouflage hunting clothes. She put on a small day pack she always kept in the 4Runner, took binoculars, pepper spray and an old 35 mm camera that had no film. With a stocking cap pulled down over her hair, she could pass for either gender at a distance, and with her GPS pendant around her neck, she set off to explore. The news chopper was gone and she could see a few police cars leaving the area on 502 headed back toward Pojoaque.

Twenty yards from the top of the hill Abby stopped, took out the empty camera and pretended to take photographs. Although photographing Penitente ruins is not appreciated by locals, it is not unheard of, and Abby knew enough local custom to talk her way through a challenge if it came. She hid behind a juniper tree and strained to hear.

One of the men was standing next to the passenger-side door talking on a cell phone. The other was seated in the front passenger drinking from a can of soda, probably laced with booze. Apparently he either had no respect for the sacredness of the grounds, or booze was more important than anything else; most likely the latter.

The man on the phone was speaking Spanish and after a few minutes Abby knew it was the archaic Spanish of northern New Mexico. She caught only a few words, but enough to know the caller on the other end was asking about a body and what kind of police were at the scene. Abby had no view of the fire scene, but she guessed FBI and ATF agents were combing the area. Soon enough, she heard confirmation of both those federal agencies by the man on the cell phone.

Abby copied the New Mexico license number on a pad she always carried in the pack. She wasn't sure about the make of the vehicle, but guessed it was a Buick or Lincoln. There was no brand name on the trunk, only faded paint, several dents and a bumper sticker saying something about Smith and Wesson.

Suddenly, the man with the cell phone said *bueno* and she thought she heard the name Ramirez before he put the cell phone in his pocket. He went around to the driver's seat and seconds later a small puff of smoke shot out of the exhaust pipe. Abby ducked down and froze; she dared not look up. She heard the car back around to the front of the ruin, turn, and slowly proceed down the road just a few feet from where she hid.

As the vehicle passed, an empty soda can sailed over the top of the car, and hit Abby on the back, startling her. Her first thought was someone had jabbed her in the back with a stick or a gun barrel. She turned slowly and heard the empty can roll off and clink its way down the hill. The car stopped and Abby heard the driver admonish the other man for trashing a holy site. Shit, she thought, is he coming back for the can? The car backed up five feet and stopped. She heard the other man hollering that the damn can was probably at the bottom of the hill. The car rolled forward and continued winding down the hill without stopping again. Abby watched it disappear into the bramble of juniper, scrub oak and large cottonwood that engulfed the dusty neighborhood.

Abby straightened up and tried to stretch cramped muscles. As she turned to start down the hill, a pack of five dogs started up. It was the usual mix of mangy mutts for northern New Mexico. Two of the pack were large, two medium and one small vicious looking heeler that led the charge. Abby whipped off her pack and frantically searched for the pepper spray. They were all barking and confused by her clothing, which still had powerful elk scent on the pant legs. They were hell-bent on trouble.

The leader lunged at her ankle just as she swung the pack and hit the heeler smack in the head, sending it tumbling backward. Quickly she fished the spray can out with her left hand and shot a stream at a gray pit bull, swung the pack back at a hairy shepherd and kicked a yellow lab in the chest before it could leap. By now the heeler was back for more and Abby gave it a full blast of pepper to send it yelping and limping down the hill. That turned the tide, and the pack ran off to look for trouble elsewhere.

Without stopping to assess her situation, she bolted the hundred yards for the 4Runner, yanked the door open while gasping for air, threw herself behind the wheel and slammed the door. Without pausing, she fired up the engine, did a near doughnut in the dirt road and headed for the highway. It was not until she came to 502 that she thought to check her pack: binoculars okay, but no camera. "No way I'm going back," she said out loud, and turned west on the Los Alamos highway for the second time that day, this time short of breath, but not worried about a potentially dangerous passenger.

When Abby entered Española, it occurred to her that a temporary cell phone for a month might be a good idea. Her involvement in this investigation had become complicated to the point that she might need to avoid detection. After a short detour and twenty minutes of signing forms, Abby had a bare bones phone for 30 days and 300 minutes of service.

At Bailey's she stopped for gas, a six-pack of Monk's lager, a rotisserie chicken and a fresh-off-the-press weekly edition of the Española Sun. The store was almost empty, and Abby was glad she didn't have to explain her hunting clothes out of season or a large tear in the left pant leg. The last rays of sunlight formed a pink backlight on the Jemez Mountains as she turned onto the Barranca road, which was empty except for a car hidden behind several trees at one of the fishing spots along the river. Abby could not see the make or color of the vehicle. At home she pulled into her parking spot by the shed and noticed a pile of new lumber that Nick had dropped off. Duster's loud meow came from the kitchen and Abby breathed a long sigh.

After a yoga routine ending with a savasana that turned into a long nap, Abby made a large salad topped with chicken, twisted out the cork on the wine and waited for the phone she knew would ring any minute.

19

A bby did not wait long for the phone to ring.

"Have you heard the news?" Carmen asked excitedly.

"I just got home, what news?" Abby said, trying to sound surprised.

"Turn on your TV."

The local evening news had just ended, but the station showed footage of a smoldering house with several fire trucks nearby. "What did it say?" Abby asked Carmen.

"A shed filled with guns and ammunition exploded, and the fire spread to a nearby trailer. The fire marshal said the cause was under investigation. But the big story is that Alberto Ramirez apparently owned the house. Of course he could not be reached for comment. So that was the house you were in, right?"

"Yes. Were there any injuries?" Abby asked.

"No, no bodies and no one around who could explain anything. Just bewildered neighbors who mentioned an old couple."

Abby said nothing.

"All right, something's going on. Give," Carmen said in that demanding tone that Abby understood all too well.

"Can't talk about this over the phone, Carm."

"I'll be there in a half hour. Make some dinner for us and have some wine or beer ready. I won't take no for an answer." She hung up.

No use trying to hide anything from Carmen even if her safety would be compromised, Abby thought. She made another chicken salad. Fish baked in paper would have to wait.

After a half hour of serious description, with Carmen staring wide-eyed while Abby talked, the wine began to take hold and small chuckles turned into giggles about the guys fleeing for their lives, and the reaction Ramirez obviously would have over a second botched kidnapping. "Only in *El Norte*" they both said simultaneously at one point and burst into hysterical laughter and tears. Later, after ice cream and cookies, they got serious again and decided on a story if one were ever needed.

The dream came again early in the morning, but this time the face was not a skull. Abby strained to identify it, but it vanished just before she woke up. Again, her pillow was soaked.

Lupe was surprised to discover her purse had been wedged under the front seat of her car. The bitch who doped her must have done it to get rid of any evidence when she had the car towed. For a moment, she considered a payback but canceled the idea as too risky. Best to play it safe, she thought, and leave.

At the motel she checked the parking lot for anyone suspicious and found only three cars all with out-of-state license plates. In fifteen minutes she had checked-out and was engulfed in thick Cerrillos Road traffic. At traffic lights she glanced at a road map and decided on Cuba, a town an hour west of Abiquiu, as a good place to hole up for a few days. Cuba was mainly a gas stop for travelers on their way between Albuquerque and Farmington, and a supply source for Navajos living on the Big Rez. Seemed perfect.

To make sure she wasn't followed, Lupe took the mountain road west of Los Alamos that skirted the famous *Valles Caldera*, the largest volcanic sump in the world. Millions of years ago an eruption and collapse of a gigantic volcanic dome created a nearly round dish-like treeless depression. Road-side pull-outs enabled travelers to spot elk and deer grazing on the lush grasses. Lupe stopped for a few minutes to soak in the peaceful grandeur of one of nature's better offerings.

An hour later in darkness, Lupe pulled into the smaller of several motels in Cuba. She got a street-level room with well-worn carpeting and an obsolete television. Lupe didn't smoke, but many previous patrons had done more than their share. She figured a few days in this dump would be all she could stand.

Lupe noticed a laminated brief history of Cuba on the only table in the room. Wouldn't hurt to see what brought people to this area in the old days, she thought; could be some of her ancestors. The historical statement said that Cuba was established in 1769 as a Spanish outpost on the north end of the Rio Puerco, where hearty people farmed good soil, raised sheep, respected traditional family values, and followed the teachings of Jesus Christ. Lupe interpreted that to mean it was a hard life with little joy. One intriguing photo in the brochure was of a woman dressed like a guacho on horseback. The caption included the word *mujerota*, which Lupe knew referred to a woman who was the equal of a male in skill, if not status. Lupe smiled; ancestors indeed.

Lupe trimmed her hair even shorter, bought a brown baseball cap with a local gas station logo that could pass for UPS if you didn't look closely, and picked up a sweatshirt that said Big Rez in large letters. With sun glasses, baggy pants, and the skills of a dancer to mimic various types of body language, she could easily pass for one of the local bros. Flying under the radar was one of her specialties.

She went to bed early Wednesday night but woke often wondering where she was. The window lacked a heavy curtain to block out car lights and the blinking motel sign cast an eerie abstract design in red on the wall. Lupe couldn't remember a worse motel room, even in Mexico.

A very cold high-pressure system had moved into New Mexico overnight, and Abby stuck close to home on Thursday, keeping a sharp eye out for anyone who didn't belong in the neighborhood. She made no phone calls, but monitored the television and internet for any news that might relate to the fire in El Rancho. One story was significant. A film showed Alberto Ramirez, a short man with a weather-beaten face, wearing rancher clothes and an old sweat-marked beige Stetson being interviewed by a young woman from one of the Albuquerque news stations. The interview was short. When Ramirez was finished giving his clipped response in a husky voice, he touched the brim of his hat and walked away. All he said was he had no knowledge of how the fire started or how the guns and munitions got into the shed, but that he'd look into it. He added that he had rented the shed to a young woman, and would notify the authorities as to her identity. When asked who was living in the house, he said that was his business and nobody else's.

Well, Abby thought, he's setting Lupe up to take the fall on the arms deal. Abby knew that Lupe would have guessed this would happen and had left the area. Abby also knew the accusation from Ramirez would eventually fall apart, but in the meantime it gave him some breathing room to do damage control. However, the Española weekly newspaper had been waiting a long time to get something on Ramirez, and Abby knew they would not waste this opportunity. To help out the newspaper, Abby sent them an anonymous snail mail letter in Spanish, describing suspicious activity at the house that burned down, which she mailed from Pojoaque that afternoon.

While driving back from Pojoaque, Abby noticed that a generic tan Subaru seemed to be following her. In Española she pulled into the first gas station on her right, watched the car go by and stop several blocks away at a taco shack. She got a partial license number as the car went by, and noticed the driver was a woman. Abby pulled out, turned back the way she had come, and turned west at the next crossroad. A mile further she pulled off to the left, parked, and watched for five minutes, but no tan Subaru came by.

Later, as she passed a pull-out for an old ruin on Highway 84, she saw the Subaru parked next to a black Mercedes. She slowed, but couldn't determine if any people were in the vehicles. An abandoned gas station a mile further down the road offered a convenient place to turn around. As she approached the turn-out, the black Mercedes pulled onto the highway in front of her. Abby copied the license number, made a U-turn and returned to Abiquiu. When she exited from Highway 84 for Barranca, the Subaru was sitting in a pull-out by the river with someone in the driver's seat wearing a large-brimmed hat. Abby maintained her speed.

Abby parked by her house, unlocked her bike from the shed, and over Duster's objections from the kitchen, rode back down the road toward the river. The car was gone. The temperature had topped off at twenty-nine degrees, and Abby was glad for the heat of exercise on her ride back. Amber light sifted through the trees, giving a false sense of warmth as the air rapidly turned cold, and Abby's hands were frozen as she put the bike in the shed. When she opened the kitchen door, Duster stuck his nose out and promptly turned back for the comfort of the house.

Abby set about stoking the fire in the wood stove as well as the kiva, and soon the house felt cozy. While mulling over a few ideas, Abby chopped carrots, potatoes and onions, and thawed roasted beef that she had prepared earlier for a quick stew. While the vegetables simmered, Abby went through a stream-of-consciousness writing exercise of what she knew about the Salazar case, what she didn't know but wanted to discover, and what she no longer cared about. After thirty minutes, she wrote her conclusion and went back to preparing dinner.

Abby tuned the television to local news and weather and sat down at the kitchen table with the improvised stew and the last glass of an inexpensive Malbec. "One of these days Duster, I'm going to cook a real meal," Abby said and sighed.

The trailer fire was either old news or she had missed the story. After several commercials, a young female weather forecaster said that a winter storm watch would begin Friday afternoon for the northern mountains. "Snow, Duster," Abby said as the big teddy bear of a cat jumped into her lap and smelled the stew. When the stew was down to the last bits, she shoved it aside and called Carmen.

"Can you talk or are you eating?"

"Yes on both, but go ahead," Carmen said still chewing food.

"I've come to a decision on this Salazar thing, and think that I've had enough."

"Oh, and why is that?" Carmen said chewing her food.

"I'm convinced that Garza killed Salazar, but not for personal reasons. I think she got paid, although her ill will toward him probably made it an easy choice."

"Okay, sounds right."

"And, I'm sure she'll never tell who hired her."

"I'll go along with that," Carmen said. "Who would you guess hired her?"

"Well," Abby said in a resigned tone, "it could have been any of five people. In fact, it might be like the Agatha Christie mystery, "Murder on the Orient Express," where a whole group of people did the deed. I really don't care any more. Problem is I'm kind of trapped or rather snared by the complexity of this thing, and need to watch my back."

"So what are you going to do?" Carmen asked.

"Not sure. Lupe Garza and I are pretty much even. We both saved each other's butts, and we did have a talk. She probably is on her way to Argentina anyway."

Carmen thought Abby sounded disappointed. "What about Roberts?" she asked.

"I don't care if I ever see him again, but I may not have a choice."

"What about Ramirez and the fire?" Carmen asked.

"He might be able to trace that to me. Remember, I gave my name to kidnappers, and the old man could describe me. But then, Ramirez has plenty of enemies. He also knows Garza has friends that neither he nor Mendoza want to mess with. I'd like to think I'm in the clear, but that may be wishful thinking."

"Humor me a minute?" Carmen asked. "If you were Garza, what would you do about Mendoza and Ramirez? I mean seriously."

Abby thought a moment. "She's careful and would not put herself at risk unless the price was right."

"You mean unless she thought she had a very good opportunity and could get away."

"Yes."

They both were silent for a long moment.

"All right then," Carmen said slowly. "Listen, snow may be coming in tomorrow. Want to ski this weekend?"

"Can't, have a date with Bob."

"Well, well." Carmen said in a husky tone. "I'll call you Sunday night if I'm not on the road. Monday night at the latest."

"I'll be here," Abby said, and put the phone back in its cradle. Before doing anything else, Abby made a note to check the owner of the black Mercedes in the morning.

Thursday morning Lupe woke up cold and angry. She was angry over being the prey and anxious for something happen. The breathing room period was over, and she wanted to turn the tables and become the hunter, but how? The cramped and dingy motel room was not an environment conducive to thinking for Lupe, who liked open spaces.

Late that morning, after a decent breakfast, the warrior woman, now looking like a scruffy local teenager, gassed up the rental car and drove north toward Farmington. En route she passed a low-budget casino run by the Jicarilla Apache tribe where she stopped for cheap food and distraction.

After passing through the small casino section she noticed a sign next to the buffet room that announcing a conference for this weekend: *"New Resort and Casino Complex."* Below the announcement was a rendition of a sprawling hotel and casino, complete with waterfall and other bells and whistles, and a short announcement of a conference for potential investors starting tomorrow at a resort hotel near Brazos. Reservations for limited accommodations were recommended.

Lupe checked the map and found the resort off Highway 64 near Brazos, south of Chama. Lupe figured this could be the investment opportunity that Mendoza had tried to get through Salazar, who at the eleventh hour had swung his weight to the Apaches. The best Mendoza could hope for now was to be a partner without controlling interest. But, Lupe thought, Mendoza would get a foot in the door, and working with Ramirez, they could control building and access infrastructure that would be essential for the tribe. Lupe bet Mendoza could not pass up the opportunity, and would attend the conference. This might be her best chance to take him down.

Lupe drove the northern route through Dulce to Chama and south to Brazos to check out the situation. She figured her boyish look in the ball cap and baggy pants should enable her to pass for a teenager to be avoided without so much as a second look. It was four o'clock when she entered the parking lot from the lone access road. A quick look around told her that conferees had not yet arrived. Piñon pines lined the approach to a log structure, with a western-style peaked roof, and large carved pine doors promised steep room rates. The view from the portal opened to a panorama of the Chama Valley and mountains to the north and west.

Quickly, Lupe walked through the lobby, guessing that a pair of solid double doors near the front desk led to the residents' rooms. The hallway for the rooms formed a loop that came back to the lobby near the bar. An exit door out the rear of the building was tailor-made for a rapid escape, although it was a keyed entrance. Parking in the back of the complex also accessed hiking trails to a nature trail and the Brazos cliff overlook a mile away. Lupe didn't like the lack of an escape road, but it would have to do.

She arrived back at the motel in Cuba at eight with a temperature in the low teens, and grabbed a take-out pizza and soda from a gas station. Thoughts of great steaks in Argentina sustained her through the ordeal of fast food. The rest of Thursday evening was spent preparing for Friday.

While Lupe was making preparations on Thursday night, Abby was taking down charts and putting the Salazar files away. If she was being followed, it would be best to eliminate all material from prying eyes. Anyone looking through the kitchen window could spot the charts if she left them up, and that could seal her fate.

The dream came again that night, and this time she recognized the face under the hood, but when she woke up she couldn't remember who it was.

20

Friday morning Lupe found what was euphemistically called a next-to-new store in Cuba and bought a woven basket and a large dark brown hoodie that she hoped would enable her to pass for a UPS driver. She filled the basket with fruit and a cheap bottle of sparkling wine from the supermarket. Early afternoon, after a favorite meal of *chile rellanos,* and thirty minutes of meditation — a ritual she practiced before a hit — Lupe prepared for the assault. She strapped the 22 to her ankle, attached a suppressor to the barrel of the Colt and filled the magazine. Identification as Wanda James, passport, money, knife, extra clip, binoculars, pepper spray canister, and surgeons' gloves went into a waist pack.

Just before the three o'clock check-in time, Lupe was positioned on the trail to the overlook high enough to see both the front and rear parking lots of the resort. Her car was in the back lot next to the rear door pointing out for a fast exit. The sky was darkening and it felt like snow. Lupe waited almost an hour for the target to appear.

Just shy of four o'clock, a black Mercedes drove up the tree-lined drive toward the entrance. It disappeared for five minutes while, Lupe assumed, the occupant and luggage were escorted to the front desk by attendants. Lupe knew Mendoza's habits fairly well and guessed he'd relax for a half hour before hitting the lobby to charm the guests at cocktail hour.

The Mercedes reappeared on the driveway to the rear of the building and parked opposite Lupe's car. Through binoculars Lupe saw a youngish man who looked about six feet tall and over two hundred pounds climb nimbly out of the Mercedes and enter the back door with a key card. Lupe was not surprised by the bodyguard, but could not decide if he was ex-military or just a burly football player. The decoy basket, pepper spray and her martial arts skills should take care of the bodyguard, unless he was wearing a gun.

On the drive to the resort Lupe checked a weather report and learned that snow was forecast for later in the evening. She thought she'd be far enough south by the time snow made the roads impassable. Initially, her plan was to take Highway 64 over the pass to Tres Piedras, connect with US 285 southbound through Española and join the steady stream of cars heading to Albuquerque on I-25. From Albuquerque she'd head west on I-40 and eventually back to Phoenix. Within a few days she should be in South America.

Snowflakes started falling on Lupe's hoodie as she walked casually down the trail looking like a lone hiker returning from the overlook. It was four-thirty when she arrived at her car. She retrieved the basket, put the Colt in the large front pocket along with the pepper spray, put on the surgeons' gloves, tossed the hood back and put on the brown ball cap. Snow was increasing, light was fading fast and for an instant Lupe thought of aborting. Commitment overruled the hesitation. She was locked-on to the prey.

Abigail woke Friday morning trying to put the dream out of her mind. After her morning routine, she called a friend at Motor Vehicles and learned the Mercedes belonged to Silas Mendoza. She slowly put the phone back in the cradle, got up and began to pace like Carmen. Worst-case scenario: she was being followed in hopes that she might lead Mendoza to Garza. Best simply to carry on with normal activity, Abby thought, but keep a loaded gun handy.

She checked the contents of the pantry and freezer and planned the menu for Saturday night with Bob. She'd make simple cheese appetizers, soup and salad while he prepared chicken marsala, one of her go-to dishes for company. They could sip wine while cooking and segue into a candlelight dinner and a rented movie.

Thursday was the fresh produce delivery at Bailey's, and Abby waited for the noon deli crowd to clear before leaving the house. After a stop at the post office and filling the 4Runner at Bailey's pumps, she breezed into the store and grabbed a hand basket.

"You look in a good mood," Bud said.

"I am," Abby said tossing her head back. "Lookn' for love in all the right places," she said and laughed.

"Tell me about it?" Bud asked.

"Just a casual dinner with a friend," Abby replied and winked at Christine, who had just finished stocking the produce case.

"Ah," Bud smiled. "About time."

Abby picked out what she needed from the produce case, selected a bottle of good wine, several kinds of cheese and topped it off with a green-chile cheeseburger from the hot case.

"Eat that here and I'll buy you a glass of wine or beer," Bud said.

"You're on. Haven't had a beer for lunch in ages. Make it a Monk's."

Bud and Abby talked about the local gossip, which included an item about a local potter who was romancing a guy half her age from back east. "More power to her," Abby said.

"By the way," Abby said, while Bud pulled up a chair, "have you seen someone in a tan Subaru that isn't local? Could have been in here more than once and it would have been in the past week? I know," Abby laughed, "only fifty tan Subarus in the area." She squeezed some mustard on the hefty burger, mixed it with the green chiles and took a large bite.

Bud raised his pointer finger. "Actually, I did see the car you're talking about. Woman about forty who was definitely not the usual 'escape to Abiquiu' type. She asked a lot of unusual questions."

"Such as?" Abby took a pull on the Monk's long-neck bottle.

"Like, are there a lot of self-employed people here, and what do they do? And, what do women do here to make a buck? And, are the people who live in Barranca all long-time locals? Oh, and did I know of anyone with an old 4Runner they would like to sell?"

"Seriously," Abby said, arching an eyebrow. They both were silent for a moment, and then Abby asked for a take-out box, apologizing for having eyes bigger than her stomach. Bud got up and walked behind the deli counter for a cardboard box and an extra pickle.

"I'll keep an eye out," Bud said and they gave each other a warm hug.

Abby paid for the items minus the free beer, and headed home thinking about the woman shadowing her in the Subaru. About three-thirty she glanced at the local paper she had picked up yesterday and noticed a small story about a conference that started today at the Brazos resort on a proposed casino-resort complex near Chama. It occurred to Abby that Silas Mendoza and Alberto Ramirez might attend that conference. If Lupe Garza knew of the event, she might try to solve a big problem. Abby sat down, looked at Duster who was looking at her and said, "You're right. I should drive up there."

Abby looked outside at the threatening weather and thought better judgment dictated staying home. Those kind of thoughts usually pushed her toward the riskier course of action. The hunt was still in her mind and the lure of action overcame a sensible decision. She rationalized it by thinking perhaps she could intercept Lupe in time and persuade her to break it off and run. Abby dressed for heavy weather, checked her handgun, tossed a sleeping bag in the back of the 4Runner, put the leftover hamburger in a take-along cooler and headed north. It was four-thirty.

Lupe walked briskly through the front door of the resort, shook snow from her head, scanned the lobby in one glance, marched up to the crowded desk while pretending to look at a card in the basket, and asked for Silas Mendoza. The clerk, who was attending to a tall well-dressed native man, did not look up and said she'd take the basket.

Lupe said, "Need a signature."

"One twenty-two," the clerk said pointing down the hall without looking away from her computer screen.

Lupe entered the hallway and paused to make sure no one was around. She approached room one twenty-two cautiously, placed the basket on the floor to the side of the door and knocked twice.

"Who is it?" she heard.

"Delivery," Lupe answered in a low voice. She stood with head down so the UPS ball cap could be seen through the peephole.

"Just leave it," the voice said.

"Need a signature." Lupe's stomach and neck muscles tightened. She was a cat ready to pounce. Adrenalin poured into her system.

The door opened slightly and the face of the bodyguard appeared. Instantly, Lupe kicked the door with her left foot, sprayed the bodyguard's eyes with the canister in her left hand, kicked him hard in the center of his chest and pushed him doubled over to the floor. She looked quickly to see if he was carrying a gun. He was not. Out of the corner of her eye she saw Mendoza frantically pawing through his bag searching for his gun. She shot twice before he found it. He coughed and rolled off the end of the bed, and sprawled on the floor, feet twitching in the throes of death.

The bodyguard, fighting to regain his breath and sight, scrambled toward a table where his gun sat in a shoulder holster. Lupe sprayed the canister once in his direction and fired a shot at the gun on the table, but could not find the will to shoot the young man. She turned, slammed the door behind her, ran down the hall through the rear exit and jumped into her car. As the car started the driver's-side window burst, sending a shower of glass over Lupe's head. Her shoulder exploded in searing pain. She floored the accelerator, turned sharply right and almost made it to the corner of the building before the rear window shattered. Still accelerating, she saw several men dive for safety and yell as she roared by, fish-tailing down the snow-covered entrance road.

Snow was falling hard, the road was a blur and she could not use her left hand except to hold the bottom of the steering wheel. At the entrance to Highway 64 she knew her only chance was to backtrack and avoid the mountain pass. She turned on the headlights and tried to clear the windshield, but snow was coming too hard for the wipers to keep up. She remembered several downhill S curves, but all she could see was a curtain of white. She needed help, and the only person she could think of was Abigail Romero. After a mile and what seemed like an eternity she felt faint. As if in slow motion, the car tilted to the right, slowly spun around and slid downhill, a chaotic dream in Lupe's fogged mind. Finally the car hit something solid and stopped. Headlights pointed upward into the thick falling snow, and for an instant it looked magical as she slipped into semi-conscious shock.

Lupe fought to regain her head and slammed her right hand on the steering wheel as she screamed into the silent night. She could feel sticky blood oozing between her skin and clothing on her left side. Her shoulder throbbed and resignation began to sap her energy. She was wounded, alone and cold. She tried to open the door with her left hand, but the door handle would not move. With all she could muster, she shoved her right hand across her body, pushed the door open and fell into knee-deep snow.

Except for twin columns of light knifing through thick-falling snow, darkness had descended on the forest and all was quiet. Her head told her to climb, but for every step she slid back as much as she gained. Finally, shock and fatigue took its toll. Lupe passed out and rolled against a tree.

Five miles before the junction of US 84 and NM 64 to Tres Piedras, Abigail was forced to a crawl in the thick snow. There were no tire tracks on the road in front of her, and as light faded she could only guess about the middle of the road. Abby remembered the resort was five to eight miles from the junction and up a steep grade. Just before the upgrade, she shifted into four-wheel drive. Halfway up the hill she saw faint lights to her left. A few seconds later headlights pierced upward through the darkness at a steep angle.

Abby put the flashers on, turned the engine off and looked down at the disabled car. She grabbed a high-powered flashlight from under the passenger seat, pushed open the door with her shoulder, pulled her parka hood up tight and walked to the side of the hill. In the thick snow, it was hard to determine the make and model of the vehicle, but it looked similar to the car Lupe had retrieved from the towing yard. Abby called out as she carefully climbed down the hill, but heard nothing. When she saw the open driver's door and broken windows she scanned the light in an arc and called out. Still nothing. Then she noticed indentations in the snow where someone had tried to climb.

A faint noise. Abby strained to hear and pointed the light in the direction of the noise. Through the thick snow there seemed to be a body collapsed against a tree. Abby plunged through the snow, slipping and sliding to a stop in front of the slumped figure. Slowly, Lupe lifted her head. Her eyes were slack and she coughed weakly. Abby sat down and put her ear next to Lupe's mouth. There was a faint breath. Abby put her mouth to Lupe's ear and said, "It's Abigail, I'm here."

"I . . . I thought of you," Lupe said and smiled weakly. "Hit . . . shoulder, can't move. Probably lost" — cough — "blood." Lupe reached for Abby's arm. "Mendoza" — her voice growing weaker — "dead. Me too, I guess."

The snow was piling up on Lupe's body, and Abby thought that in the hoodie she looked like St. Francis resting peacefully against a tree.

"Come full circle," Abby whispered to herself. "I'll get you out," she said firmly. "Hold on."

"Tired," Lupe said with effort. After a moment she looked up at Abby. "Be true to yourself, *cazadora*." She closed her eyes and let out a single long breath.

Tears streamed down Abby's cheeks and salt trickled into her mouth. Lupe did not look up. Slowly her head dropped to her chest and her hold on Abby's arm went limp.

Through watery eyes Abby became aware of flashing lights on the road above. A bright beam from a flashlight came to the edge of the hill and scanned across the disabled vehicle.

"You okay down there?" Abby heard from behind the light.

"No," Abby shouted. "Injured woman."

A New Mexico State trooper slid down the hill with his flashlight held overhead to illuminate the largest possible area. He skidded to a stop and fell back just short of Abby. He righted himself and shined the light on Lupe, her body awkward, no longer a peaceful St. Francis in repose.

"I think it's too late," Abby said.

An hour later, after an ambulance had taken two dead bodies to Española, and Abby had given her statement to the police and had been released, she drove carefully on a snow-packed highway back to Barranca and a sleepless night. There was no tan Subaru, and Abby didn't care — about anything.

21

It snowed on and off all night. Abby spent most of it drinking decaf tea, stroking Duster's silky fur, and looking out the window at snow swirling about in the security lights, which came on with each strong gust of wind. Her mind was a blank and she felt empty, as though a burden had been lifted, but with no feeling of liberation. Her world stood still, suspended without meaning or purpose. She didn't know how long this went on, but bit by bit she became aware the view out the kitchen window had gone from dark to gray. Abby took several deep breaths, urged herself upright and went to bed for much-needed sleep.

Several hours later the phone rang somewhere in the distance. It was Bob.

"Abigail, how are you this fine morning? You should see the snow on the rocks; winter wonderland at its finest."

Abby was silent trying to clear her head.

"Are you all right?" Bob asked concerned.

"Yeah, just had a rough night. I'll fill you in later, but I'm okay, at least physically."

"Abigail, this doesn't sound like you." Bob paused waiting for a response, but none came. "Anyway, we are snowed in at the ranch. The chief has decided he doesn't want the roads full of ruts after the snow melts today, so we're locked down except for emergencies, until tomorrow. I'd love to have you come out, but . . ."

Abby interrupted. "No problem, I'm in no shape or mood to go anywhere today. I'll be back to normal by tomorrow and we'll cook dinner together," she said hoarsely.

"All right," Bob said. "Sunday it is." He knew better than to push her into explanations at this point, so he simply described the beauty of the snow on red rocks and the flocked trees. He did have *joie de vivre*, Abby thought and smiled to herself.

An hour later, after a poached egg, green chiles and a dab of butter floating on a bowl of grits, the phone rang again. Abby knew it couldn't be Carmen, so she glanced at the caller ID and saw the name D. Roberts. Immediately, Abby went into full alert.

"Good Morning Mr. Roberts," Abby said with no cheer in her voice.

"Morning, Abigail. I hope you are enjoying the snow."

"Yes, it's lovely." She didn't offer anything more.

"Well, I'm calling because of the shooting last night."

"Yes, I heard," Abby said tersely.

"The news this morning said the dead woman, Wanda James, was part of a drug war, that she was connected to a Mexican drug cartel." Roberts paused for a response.

"I'm not surprised they would say that," Abby said.

"So, you think differently?" Roberts asked.

"Frankly, Mr. Roberts, I don't really care anymore. This whole business is wretched. I'm tired of corrupt politics and people who turn a deaf ear. As for drugs, it's the scourge of northern New Mexico, and I'm sick of it."

"Yes, yes, I quite agree."

Bullshit, Abby thought, you're part of the problem.

"I'm curious, Abigail, were you ever able to find Lupe Garza?"

Abby took a deep breath. "Mr. Roberts, I never learned anything about the Salazar murder. I'm sorry I can't give you a report on the period that I worked for you, but there is no report to give. I believe you have my discounted bill, but again, I came up empty. No doubt the police will piece things together. Now if you'll excuse me, I have things to do."

"All right, Abigail. Thanks for your time, and my check will be in the mail soon." The line went dead. Abby knew she'd never see that check.

She turned on the desk computer and began to scan local and national news for stories on the shooting. Roberts was right about the drug war news angle, and he surely knew Wanda James was Lupe Garza. With his connections, Abby thought, he'd find out Abigail Romero was the last person to talk to Lupe Garza.

Abby sat down at the kitchen table with a yellow pad, and wrote, 'Worst Case Scenario' at the top of the first sheet. With grim resolve, she began to list the possibilities: Roberts knows Abby with Garza at the end; if he hired Garza for the hit, he'll need to find out if Garza confessed; both Roberts and Mendoza hired tan Subaru; Subaru is detective, hired killer, or both; Roberts might think he needs to silence Romero — soon; if Subaru is here, Roberts will come today; Ramirez revenge for fire; can anyone help? No. Not a bright spot in the bunch Abby concluded.

The yellow pages for Santa Fe listed five investigation agencies in addition to her own. She had never bothered to check out the others as her business was different. Examining each entry carefully, she looked for the one Roberts and/or Mendoza would select; not a high-profile agency, but a one-person firm that needed the work and wouldn't ask questions. She settled on Discreet Inquiries, Inc. Abby jotted down the number along with the numbers of two other agencies. She put the temporary cell phone, binoculars, hand gun and water bottle in a pack and set out on foot to find the tan Subaru.

After a fifteen minute walk up the hill to the south of her house, she found the same spot where she had observed Myron Galton doing his reconnaissance of her house last summer. From this vantage Abby could see the road leading to Barranca and several places where the Subaru would park in order to keep tabs on Abby's movements. The bright snow helped distinguish anything that was not snow-covered. In seconds she spotted the Subaru parked in a pull-out next to the river.

The county had already plowed the main road, and cleared the pull-outs. Lucky break for the Subaru, Abby thought, although the lady detective's car stood out. "Time to roll the dice," Abby said quietly. She looked across the river at the splendor of Red Mountain spotted with fresh snow and wished she was in a frame of mind to enjoy the spectacle.

Abby dialed the number of Discreet Inquiries. She knew all she'd get would be an answering machine, but after the shooting last night, Abby figured the person in the Subaru would check calls often this morning. After the greeting, Abby said, "Have important news on Lupe Garza," gave her temporary cell number and hung up.

Abby wanted to know if Silas Mendoza was part of the contract to kill Alfonso Salazar, but she reasoned it would be a long shot to get any supporting evidence. Besides, it was always possible contractors made separate deals with Garza, independent of the others. Regardless, the fact the Subaru was near Abby's house this morning meant that the Discreet Inquiries detective was in contact with Roberts, unless she was working with agent Smith and ATF. The feds angle hadn't occurred to Abby until now.

Abby's temporary cell phone rang. Abby opened the line but did not speak.

"Hello, this is Discreet Inquiries returning your call." The voice sounded older than Abby and neutral in tone.

Abby spoke slow and firm. "I'm in a position to see your car, and I know you are working for Darien Roberts. You're driving a tan Subaru with a New Mexico license that begins DCY. Are you prepared to be an accomplice to murder?" Abby hung up.

The gamble paid off. A minute later the tan Subaru moved from the pull-out and proceeded toward Abiquiu. Immediately, Abby called Bud Bailey at the store.

"Bud, I need a favor," Abby said. "If you see the tan Subaru in the next ten minutes, please call me at this number."

"Sure, we're a little busy, but I'll do what I can. You okay?"

"Yes, for now. Are there any sheriff's deputies in the store?"

"Two," Bud said.

"Tell them to be on the lookout for the tan Subaru and a BMW sports coupe. No reason other than chronic speeders."

"Okay," Bud said, "but you know these guys might be escorting prisoners."

"Right, but it might help," Abby said. Escorting prisoners, Abby thought, another waste of law enforcement time in this county; a stupid policy that won't change.

"You sure you're okay?" Bud said again.

"Not to worry. Talk to you later."

"I've heard that tune before," Bud said, in the droll tone he was famous for.

"Right again, Mr. Mayor, but no time to kibitz." Abby put the cell in her pack and thought about her next move. Still working from the worst case scenario, Abby reviewed the possibilities: the Subaru detective would call Roberts, resign from the case due to some emergency, but tip Roberts off that the Romero woman was on alert. In that case, Roberts would not show, at least not today. But, it was also possible the detective would be concerned over losing her license if it ever came out that she was in collusion with Roberts. In that case, she either would not mention anything about Romero or tell Roberts that Romero was home, all was quiet and she was leaving. With that scenario Roberts could appear within an hour. It was just past noon.

Abby was cold and started back for the house to warm up and hatch a plan. She knew the sensible thing would be to call the Rio Arriba County Sheriff and make a case for needing protection the rest of the day. However, the explanation alone could take too much time, and the problem with Roberts would not be resolved. *The skull was grinning, and Abby knew it.* Like an alcoholic craving a drink, Abby prepared for a showdown with Roberts, or Ramirez, or maybe even the feds.

By noon the sun had done its inevitable job on the unpaved roads, which were now muddy, and the remaining snow was but a faint suggestion of what transpired the night before. Abby hung her coat on the hook by the door and dropped her pack on the kitchen table.

Abby wrote a note: "Mr. Trujillo. Out for a run and errands. Back by five-thirty. Leave the package by the door." She taped it to the outside of the door window and left the box outside next to the door.

Abby dressed in the hunting clothes she wore during the rescue of Lupe, picked up the day pack and started up the hill. The observation spot was in sunshine and the warm rays off the bright snow felt good on her back. Several dogs wandered by but fortunately they were not up for play or anything else. Birds fluttered in the wet snow getting a refreshing bath, and a squirrel busied itself looking for food buried before the onset of winter.

After an hour, a BMW coupe appeared on the road and a shot of an emotion Abby could not immediately identify ran through her: fear, exhilaration, or perhaps both. Abby was both hunter and prey. The car parked at the bottom of the hill below Abby's house and a figure in a fedora hat, dark glasses and a parka climbed out, looked around, and started up the hill towards her house, head down as though in thought. Roberts' appeared to be a troubled man.

Abby stayed put and watched. Roberts approached the house cautiously. He looked in the 4Runner and inspected the door on the shed, which was padlocked. He looked at the note on the kitchen door and then looked down and saw the box, which meant she had not returned. He walked around the house and looked in several windows. Satisfied that Abigail was not home, he walked over to the trees on the south side of the driveway, and stepped behind the largest one he could find. He stood there ten minutes before he left and walked back to his car. After another five minutes he drove slowly toward Abiquiu.

Roberts' actions told Abby everything she needed to know. She dialed the number of Bailey's General Store. Bud answered.

"Bud, it's Abby. Do you know Darien Roberts if you see him?"

"Sure."

"If he comes in the store, would you call me?"

"Give me that number again," Bud said. "And Abby. . . "

"Yes."

"Oh, never mind," Bud said in a resigned tone. "By the way, the deputies were escorting prisoners and they are headed north."

"At least they are in the area," Abby said, and gave Bud the phone number again."

Inside, with an eye on the driveway through the kitchen windows, she made a deli turkey sandwich and hot tea. She placed a new greeting message on her answering machine and set it to answer on the first ring. Finally she put a long stout rope on the table. Abby had a plan, but plans can go south in a hurry. She'd take it as it came, and trust her instincts and reactions. Abby tried to stay awake while sitting at the kitchen table, but failed.

Late afternoon, the phone jolted Abby awake.

"He's here," Bud said.

"Call me when he leaves if you can. Same number," Abby said.

Abby put Duster in the bedroom and shut the door. He howled for a minute and then gave up. She turned on the radio, put on the hunting parka, put the handgun in the right pocket, the pepper spray in the left, the cell in a pants cargo pocket, took the note off the window, put the box out of sight, turned a light on in the main room and turned off the kitchen light. Abby walked across the driveway and stood behind the same tree Roberts had used earlier. The driveway was now completely in shadows and light was fading fast.

The phone vibrated in her pocket.

"He just left and headed your way," Bud said. "Let me know if you need 911."

"I'm good, and thanks," Abby said and hit the end button.

Roberts drove up the hill slowly, and turned around in the driveway with the car's front pointing down the hill. He climbed out and closed the door quietly while surveying the area. Abby remained hidden. He walked toward the kitchen door with his right hand in the front pocket of the parka. He saw that the note on the door had been removed and the box was gone. He looked around and called out.

"Ms. Romero." The sound soaked into the silence.

Carefully, he tried the knob on the door. It turned easily. He eased the door open and cautiously stepped inside the dark kitchen.

Abby quickly dialed her home phone number. The ring startled Roberts and he froze. Immediately Abby's voice came on the answering machine.

"Mr. Roberts. Put both hands on the edge of the counter and move your feet back. Do it now!" the message said loudly.

In the time the message took to play, Abby ran to the kitchen door, flung it open, pointed the pistol squarely at Roberts, held the pepper spray ready to use and flipped on the lights.

"Keep your hands on the counter and move your feet back. I'm dead serious."

Roberts sighed and complied without saying a word.

Abby shoved the pistol and spray can in her pockets, moved swiftly behind him and yanked his parka down over his arms pinning them to his sides. She grabbed a chair and shoved it hard against the back of his legs forcing him to fall back into the chair. Next she threw two loops of rope around him holding the end tight. Abby was breathing hard, and she coughed several times trying to regain her wind.

"You seem to have anticipated this." Roberts said spitting the words out.

Abby dropped the rope and walked around to face him.

Harshly she said, "Let's dispense with any pretense. You think I know something that can hurt you. I don't."

Roberts looked at her at first in bewilderment and then in pinch-faced hatred.

Abby continued. "Did you know that Mendoza also hired the woman in the Subaru, or were you and Mendoza working together? Never mind," Abby retrieved the pistol and spray can from her pockets and stepped back. "Mendoza is history."

Robert's looked puzzled, which made Abby wonder about Mendoza.

Abby looked at Roberts with the exasperation of a person finally fed up with game playing. "Lupe Garza and I never talked about Salazar, and I never asked. Any of four people, which includes you, and perhaps all four could have killed Salazar. As I said over the phone, I don't care any more." Abby didn't want this to escalate, but the ill feelings she had for this man made it difficult to restrain herself.

Abby continued as calmly as she could manage. "The mistake you made was having me followed from the start of all this business. I'm making no accusations now or ever." She paused to see if that registered with him. She couldn't tell. "I'm sure you know that even if Garza did divulge something to me, a sharp lawyer would have it quashed. But, she did not, and you'll have to take my word for that. The only person you possibly have to fear is your wife, or maybe Ramirez." Abby stopped again and tried to read Roberts. His face had gone from red to white with no expression. Perhaps he was paralyzed with all this, Abby thought. Then again, he might be waiting for a chance to get his gun.

Abby went on, "I suggest you say nothing. I won't even search you or take your gun." Abby did not want her fingerprints on his gun, and she hoped she could get him to leave thinking he had achieved what he came for. "But there is a sheriff's deputy ready to intercept you on the road if I don't call within the next ten minutes."

"I doubt that," Roberts spat, although the look on his face was one of defeat.

"Are you willing to gamble?" Abby asked. "Ten minutes, Mr. Roberts. You just got off lucky. Better move." Abby stepped behind him, flipped off the rope and stepped behind a support pillar in the kitchen. She pointed her pistol at Roberts' back as he went through the door.

"Oh, one last thing," Abby said. "If no next of kin shows up I'm sending you the bill for Lupe's cremation."

Roberts walked to the BMW, sunk dejectedly behind the wheel and disappeared down the muddy road.

Abby took several deep breaths, let Duster out of the bedroom, put the revolver in her pocket and walked up the hill to watch her house until she felt safe enough to return. She was surprised to see a sheriff's deputy cruiser on the road moving toward her house. Abby walked back in time to explain to the deputy that she was worried about a burglar, but everything was okay, and thanked him for his effort. As soon as she entered the house, she called Bud, thanked him and said she'd explain in detail later.

Duster was looking out the living room window and howling in a low tone that meant he was troubled by something. Abby knew it was not a good idea to ignore Duster, but nothing seemed out of place or unusual. Abby wondered if Roberts had made his way back on foot and was lurking somewhere. With pistol in hand she cautiously looked through all the windows and took a tour around the outside of the house, where she flushed a feral cat from the portal. That was Duster's concern.

Abby wanted to build a cheery fire in the kiva and enjoy a shot of good whiskey, but all she could manage was a can of chicken noodle soup, saltines and the last dregs of white wine. Abby was spent.

Sometime after midnight Abby heard a noise on the portal, but in her groggy state it seemed like a dream. Duster was on alert, so something had happened. She sat up. A light breeze caressed one of the wind chimes and the feral cat meowed from the portal. Duster was at the window in a flash. He let out a low howl and Abby heard the cat scamper across the portal and into the bushes. Duster came back, rubbed against Abby's arm and purred loudly. Abby slept soundly until first light, without any dream she could recall.

22

Early **Sunday morning** Abby drove a quick tour of the roads around her house to see if a tan Subaru or BMW coupe had returned. Neither had. She made a bagel with smoked salmon and cream cheese, and on her second cup of coffee called Bob to confirm his four o'clock arrival. As the day wore on, she did little except prepare for the evening, mainly by building anticipation. A Sunday-style news program had shifted from the death of Silas Mendoza and Wanda James to the politics of the winter legislative session. The Salazar affair and all of its tentacles were receding from Abby's thoughts.

Bob arrived promptly at four with a bottle of Hatch Green Chile white wine and a cherry pie from Bailey's. He hung his coat on the hook by the door and with a big smile gave Abby hug and a kiss that started out polite. Abby leaned into him and turned the kiss into something more than polite. Within seconds the embrace turned into a full passionate assault that could not be turned back. Abby pulled him into the bedroom with clothes coming undone and being flung to the side. He asked her in a hoarse whisper if he needed a condom. Yes, she whispered, and for the next fifteen minutes the only sounds were of joy and surprise by both.

They lay in each other's arms under the big yellow comforter, both smiling, chuckling and saying things they would never remember, but knowing the moment would be etched in their memories for a long, long time. Neither of them was in a hurry to move.

Finally, Bob said, "Here's to spontaneity, and something I've thought about and hoped for since I first met you."

"Fine wine must age," Abby said. "And you certainly have aged well *señor.*"

Abby said he could use the bathroom first, and he declined in favor of savoring one more look at her *au natural.*

Food preparation consisted of a lot of bumping into each other and playful pats along with finishing most of the wine before dinner. Bob found several light-jazz guitar CDs and sometime close to eight o'clock they collapsed on the couch with coffee and cherry pie.

"I hate to spoil the evening, but if you want to talk about Friday night, I'm here," Bob said. "I heard the news and would not be surprised to learn that you were the passerby on the highway that the news mentioned."

"I was, and it was about as traumatic as it gets," Abby said with damp eyes.

Bob remained silent, waiting for Abby to continue.

Abby sat on the edge of the couch and looked straight ahead. "In a strange way, we bonded. Putting aside Garza's profession and a sexual preference I don't understand, we realized we were kindred spirits of sorts. We are, or were, hunters."

"Help me understand that?" Bob asked turning toward her.

Abby faced Bob and spared him the common understanding about hunting and went on to describe an attitude about pursuit and capture or resolution.

"It's the attitude that motivates me in my research and investigation. I've had it since I was a child, and cannot explain how I got it. My father knew it and seemed to understand it. Lupe Garza had the same attitude and she knew I had it the moment I chased her out of the pueblo. It seemed inevitable we would gravitate toward each other." Abby had moved to the end of the couch, leaned against the arm and put one knee up on the cushion to face him comfortably.

"But you never could have been friends," Bob stated rhetorically.

"True," Abby said. "I'm sure we both understood that. If she hadn't died, she'd have gone to South America and we'd never have crossed paths again."

"South America!" Bob said. "How do you know that?"

So much had happened in the past few days that Abby had forgotten Bob knew nothing about the rescue, the fire and the talk in the café.

"Well, this is a long story," Abby said.

"I'm good for a long story," Bob said and leaned back against the arm of the couch. "We could open another bottle of wine, or have decaf tea?"

"I'm for tea," Abby said. They moved to the kitchen table.

For the next hour Abby described in detail what she knew of the events that lead to the shooting in Brazos and Lupe's death, but left out the confrontation with Roberts. When she finished, Bob knew Abby was exhausted. The fire was nearly out and the music had stopped a long time ago.

"Come to bed with me," she said softly leaning toward him. "I don't want to be alone tonight."

Abby slept soundly in Bob's arms and found his soft snoring a comfort. Duster managed to find room on the bed, but left when the two of them explored sexual pleasure once again in the early dawn.

When the sun's bright rays made their way through the kitchen window they made French toast together with sausages and coffee. Bob called the museum and told them he'd be late. Duster seemed accepting of the unusual morning situation, but behaved as well as cats do when their routine is slightly out of kilter. Abby put on the classical music station and they talked about taking a skiing trip together before April. Both agreed that Telluride would make the best destination as it had uncrowded black diamond trails. Bob left before noon, and each of them knew without saying it that a corner had been turned.

Abby spent the afternoon taking naps and reading. As the western sky turned a reddish hue, Carmen called.

"I just heard the news. You okay?"

"Yes, I'm fine now. It was a rough day or so, but I'm back to normal. Can you come over tomorrow night? I have lots to tell you. Too much to start now, and I need to sort a few things out in my mind."

"Sure. Need anything?"

"Yeah, stop at Garcia's on your way home and get some tamales: *pollo*. I have wine and beer."

"Done. See you at the usual time."

Abby called Bob to say goodnight and tell him Carmen was coming over for dinner Tuesday night. Bob said the week looked busy, but perhaps they could get together by Friday or Saturday at the latest.

"Sounds good," Abby said. "I'll miss you."

Tuesday morning the phone rang early, at least by local custom. It was Bud Bailey.

"Abby, there is a guy here from Alcohol, Tobacco and Firearms who is asking for directions to your house. What should I tell him?"

"Put him on if you don't mind tying up the phone," Abby said.

"Ms. Romero, I'm Agent Jack Smith and I have a few questions regarding the shooting in Brazos. May I come out to your house?"

At least it wasn't John Smith, Abby thought.

"I'd rather meet you at Bailey's," Abby said. "I can be there in twenty minutes."

"Okay, that will work," Agent Smith said.

Abby arrived twenty-five minutes later. She saw a clean black SUV in the parking lot with government plates and guessed that Agent Smith would be dressed accordingly. He was: leather jacket, aviator glasses, polished cowboy boots and gray Stetson, no gloves, tall with short blond hair — the whole nine yards, Abby thought.

Agent Smith offered his hand and ushered Abby to a side-room table. Bud brought Abby a cup of coffee, and gave her a 'what-kind-of-trouble-are-you-in-now' look. Agent Smith put a small recorder on the table and got right to the point.

"I have a few questions about the death of Lupe Garza, aka Wanda James. I understand from the police report you were at the scene when Ms. Garza died. Please tell me everything—how you happened on the scene, what happened and anything else you remember." He pressed the record button.

Abby swallowed some coffee, cleared her throat and started in. "I was on my way to the Brazos resort for the conference on a new casino in order to drum up a little business." Abby looked at Smith to see if the pun made any impact. It did not. She handed him her business card. "I thought perhaps the Jicarilla tribe might need some spade work on title searches and the like. But the snow was so thick I had decided to give up and was looking for a place to turn around. That's when I saw headlights pointing up from the side of a hill."

Abby went on to describe finding the woman slumped against a tree. "The state trooper arrived almost right away and took over." Abby looked passively at Agent Smith.

"What about the gentleman that Ms. Garza allegedly shot? Can you tell me anything about him?"

Abby shifted in her chair and looked over Agent Smith's shoulder. "Only that the man was a property developer, which puts him in the category of people I try to avoid." She looked back to Agent Smith's eyes.

"Yeah, well, apparently there was something going on there. Did you have an appointment with him at the resort?"

Smith was no longer looking directly at Abby, having given up on getting anything useful.

"Heavens, no." Abby shook her head, chuckled and gave Smith a 'next question' expression.

Agent Smith pushed his chair back, clicked off the recorder, adjusted his glasses and stood up. "Well, if you think of anything at all, please call me." He took a card from a pouch in his shirt pocket and handed it to Abby. As Smith turned to leave, he stopped and asked, "Do you know anything about the house that burned in Pojoaque?"

Abby had been waiting for that question. "You mean the one the other day the news said had a stash of arms?"

"Yes." Smith studied Abby.

"No, I don't. But then this is northern New Mexico, Agent Smith. After a while nothing surprises you." Abby smiled wryly.

Smith looked at Abby with no expression for a moment. Then he raised an index finger to the brim of his hat and said, "Give me a call if you think of anything."

Abby could have sworn he winked, but she couldn't tell for sure because of the dark glasses. She watched him as he exited the store thinking that Agent Smith knew he did not have the whole story, but didn't know what else to ask. Abby watched the black SUV pull out on the highway and waved a small goodbye with her fingers.

Bud watched Abby wave goodbye and chuckled. "Thanks for the pick-me-up, *señorita*. Never a dull moment when you're around," he said and walked to the back of the store without waiting for a retort from Abby. She picked up a few groceries, and as she approached Bud, who was back at the cash register, he pulled his glasses down to the edge of his nose and looked over them into Abby's eyes.

"Well?" he asked.

"Just routine, man," Abby said.

"Yes, and *Bob's your uncle*," Bud said followed by his own brand of wry smile.

Abby laughed, paid for her groceries, and said, "More later, *muchacho*."

When Abby arrived home she looked around the house wondering how to kill the rest of the day. She needed to hustle up some work. She put out an email to her best clients, checked the LinkedIn site where she found one inquiry, and did a little tax preparation work which she always hated. By three o'clock she was bored stiff and went for a run.

Several eagles, majestic in their white heads and large chests, were perched in the tall cottonwoods along the riverbank. Abby slowed, and as she did, one of the birds lifted off and glided silently above the water for what seemed like too much time to stay aloft without beating its wings, snatched a fish from the water and flapped away with the squirming prize in its talons.

"Wow," Abby whispered. "What a great place to live."

23

As Abby started to preheat the oven for the tamales Carmen would bring, Candace Roberts called.

"Hello, Ms. Roberts, what can I do for you?" Abby said cheerfully.

"Ms. Romero, I . . . I would like to meet with you. It's urgent. I've learned something disturbing and thought you might be able to help me understand."

"Can you be more specific?"

"Well," she paused. "I came across several photographs that were apparently taken at the Pueblo in Taos. You are in one of the photographs."

Abby stared out the window, speechless for a moment. "Describe the photo," she said trying to sound matter-of-fact.

"Well, it's. . . it's of the shooting scene. They were in Darien's phone camera." Candace's voice was trembling.

"Can this wait until tomorrow?" Abby asked raising her voice. "I have company due any minute."

"Yes." Candace sounded frightened, and Abby understood why.

"Will you be all right, Ms. Roberts . . . until then?" Abby asked.

"Yes, yes, certainly," Candace answered without conviction. "Would Mucho Gusto be, ah, satisfactory, say one o'clock?" Candace was doing her best to sound stable.

"I'll be there at one. And Ms. Roberts, don't read too much into the photo. We'll go over it." Sometimes a lie can buy time. Abby hoped this was one of those times.

Abby's thoughts were interrupted as Carmen's car came to a stop. She rushed through the kitchen door with a brown sack that smelled heavenly. "They're in foil, so let's put them in the oven." Carmen opened the oven door to a preheated oven and grinned. "You're on the ball *hermana,* as usual."

"Wine or beer?" Abby asked.

"Beer. What have you got?" Carmen opened the refrigerator door and smiled as she pulled out two Monk's longnecks. "Okay," Carmen said as she looked Abby in the eye. "I want to know if you are really all right." She put the bottles on the table and held Abby by the shoulders as she looked deep into her eyes. "Fair," Carmen said. "It must have been awful," she said after a short pause. Duster took all this in, flicking his tail in excitement.

Carmen took a long swallow of the Monk's and waited for Abby, who was leaning against the kitchen table.

Abby shrugged her shoulders and sighed. "I thought Lupe would be gone, but when I saw the report on the conference in Brazos, I knew she'd try to settle the score." Abby paused. "I had to try something, but I was too late. Probably couldn't have done anything anyway. She died holding on to me." Her voice broke. Duster rubbed up against Abby's leg and purred.

Carmen wrapped her arms around Abby, but she didn't cry.

After a few seconds Carmen let go and they sat at the table across from each other.

"I've pretty well worked through all this, but it was strange," Abby began. "I think I finally have a better handle on this 'hunter' thing I've been grappling with for so many years. Lupe was cut from the same cloth, and we both recognized it in each other. We didn't solve anything, and I never got the answer I thought I was looking for about the turning point."

"You mean what worried you about . . . well, you know," Carmen said.

"Yes," Abby said. "I guess there was a kind of osmosis between the two of us. So," she continued, "there was no solution, but a kind of catharsis. And, it's over."

"Good," Carmen said.

"And then Sunday, Roberts came over."

"What!" Carmen blurted and stood up.

"He called first thing in the morning," Abby said.

"Why?" Carmen asked, sitting back down.

"He must have found out that I was the last person to see Garza alive. I'm sure he wanted to know if she confessed and fingered him for the contract on Salazar. He didn't ask, but that's what he wanted."

"So then what?" Carmen asked leaning across to touch Abby's arm.

"When he hung up I went out to find the Subaru that has been following me. I did and called the woman detective on a temporary cell phone."

"Wow, you were way ahead of the curve, girl."

"Fortunately." Abby leaned back in her chair. "Anyway, I figured that if Roberts thought I knew that he had contracted for Salazar's death, he'd come after me, and I was right. So I called the detective and said that I had info on Wanda James. When the detective called back I asked her if she wanted to be an accomplice to murder? She drove away immediately. So then I just waited for Roberts to show."

"Ohmygod,"Carmen said putting her hands to her head. "He came here? He came to . . . to silence you?" She stood up again.

"I was ready for him, although I wasn't sure whether it would be him or someone for hire, but he probably thought quick action was necessary. Besides, I'm pretty sure he doesn't like me and wanted the pleasure of shutting me up for himself." Abby described the trap she set for Roberts, how she handled it and his reaction.

"Are you sure he won't try again?" Carmen eased herself back onto the chair without taking her eyes off Abby.

"Yes. I'm sure he knows he's safe from prosecution. But there is a giant loose end in the name of his wife." They both leaned toward each other.

"What do you mean?" Carmen asked.

"Candace Roberts called just before you arrived. She said she found several photographs taken at the pueblo, and one of them had me in a frame. The only way that could have happened was that Roberts was photographing the murder, and I appeared because I was following Lupe. Candace will figure out that her husband killed her lover. I'm meeting her tomorrow for lunch, and I'll bet by then she'll have reached a decision."

Carmen gasped, and sat back.

"Oh, and an agent from Alcohol, Tobacco and Firearms came here to grill me about Lupe. They'll probably hang everything on her. Ramirez will see to that. Ramirez, Mendoza, and Salazar won't have their names tarnished, and El Norte escapes again." While continuing to talk, Abby got up, took the tamales out of the oven and put a bowl of room temperature green chiles on the table. She wrapped the package of tamales in a towel and placed it on the table along with three plates, one for the cornhusk wrappers.

"So what do you think Candace will do?" Carmen asked. "I mean she's Anglo, not *Norteña*"

"I don't know how much Salazar really meant to her, but I'm guessing it was more than we might think," Abby said while opening a tamale. Carmen took the cue and unwrapped two tamales, placed them side-by-side and covered them with chopped green chiles.

"Are these Nick's?" Carmen asked referring to the chiles.

"*Sí, señorita, mucho . . .*" Carmen put up a hand to stop Abby.

"Next time I come over I'll bring you some of the super-hot chiles from my uncle's garden. I think he puts hot sauce in the soil." Abby laughed. "Okay, back to Candace Roberts," Carmen said before taking a forkful of tamale.

Abby continued. "I have no idea what Candace will do, if anything, and what you suggest about her — not acting in haste — seems right, at least based on what I've seen so far. But," and Abby shook her fork lightly in Carmen's direction, "you know the old saying about a woman scorned. And in this case the scorn was as extreme as it gets. Roberts killing Candace's lover and having Lupe Garza — his former lover — do the job might be more than she is willing to live with. As a form of revenge, divorce may be too meek." Abby took a drink from the bottle and went back to her tamale.

Carmen stared at Abby, unsettled by what she just heard. "Your meeting tomorrow with Candace is to confirm her suspicion about her husband, *que no?*"

"Yes," Abby said.

"How are you going to handle it?" Carmen asked.

"I'm not sure. It'll depend on her. I don't want to be an instigator."

"But there should be some justice in all this," Carmen said emphatically. "I mean, Salazar may have been a first-class bastard, but he didn't deserve to die!"

Abby sighed. "Yes, I agree, but there is no way the legal system would be able to serve justice without a confession."

Carmen shook her head in dismay.

"There is one other thing," Abby said.

"I hope it's good news," Carmen said.

"It's very good," Abby said, grinned and cocked her head.

"Yes," Carmen said dragging it out and leaning forward.

"Bob Janovich and I are no longer just friends."

Carmen jumped up, did a turn-around dance with hands in the air and shouted, "Hallelujah." She sat down, grabbed Abby's hands, looked her in the eyes and asked, "Was it good?"

Abby widened her eyes, grinned and jiggled her shoulders back and forth.

"That good!" Carmen sat back and fluttered her eyebrows Groucho Marx-style.

They spent the next hour with Carmen pressing Abby for the kinds of details about Bob that are important to women, and when could she meet him. Finally Abby almost pushed Carmen out the door and called it a night.

Wednesday morning Abby did the usual routine and added a morning bike ride to the post office. The sky was one of those iffy colors indicating the weather could go in any direction later in the day. Abby decided to dress for foul weather just in case. She added an hour to the departure time to pick up food for Duster and a few staples. Abby had no plans for the rest of the week. Despite pleasant thoughts of Bob, she still felt flat from all that had happened with Lupe and Roberts. Perhaps a hike and an evening with Bob would be the lift Abby needed. She decided to call him when she returned from lunch with Candace.

Abby arrived at Mucho Gusto ten minutes early and took the same window seat she had the last time they met. Abby told the waitress she was expecting a guest within a few minutes, but wanted a cup of chai while she waited. There were only two other couples in the restaurant, both middle-aged women, and given the time of year, Abby guessed they were locals. She wondered if this would bother Candace. Abby glanced at the local art hanging on the beige walls, and decided none of it would fit in her home. Abby had never developed a taste for painting, other than to admire Georgia O'Keeffe's work for its drama and innovation.

At several minutes past one o'clock, Candace's Lexus appeared in the parking lot. She walked head down as though rehearsing what she would say. As she came through the door, Abby stood and waved her to the table.

Candace Roberts was dressed for anonymity with dark glasses, a pull-down felt hat, wool jacket, slacks and dress leather boots — no flashy jewelry. She forced a smile and took off the dark glasses. Abby waited for her to speak. Through pained eyes, Candace looked at Abby not knowing where to start.

Candace opened her purse and took out one photo printed on plain paper and handed it to Abby. Abby examined it carefully without speaking. A waitress approached the table and Candace waved her away. The photo was grainy due to the paper, but clear enough to show a man in a long coat crumpled on the ground. At the right edge of the frame Abby, in a ski jacket was starting to run towards the fallen man. A monk was moving away at the extreme left edge of the frame.

"You can imagine how disturbing this is," Candace said with tears in her eyes. "I am terrified of why Darien took this photo. It could be coincidence, but . . ." She let that thought trail off and looked down at the table. The waitress stood off to the side waiting for a signal. Abby wanted to say something to break the ice but couldn't think of anything appropriate. Finally, Candace said, "I'm not hungry, but I could use a cup of hot tea." Abby called the waitress over. Abby ordered a *quesadilla* they could share.

"What can you tell me about that night?" Candace asked, her voice shaking slightly.

Abby began with a general description and Candace tried to listen, but seemed gripped by fear. "There isn't much to tell, Ms. Roberts. I was following along with the crowd when I heard two shots from a revolver. It coincided with rifle shots from the pueblo guards. Have you ever seen this event, Ms. Roberts?"

"No, and I certainly won't."

Abby continued. "After hearing the shots and seeing the man fall, I noticed a monk starting to run away from the crowd and I followed. A block or so past the entrance the monk tried to run me over. I walked back, met my companions, gave my story to the police and left. I'm afraid that's all I know." Abby paused while the tea was delivered. "Just to be clear, Ms. Roberts, I never saw your husband, but one of my companions did."

Candace Roberts took a sip of tea, looked out the window and sighed. "He told me he had an art reception that night, and since I hate those things I told him I'd rather not go. Of course he knew I would not go. So . . . " she stopped and cleared her throat. "I never thought anything about it until I asked him the next morning if he had heard the news about Alfonso. He claimed he had not, but seemed legitimately upset after I described what happened."

Candace paused while the waitress put the *quesadilla* cut in quarters on the table with two plates and backed away. "We attended the funeral and he said all the right things." Candace let out a long slow breath and took a small bite from one of the wedges.

"If you don't mind my asking, how did you discover the photo?" Abby asked.

"Saturday, Darien went out to take photos of the snow at Ghost Ranch. He said he took some good shots with his phone camera he thought could be used to develop several paintings. That evening, I saw his phone lying on the desk, so I took a look. There were no shots at Ghost Ranch but there were a half dozen taken at the Taos pueblo. Five of them showed Alfonso, and two had the monk in the frame, but none showed the monk's face. Darien was busy doing something else, so I emailed the photos to myself."

"I couldn't look at them for a whole day, because . . . because . . ." Tears welled up in Candace's eyes again. "I haven't said anything to him yet. I just don't know what to do." Her shoulders sagged and she looked away with empty eyes.

Abby sat back and looked at Candace Roberts with compassion.

Candace collected herself, squared around to look at Abby and asked, "Are you still trying to find out who killed Alfonso?"

Abby looked down and took a drink of tea. "No," she said looking up at Candace. "I'm through with that," and gently put the cup down.

They both were silent for a moment before Candace asked, "Do you know who shot him?"

Abby paused just long enough to let Candace know that the answer would be a half-truth.

"No," Abby added, "but I have a few theories. Even if they are true, nothing could come of them." Abby wished she had not said that. She covered by adding, "Two suspects are already dead."

Silence.

"Do you think the killer might have been hired by my husband?" Candace asked looking hard with hatred.

Abby had hoped Candace would not ask that question. She looked at Candace a long moment and leaned forward with her hands under the table. "Ms. Roberts, a person in my business speculates a great deal but acts only when there is hard evidence. There is no hard evidence in this case. Believe me, I've looked, and so have the police. Unfortunately, this case will never be solved. The Martinez boy will probably be released soon. Nobody seriously believes he did it."

"Oh, I knew that the day it was announced," Candace said exasperated. After a moment, she slowly leaned in toward Abby and asked in a hushed tone, "What would you do in my situation?"

Abby had known she would have to deal with that question and had come up blank in rehearsal while driving to lunch. She pursed her lips and then said, "I wish I could give you some worthwhile advice, but I honestly can't think of any. I really don't know what I would do." And she didn't.

There are no rules for a woman's response when a husband kills her lover. In almost every culture, a wronged male has the right to administer justice. A woman in the position of being wronged by a husband is supposed to forgive and take steps to mend the relationship. A woman who loses a lover to a husband's wrath is supposed to suck it up and go on as though it never happened.

Deep down, Abby thought that Candace would not suck it up. Somehow Candace Roberts would get revenge, just as Abby would if she were in the same situation.

Driving out of Santa Fe, Abby could not get the look on Candace Roberts' face out of her mind. It was the look of a person both terrified and deeply angry. Abby knew the next few hours for Candace would be critical for her future, and possibly her husband's future as well. Abby knew she should not feel responsible, but she did, and she knew she had to do something; she could not simply walk away at this point. At the bottom of Opera Hill, Abby exited for an underpass and headed back to Santa Fe.

24

As Abby drove into Santa Fe, amber winter light of late afternoon flooded the hillside, setting adobe condos clinging to the hillsides aglow. She was unsure what to do other than to start at the Roberts' gallery. She found a parking space on a side street near the gallery. Abby unsnapped the pistol from the holder under the seat, checked the magazine, and put it in her jacket pocket. She put enough quarters in the meter to cover the time left for the day. It was past four o'clock, and the gallery closed at five. She felt Lupe Garza's presence and wondered what Lupe would do. In fact, Abby wondered, what was she doing herself? Was this to confront Roberts, save him from Candace, protect Candace, or worse, to engage in the unthinkable? All she knew for sure was she was in a hunter's mode, fully alert.

She pulled on thin gloves, pulled the stocking cap over her ears, left the 4Runner unlocked in case she needed a quick getaway, and walked up the sidewalk opposite the gallery. No one appeared in the gallery as she passed, but she caught sight of her reflection in the window and it was startling. Who was this person? At the corner she paused, and felt an altered reality snap into place. She turned around, walked back a few steps and went into a fashionable clothing store with a street-side window diagonally facing into the Roberts gallery. A stoic unsmiling Abby told the clerk she was killing time and would like to browse.

Minutes later, Abby saw the ever-stately Amanda Archuleta glide by the front window of the gallery. She seemed to be talking to someone over her shoulder. Darien Roberts appeared briefly before they both disappeared from view. Moments later, Amanda reappeared and placed an object in the window. It looked like a small sculpture of a bird.

Light snow began to fall as the afternoon light faded. The street was empty. Abby paced back and forth while she looked across at the gallery. Finally, the clerk asked if there was anything in particular she could show Abby.

The clerk's question jolted Abby. "No," she said embarrassed. "I won't take much more time. You certainly have a nice shop, and I do like the new spring fashions. Brightens up the place during these drab winter days, doesn't it?" The clerk smiled and busied herself preparing to close the shop at five. Abby began to have second thoughts about staying any longer.

At four-fifty, Candace Roberts, dressed in a dark coat and felt hat, walked rapidly up the street from the direction of the dry riverbed to the south and entered the gallery. Amanda came to the front and greeted Candace with a slight bow. Candace appeared to wander around looking at the art. Five minutes later Amanda left the gallery by the front door without locking it and headed up the street toward the plaza. Probably meeting someone for a happy-hour drink, Abby thought.

When Amanda was out of sight, Abby thanked the clerk, left the store, renewed her focus and jay-walked across the street past the gallery slow enough to get a good look inside. Candace was in the back talking and gesturing, apparently to Roberts who was out of sight. Abby stopped at the end of the gallery out of sight and strained to hear. Someone moved toward the front door. Abby turned away and heard the dead bolt on the front door click into place. Abby could hear voices, but could not make out the words. Suddenly, Candace's voice rose.

"You can't just walk away from this!"

Abby ran down to the end of the street, turned left and stopped short of the alley.

"This is not the end." Abby heard as Candace slammed the rear door to the gallery.

Abby ducked into a shallow doorway and waited. Seconds later Candace, moving so fast she almost stumbled, raced out of the alley, across the street toward the walking path bordering the riverbed, and vanished behind several pine trees. Wind gusts swirled snow in a chaotic pattern and Abby shivered. A cramp tightened between her shoulder blades, but she held her position, knowing Roberts would appear soon. Amanda had told Abby that Roberts often walked the riverbed from his home in the *Acequia Madre* neighborhood to and from the gallery.

Hearing rapid footsteps coming down the alley, Abby pressed tightly into the doorway. Roberts emerged hunched over with a fedora pulled down over his eyes, his normal easy stride replaced by a straight ahead charge without looking for traffic. Candace was nowhere in sight as he disappeared behind parked cars. Abby could see his head bobbing as he moved without caution up the path to the left, apparently heading home. Abby followed at a safe distance, the light almost gone.

The walking path along the riverbed extended for almost two miles from its northeast point to Abby's left, past where she now stood, to several miles below and to the right in a meandering line along Alameda Street. The path tunneled under the major cross streets enabling walkers and runners to move without stopping for traffic along the full length of what amounted to a narrow four mile-long park. Bushes and trees flanked the path and riverbed on both sides, muting traffic noise. As dusk gathered around 'the city different,' the river walkway became a ghostly hollow of dark shadows.

Abby caught fleeting images of Roberts whenever an overhead streetlight captured his hunched silhouette. She followed quietly, stopping briefly in the gathering darkness to remain hidden. After crossing under *Paseo de Peralta*, the path lost its pristine parkway appearance and became a jumble of overgrown trees and bushes. Roberts dissolved into the dark bramble and twisted contours, and Abby slowed her pace in case he had stopped. The walkway was empty. Street noises grew faint and well-spaced streetlights cast an eerie glow over a canopy of barren branches.

Abby pressed on in her *cazadora* mode, feeling the rush of the hunt, only this time it was different — *a turning point threatened*. Her hearing sharpened as her eyesight adjusted to the darkness. Automatically, she pulled the glove from her right hand with her teeth, stuffed it into her left pocket, closed her right hand around the handle of the pistol and pushed the safety button off. The snow had stopped, but the wind created a soft white noise through the trees.

Abruptly, the dark silence was broken by a voice, a woman's voice, shrill and menacing: " . . . gone far enough." Abby ran ahead into a small opening. Candace Roberts stood off to Abby's right, pointing a small revolver unsteadily at her husband, who was backed up against a park bench only ten feet away from his wife.

"Don't be stupid," Roberts yelled. "You'll only . . ."

"Shut up you bastard," Candace shrieked.

"Candace, put the gun down," Abby shouted.

Candace whirled in Abby's direction, and in that instant Roberts drew a small revolver from his coat pocket and pointed it at Abby.

"Romero, you meddling bitch," he snarled. "You're through."

Abby instinctively pulled her gun and dropped to one knee just as Roberts fired. With no pause Abby put the sight of the barrel on Robert's right shoulder, but as she started to squeeze the trigger, a loud pop sounded to her right and Robert's head jerked back violently. He arched backward and crashed against the park bench, crumpled forward, and sprawled on the path in a grotesque twisted shape; his revolver lay on the ground inches from his outstretched hand. Candace screamed just as several voices from across the street yelled.

"Call the police and an ambulance," Abby yelled back. She rushed over and took Candace's gun in her gloved left hand. Men rushed in from several directions and Abby shouted at them to stay back. She put her own gun back in the jacket pocket, not sure if she actually had fired.

"This is a crime scene. A man may be dead. Wait for the police," Abby yelled. Everyone stopped. Abby drew closer and saw the unmistakable posture of death: Roberts' vacant eyes and bloody face pointed skyward. Blood trickled out from his mouth into a narrow ribbon that ran down his neck and soaked into his expensive mauve shirt and wool jacket.

A siren wailed and flashing lights appeared in less than a minute. Candace Roberts stepped over her husband's body, sat down on the bench and started to cry; softly at first, and then harder until she was sobbing uncontrollably, convulsing for breaths that wouldn't come. Abby put a hand on her shoulder, which didn't halt the outpouring of grief that had been held inside for too long.

The snow began again, with large soft flakes muting the flashing lights. Abby looked for a place to sit down, but there wasn't any.

The next four hours were like a bad dream to Abby. The hollow sound of police work in an old building with lousy acoustics, the smell of burnt coffee, crude laughter, chairs scraping and squeaking and phones ringing with all manner of bizarre ring tones. Abby answered questions through a fog, and of course the questions came again and again with monotonous repetition. She had no idea what story Candace was telling, but no doubt she had called her attorney and was offering little or nothing.

Abby's story was basically the truth without going into much detail. She said she had worked for Roberts investigating the death of Alfonso Salazar, but had finished without a conclusion. She mentioned having lunch with Candace Roberts that day and seeing a photo Roberts apparently had taken at the murder scene in Taos. When police asked about the significance of the photo, Abby said she was concerned that Candace may have thought her husband had something to do with Salazar's death, although she never said as much at lunch.

When police continued to grill Abby about her reasons for following Roberts, she simply said she was concerned for the safety of both of them; flimsy reasons, but ambiguity was the best strategy at this point. When the police looked at her gun, they saw it had not been fired, and returned it to her. Abby had given the police Candace's gun, and Robert's revolver was retrieved by the police at the scene.

Just before midnight, Abby was driven to her 4Runner by a black-and-white. No words were exchanged. Before leaving the station she was advised to remain in the area and retain an attorney for a possible court appearance. She was not charged.

Abby drove home slowly in light snow on a pitch-black highway with almost no traffic. Thoughts were few. Once again she felt empty and alone. She had no feeling of relief, no catharsis over a potential turning point, no sense of justice, not even a feeling that it was over, just more sadness, sadness that all started on the holiest night in the Christian world.

Abby managed to get four hours of sleep before the phone started to ring. The media demanded feeding but were disappointed when Abby kept telling them on the advice of counsel, she could say nothing. She knew the media would have a field day speculating about Roberts, Garza, Mendoza, and Salazar. It would be a mystery writers would dig into for decades. More stuff for the legends of 'the city different,' a place that defies logic, and has the charm that has gone with mystery and evil deeds for over two centuries.

At noon Carmen called to say she'd heard the news and would be over after work. After a late breakfast, Abby called Nick, her mother and Bob in that order. Nick became quiet when Abby told him her story. She knew how difficult it must be for him to be guardian of a godchild that kept tempting fate. She wished she could release him from his role, but no one could do that. Abby asked Nick if they could renew their monthly Sunday evening dinners, although she warned him there would be three at the table. Nick said that would be nice. When Abby called her mother, she was surprised her mother had not heard anything about Roberts' violent death. This enabled Abby to forestall any detail and deal with it later. Bob already had most of the news.

"Do you want company tonight?" Bob asked.

"Yes, but Carmen is coming over," Abby said apologetically. "Do you want to meet her?"

"Yes, but tonight might not be the best time. Call me when you can. I'll miss you."

"Bob."

"Yes."

"There is something you should know."

Bob waited.

"I would have shot him. Candace fired first."

Bob was silent. After a moment he said, "Sounds like you showed good judgment given the circumstances."

Abby was silent.

"Abby."

"Yes."

"What do you think a police officer would have done in the same situation?"

"Thanks," she said. "I'll call you later."

Shortly after six, Carmen's red Ford pulled up next to the kitchen door. She came in carrying two grocery bags and put them on the kitchen table. Abby eased the door shut and walked over to Carmen, who wrapped her arms around Abby and held her tight without saying anything until she finally whispered, "I'm all right . . . really."

Carmen stepped back and looked into her eyes. "Are you still *mi hermana?*"

"*Sí.* Nothing's changed, except a lot of sadness.

Carmen frowned with sympathetic eyes, walked over to the table, opened the grocery bags and took out a rotisserie chicken with small tortillas and a six-pack of Bud Light long-necks. "*El Norteño* comfort food," she said and laughed. "Got plenty of wood? Thermometer is dropping to zero tonight. Let's build a fire now." Duster jumped up on the table, stuck his nose in the bag with the chicken, made a short trilling noise, and looked at them both as if to say, "Let's eat."

"No, Buster boy," Carmen said laughing. "Let's have a beer first," and she opened the drawer she knew held the bottle opener. Abby stacked wood in the kiva fireplace, squirted lighter fluid at the base of split logs, opened the damper and tossed in a lighted match. In minutes Carmen had carved the chicken, found paper plates, and the two friends sat in front of the growing fire with cold food, beer and the comfort of each other.

Carmen told Abby the gossip about Roberts at work that day. Most of her women co-workers had a story about Roberts. Candace Roberts came out a hero, and everyone hoped that she'd get off on self defense. Given that two judges in the First Judicial District now were women, the consensus was that Candace would walk. Everyone at work wanted to know how Abigail fit in the picture. All Carmen told them was that her friend had worked for Roberts investigating the Salazar murder.

After an hour or so, in a predictable lull in the conversation, Abby said, staring straight ahead and without warning, "I had him in my sights, but Candace beat me to it."

Carmen took a long drink from the longneck and they both looked into the fire.

25

The **outside thermometer** registered minus one Thursday morning, and Abby added extra wood to the living room stove and turned up the heater near the kitchen table. At precisely 8:30 the phone rang. Caller ID said A. Ramirez. Abby answered as though she did not know who was calling.

"Hello. Abigail Romano here."

"This is Alberto Ramirez. I'd like to discuss some business with you."

Abby noted he did not use Spanish with her, which meant this would not be a friendly conversation.

"What about, Mr. Ramirez?" Abby returned the formality in kind, and she was sure Ramirez understood.

"I won't discuss it over the phone. Please come to my ranch later today, three o'clock."

"Mr. Ramirez, if I come to your ranch I'll bring someone with me. If we meet in public, say at Bailey's in Abiquiu, I'll come alone."

The line was silent for a moment. "All right, Bailey's at three." The line went dead without him saying *bueno* or goodbye.

Before putting the phone back in its cradle Abby called Bailey's and asked for Bud. She breathed a sigh of relief when she heard his voice.

"Bud, it's Abby."

"Yeah, what's up?"

"Will you be in the store at three this afternoon?"

"I think so, let me check my book. Yes, I can be. Why?"

"Alberto Ramirez wants to meet me, and I need a friendly person nearby."

"Sure, no problem. I know Alberto. We're on good terms."

"Good, see you at three. Thanks."

When faced with an unpleasant task or situation, most people dig into one or more of those unpleasant jobs that are putt off for as long as possible: jobs such as cleaning the stove, or the garage, or the bathroom, or taxes. Abby spent the next four hours on her taxes, the bathroom and Duster's litter box. By one o'clock she was zonked and needed a twenty minute nap. She set the alarm just in case, and it was a good idea, as when the alarm went off she was sound asleep. After a quick shower, she dressed in denim and wore her dress Stetson. She had never met Ramirez, but knew he was a no nonsense gruff old rancher who was accustomed to getting his way without argument. Abby had no intention of playing the coy submissive woman.

Abby backed the 4Runner to the parking rail at Bailey's five minutes before three. The lot was empty except for Bud's pickup with the bumper sticker that said, "I whizzed at Bailey's General Store — Abiquiu, New Mexico," which always made Abby grin. Thin gray clouds formed on the western horizon, and Abby thought it would be a blazing sunset. She left the 4Runner unlocked, for a quick entry if needed. Abby went straight to the deli and took a chair facing the front door. The store was empty. Bud must be in his hideaway in the back, she thought.

After five minutes, Bud came out from the back, waved at Abby, went behind the counter, picked up some papers, looked around and gestured with both hands indicating, 'no show?' Abby shrugged, and Bud walked back to his office. Abby got up from the chair and walked to the front door. The parking lot was still empty. As she stood there everything suddenly went into slow motion and she said loudly, "Oh my God!" bolted out the door and into her truck.

Tires screeched as the 4Runner tore out of the lot and onto the highway narrowly missing a car turning into the post office. Abby screamed "No, No, No," and pounded the steering wheel. "Duster, Duster, Duster!" Abby yelled. "Oh, Duster." Abby gunned the 4Runner to the limit the road would allow as she raced along the curved river route. When she was several hundred yards from the bottom of the hill she saw it. Black smoke billowed above the tree line. "Duster, my boy." Tears were streaming down Abby's face. She raced up the hill and skidded to a halt just before her driveway. Bluish-orange gasoline flames engulfed the shed.

Abby ran toward the house which was still unharmed, opened the kitchen door and saw the horror on Duster's face. She grabbed the fire extinguisher from under the sink. Frantically she pulled out the pin on the lever and ran back toward the shed. A white cloud of foam exploded in front of her, but the heat was too great to get close enough to the shed to do any good. In frustration she threw the extinguisher to the side, turned, and ran back for the garden hose. Crying and screaming in anger she tried to get the hose connected, but when she finally got it screwed on, she discovered the hose was frozen.

Abby stood there holding the hose, and watched the shed fall into a pile of hissing, steaming embers when they hit the surrounding snowbanks. The new lumber Nick had piled neatly next to the shed had become a mass of smoking charcoal. Her bicycle stood in the center of the carnage like a strange metal sculpture slowly twisting into the shape of a writhing skeleton.

Abby stood stunned, holding the impotent garden hose, with only one thought in her mind.

El Norte.

Printed in Great Britain
by Amazon

22697478R00146